The Land Beyond the Sunset

A Celtic America Called Eirgalon

(Book 1 of the Chronicles of Eirgalon)

by

Joel Kreger

2

Dedication

To my wife who always believes in me,

my children who always give me inspiration,

and my grandchildren who always bring me joy.

Table of Contents

The Land Beyond the Sunset

Prologue

By mere inches do the gods shift, ere so slightly, the flight of a single solitary arrow, and so is altered the course of human history.

In realms which lay beyond domains of men, exist such beings called by mortal man, "the gods." Be they gods or demons in the thoughts of men matters little, for truth be told, to some they may be gods and to some they may be demons. Be that as it may, at times they touch the human world, and in their touching they move and turn that world into different outcomes and alternate timelines.

One of these beings was known as Gluskabi and he was given glimpses of foresight not all gods are given. He viewed the timeline of his people in the western continent. Saw them prosper, grow, and flourish for a time. Looking further down that timeline, he saw them greet the Europeans, and then diminish, becoming but mere side notes in the course of that history. He pondered how he might change this outcome. He peered down alternate timelines of what might be, and conceived a plan. He made conversation with Loki of the islands and lands to the east. Now Loki was known to be a trickster and he was intrigued by the suggestion that Gluskabi made. Could the flight of one mere arrow change the course of human history? As Gluskabi bid farewell to Loki he smiled inwardly, for he knew he had planted a seed of mischief and that Loki would produce the fruit.

That moment of the arrow with altered flight came when the troops of Harold Godwinson met those of William of Normandy on October the 14th, in the year of 1066 by Western reckoning. There it was that Loki acted. With but the merest puff of wind Loki moved the flight of an arrow, a single solitary arrow, and immediately the future that would be, became a different future. Now it was Harold, son of Godwin, who rode triumphant from the battlefield rather than dying from an arrow through the eye; and William, now no conqueror, lay a casualty dead upon the soil of a foreign land. Harold, blood of northern Viking kings and Celtic royalty ruled this land. Ireland remained free of Norman influence. As decades and centuries passed, Northern civilization flourished east through Scandinavia, the German lands, and Russia; as it also did across the western seas into the newly colonized territories of Vinland and Markland. The climate of the North Atlantic cooled, but rather than retreating from western struggling lands, this stronger northern culture, a combination of Viking and Celtic peoples, expanded both southward into the lands of Europe and, in similar fashion across the Atlantic, they expanded southward into the fertile country along the eastern seaboard of that land they called Eirgalon - the land beyond the sunset.

Chapter 1 - The Lake at Dunsheelin

He felt a momentary flicker of embarrassment as he moved from the deep water towards the shoreline where he had dropped his clothes. This was so unlike him. He didn't normally disrobe completely before running into the lake for a quick swim, but something today had beckoned him and he had, without much thought or foresight, peeled off every stitch of clothing he had been wearing, tossed them into a pile by the nearest tree, and then gone running into the water to rinse off the sweat of his work on this sultry summer day.

Having pleasantly rinsed and refreshed himself, and now thinking of his total lack of clothing, he began walking out of the water. As he emerged from the water one could see, if one was looking, that he was a healthy young man of solid build with muscles grown strong by physical labor. The water streamed off his wavy black hair and through his beard, which covered the square cut of his jaw. His skin was tanned to a soft bronze by the summer sun. He was a fine physical specimen of the Nordic-Celtic people who now shared this land of Eirgalon with the original Wabanaki people.

He was striding forward waist deep in the water and shaking the water from himself when he looked over to the tree where his clothes should be.

An exclamation burst from his lips, "What the..." and quickly he moved toward the tree.

He was splashing knee deep through the water and

picking up speed when she stepped out from behind the tree holding his clothes before her.

Her soft feminine voice, filled with playful teasing covered over with a false veneer of innocence, lilted over the water to him, "And would you be looking for these?"

In what he felt was in all likelihood one of the fastest reactions of his life, he threw himself down into the knee-deep water and then righted himself into a sitting position. He looked back up and saw that she had stepped away from the tree and closer to the shoreline.

There was no mistaking the gleeful smile on her face and laughter in her voice as she teased him, "Would these dirty and sweaty clothes be belonging to you? I happened to find them by yonder tree and I thought that some poor soul must have been so overwhelmed by the reek of them that he had simply discarded them there."

There she stood, Leesha. She had been his best childhood friend. The one he had played childhood games with, and with whom he had caused all sorts of trouble, much to the elders' chagrin. They were always good at playing practical jokes on each other as well as on their friends. But at this moment, as she stood on the lakeshore with the sunlight shining on the soft brown hair and the gentle breeze moving her loose summertime gauzy dress, she appeared as anything but his prankster partner. She was suddenly looking so appealing. He was seeing her as something more than a childhood friend. He realized that he wouldn't be jumping up anytime soon and running to her to grab his clothes, as he might have in years past.

"What's the matter, Sko? Someone come along and

tie your tongue before they stripped you bare and threw you in the lake?"

He was completely tongue-tied and didn't know how to respond. He was surprised, annoyed, aroused, and confused. Finally, totally lacking any semblance of eloquence he stammered, "Aw, Leesha, what are you doing? You know those are my clothes."

Her laughter bounced through the short distance that lie between them as she said, "Well, now that you mention it, they do look a wee bit like the clothes you were wearing when I saw you out there working at putting up the hay for the cattle. Phew, and lordy, but they sure do smell like you too!"

"You know they're mine! Just give them to me!"

"Well now, you'll not be expecting me wade out into the lake and get myself all wet just to hand you this pile of smelly rags. Why don't you just come and get them?"

With a growing frustration, Sko blurted out, "Because I can't right now!"

"What? A big healthy guy like you can't pick yourself up and . . . ohhh . . . I see. Could it be that your proud manhood won't let you?" She smirked from ear to ear as she said this, while his face blushed brilliantly.

To his dismay, he heard other voices coming from far down the shoreline, and then rounding the point, which jutted out into the lake, appeared two of his other friends walking towards him along the shoreline. It was his close friend, Karl, with Enat, the sister of his current sweet adversary, Leesha.

With a rush of words and pointing to the distant couple, he blurted out to Leesha, "Please, just quick drop the clothes and turn away so I can get out before they get here. Please!"

"Oh well, if I must. I'll just drop them here and walk away. I wouldn't want you to be embarrassed in front of those two." With that said, she did indeed drop them. True to her word she also turned and started to walk away.

Sko jumped up and quickly ran out and started pulling his pants on. Leesha hesitated and then stopped, turned back toward Sko to ask a question.

"Now don't you think it will look strange to those two, when they see me walking away and you pulling on your pants? What will they think we have been doing?"

"They won't think anything," he exclaimed as he was now struggling with his shirt.

At that moment Karl's voice could be heard shouting in the distance, "Hey, you two! What's going on?"

With a devilish grin Leesha whispered, "So, Sko, what we will be telling them? Will we tell them that you had stripped down to show me that manly body of yours, or that I was trying to take advantage of you? Which sounds better to your ears?"

"Neither one. At least I know the first isn't true. But maybe the second has some truth to it," he said as he finished putting on his shirt.

She raised her voice, projecting it toward Karl and Enat, "Well, a fine day it is. Are you two out for a late afternoon lover's stroll?"

That brought a quick retort from her sister, who looked to be nearly a mirror image of Leesha except for the honey blond hair cascading over her shoulders, "No more than you, by the looks of it! But really what we came for is the two of you. Father wants to see the four of us, along with Neal and Teite, all together. And by all accounts he wants to see us as soon as possible! Have you seen either one of them - or have you been too busy doing some skinny dipping."

Leesha snorted a laugh, "Not I. Don't look at me. But this big lummox here. Well, that's another story."

To which Skoth quickly blurted out, "I was just rinsing off after the sweaty job of putting up that cutting of hay, which, I might add, would have gone much faster with Karl's help! Now, what was it you were saying about the Chief?"

Sure, there were some who thought that Sko was a wee bit slow in speaking sometimes, but there was great depth of intellect beneath that naive looking expression he often wore, and he knew well how to change the drift of a conversation when needed. Leesha smirked in the amusement of this as she stood to the side, but left herself be silent so as allow it to happen.

Karl took the bait and replied, "She said the Chief wants to see us!"

"That's what I thought. Must be something important if he is tracking us down in the middle of the day."

"So finish getting dressed and let's go."

"What about Neal and Teite? You said he wanted to see them too."

"That's right. We'll go get them. They must be down at the Academy. They are such bookworms. Meet you at the Hall."

With brief farewells the couple then went off down

14

the trail to the Academy. After they were out of earshot, Leesha and Sko started walking down the shore back towards Dunsheelin. It was the primary settlement of the people and what some might call the center of government on that long island called Fada Innis. Sko was still annoyed about her grabbing his clothes but was trying to joke with her about it as they walked. However, their inner thoughts dwelt upon what the summons from Chief Unaine might be about.

Several minutes into their walk the walls of the Dunsheelin could be seen rising in the distance. They cut back from the shoreline path to the main road and walked past several homesteads and crofters' houses sharing greetings with those they passed. It was obvious they were known by all. As they neared the stonewalls of the fortress, Leesha started giving some directions, "Sko, you may have rinsed off, but those clothes are a stinking mess. You'll be wanting to go to your room and change into something a little more presentable before you meet the Chief. I've got a few things I have to do myself, and I'm sure it will be a while before Karl and Enat are able to find Neal and Teite and get them there, so I'll meet you outside the great hall in about an hour."

Sko smiled, and jokingly said, "Yes, my queen. I shall do all you command. Pray tell, would there be any other task I may do for you? Perhaps you would like me to escort you on your errands, so that no one takes advantage of you," and then with an exaggerated smile, "or you of them?"

Leesha was not to be put off, "Oh, go on with you now. Get yourself moving, ya big oaf, or for sure the Chief will be most annoyed," and with that she left him there as she quickly moved off on a mission of her own.

Sko wondered what she was up to. She was always up to something. Ah, well, he had his own self to take care of, so it would have to remain a mystery as to what she was about. So without any more thought about her, he turned and went to his room to get himself ready, still thinking about what this summons might be about.

Chapter 2 - The Meeting in the Great Hall

Even after taking his time to put on some fresh clothing and make his way to the Great Hall of Dunsheelin, Skoth found himself the first to arrive and the door closed. The Hall's guard for the day, Erik, was lounging in the chair to the side of the door and did not deign to stand at Skoth's approach. The duty of being the Hall's guard for the day was an honor, to be sure, but it didn't involve a great deal of physical labor, nor was it a duty that required a great deal of formality. The primary functions of the position were to make sure the Chief wasn't disturbed when he wanted privacy and to keep peace among any petitioners who came before him seeking to have him judge their dispute. Erik was one of the long-time trusted men that the Chief relied upon, for although he was rather uncouth and notably irreverent, he could be counted upon to be level-headed and even exert a calming influence upon people who were emotionally charged.

He was intent upon the small figurine he was whittling with his dagger, but did briefly raise his eyes and give Skoth an almost disdainful look, before dropping them again to focus on his carving.

Giving voice to his attitude, Erik said, "Well, if it ain't the high and mighty Sko himself, come to honor us with his presence."

Sko was used to Erik's demeanor, but the elder Celt

(for that is what they called those who were descended of that mixture of Nordic and Celtic people from those isles far to the east) always seemed to know just what to say to unnerve the younger man.

"C'mon, Erik," Sko replied, "You know the Chief sent for me."

"Sure, I do. But for the life of me, I can't figure out why," he said with a teasing sneer.

"I bet you do. Or at least I bet you have some idea about what is going on. Why don't you fill me in? That way I won't come off as quite the big fool that you always seem to say I am."

That got a chuckle out of the guard but no response because it was then that the group of young folk that had been called to the Chief appeared rounding the corner. It included the Chief's daughters: Leesha, Enat, and Teite, as well as the two young men, Karl and Neal.

With feigned heaviness, for although in his fifties Erik was still fit and limber, he rose to his feet and greeted them, "It is about time you folks showed up. I was starting to think I'd have to spend the next several minutes talking with this idiot."

Leesha was quick to respond, "I know what you mean. Sometimes he can hardly make a coherent comment."

"Right you are," chuckled Erik as he moved forward, banged stoutly on the door twice, and swung it open for them to enter. He held the door open while the six of them filed in. He was starting to pull it shut and resume his guard position when Unaine's voice carried out from the far end of the hall, "Erik! I want you in here also. Close the door and join us."

Sko was the last one in and therefore the closest to Erik, so only he could hear what Erik muttered under his breath, "Geez, what the hell does he want me for? What sort of trouble am I in for now?"

There was, of course, no reply to be made, but Sko smiled to himself at the knowledge that there were some things that could get under the skin of the elder warrior.

Chief Unaine was sitting at the head of a large table near the hearth of the

Great Hall where only a small fire was burning. There was no need of a fire in this warmest of seasons but tradition held that there should always be a hearth fire burning in the Great Hall of the Chief who led the fair folk of Fada Innis, and so there was. From his seat facing them, he motioned for them to join him at the table. As they approached the table two of the high-backed chairs on the near side of the table made scraping noises as they were pushed back and their occupants turned and rose to greet them. One of them was a young man of their age, Tkaden. The other was an older man of the Wabanaki who they had met before, Dakatomi.

Unaine spoke the words of introduction, "I'd like you to meet the representatives of our neighbors to the north from the Wabanaki lands. This young man is the son of one of their primary chiefs, and he goes by the name of Tkaden. Our other guest is Dakatomi, whom you may already know, since he has visited us several times before and spent some time with us."

Handshakes and greetings were exchanged among the group, and then Unaine invited them all to sit around the table. He also beckoned his chief advisor, Theofinn, over from where he had been working at a desk to the side of the hall. Hair and beard whitened with age, and with a tall frame that was hunched over with the weight of many years, the druid scholar made his way to the table.

When all were seated, Unaine began, "I know you are all curious as to why I called you all here. I ask that you be patient and don't interrupt me." With this statement he looked directly at Leesha, and she gave him a pout face in mock defiance. He hesitated, but then went on.

"For many years Theofinn and I have discussed and debated some of our ancient prophecies. Seldom have we come to agreement as to what they might mean. However, we think we might have some idea about how one that the seer Thorfall put forth hundreds of years ago. It goes like this:

> *The arrow's flight replaces death with life*
> *a double week of generations and new lands are*
> *filled with strife*
> *the east moves west and north moves south*
> *unite as one to meet the test*
> *beware the sunset lox*
> *a sly and wily fox*
> *a youth, son of bold*
> *must lead the fold*
> *a kingly role to search and find*
> *the key to guard our humankind*

Theofinn, would you tell these young ones what we think this portends."

Theofinn, voice gravelly with age, continued the story, "Now, Thorfall was an old man when he wrote that, but men would say that he was one who conversed with the gods of our lands, old and new, east and west. It is recorded that oft he spoke of that battle in his youthful days, when as an aide to good King Harold Godwinson they repelled the invading Normans led by William. That battle was known for the ferocity of our men, but also for the deaths inflicted by the arrows of the Normans that fell like rain upon our men. It is said that the gods whispered to Thorfall that they had touched just one of those arrows - one that would have killed King Harold - and left him to live and to have the victory. We think that is the first line. The gods changed the course of our history by touching that one arrow."

He paused for effect, and then went on, "A double week of generations brings us to our time, and we have settled these new lands of Eirgalon, but there is much conflict here. It may be that this is the test of our time. Do the gods wait to see it we can overcome our quarrels and conflicts and unite as one?" And then with casual toss, as if throwing dice, he tossed a single rune onto the center of the table. It landed face side up and all could easily make out the marking. The rune carried the marking of the king.

No one spoke for several moments.

Theofinn spoke, "In a Ritual of Quest the runes were cast. They have been read. In response to that reading, Chief Unaine commissioned me to make this special runestone and to consecrate it with a reading of that prophecy. It has been invoked. Now comes the decision. To whom shall the King Rune be bestowed?"

Erik, always the practical one, interrupted at this point, "I'm not debating anything you wise folks are talking about here. I'm just a simple soldier. Little do I know the minds of the gods and the interpretation of prophecies, but I'm not sure why we're talking about this with those two here," and he pointed at the Wabanaki men.

"Ah, yes," said Unaine, "Our good friends. It seems our Wabanaki friends have heard a similar message. Dakatomi, would you enlighten our folks with your story?"

Dakatomi turned to Erik, "As I told your chief, before he died, my father, eldest shaman of our people, was visited by Nokomis. That ancient spirit, Grandmother, we call her, came to him and told him something very similar. For some time now we have been discussing what this might mean for us. We too see the world around us, and we too see the conflict and strife that grows among our people and with the clans of your people. Do you not wish us to share the future with you as we share the present? Would you wish us be gone?

Now Eric stammered an apology, "No, no. I've had my issues with a few of your folks, but by and large you people are a good folk. I just wasn't sure why you were here."

Smoothing the troubled waters, Unaine stepped back into the conversation, "Erik, you are a good man and that was a worthy question, but if you had just refrained from interrupting you would have heard it all," he paused, "and I thought it would be the younger folks who would be interrupting. Ah, well, does anyone object to hearing the rest?"

Between the three elder men, Unaine, Theofinn, and Dakatomi, the rest of the story was laid out: the strange visit of Nokomis to the Wabanaki people, the struggle to interpret what she meant, the debate in the druidic circles over Thorfall's prophesy, the growing inter-tribal disputes within the Wabanaki tribes and within the Celtic chiefdoms, and the ever-increasing dissention between the two sets of people. New to the ears of the young folk was the information of the growing threat from the west. The Skraeling people from west of the great River Mahakentuck were said to be unifying under the leadership of one man, who had the ambition to attack and destroy the Wabanaki and Celtic lands. If that were true, then no single village or chiefdom of Wabanaki or Celt could stand before them for those western nations were deemed to be strong.

Then Unaine, King of Fada Innis, reached out to the center of the table and gathered into his hand the King Rune. He turned it over in his hand and rubbed it between his thumb and forefinger, looked at it for several moments, then lifted his eyes and looked around the table. He set it back on the table before him and then he spoke.

"So, now we come to it. The time has come for us to bestow this rune to the youth of whom the prophecy speaks. To give it to the one who must lead us. Who shall that be? Who will find the key? Who will be our High King of Eirgalon?"

All eyes were wide, but none spoke.

Dakatomi spoke, "Seated at this table is a young man of our people, a man of west and east, a son of Wabanaki and Celt. I believe it to be him. I say, Tkaden. But others say otherwise."

That young man, who to this point had spoken nothing but greetings, said, "I claim not the mantle given. I

23

gained no sign of this in the vision quest of my manhood training. I know our shaman sees things others cannot, and I am willing to serve my people. But I know not that I am the one."

Leesha, who had been holding her tongue for a long time finally spoke out a question, "I am curious. How is it that you are also of us?"

"I am a Wabanaki, it is true. My father is a chief and my mother is a wise one. My father comes from a long line of Wampanoag leaders. It is from my mother that I share your blood. Her mother was from your people."

Theofinn said, " And there is no question about that because Maedrid, his grandmother, is my sister. While I haven't had many occasions to see this remarkable young man, I know that he is indeed who he says he is, and I can see my sister in those eyes. He is most definitely one of us, as well as he is Wabanaki."

Another question from Leesha, this time directed to Theofinn, "So are you saying he is the chosen one?"

"Not at all. Dakatomi may think that, but I think it is another."

Teite, the eldest of the king's daughters and the most scholarly, now spoke up, "Well then, Master Druid, you must have reasons you haven't shared with us. Perhaps you can explain."

Through all this King Unaine of the Fada Innis Celts (though he preferred to be called simply "Chief") smiled in enjoyment. His three daughters were a delight to him: Teite, the eldest, blonde of hair and blue of eye (a younger image of her mother) who was a scholar in her own right; Leesha, brown hair and flashing brown eyes with a quick wit and boundless energy: and Enat, a younger version of Leesha, but with blonde hair and with a bit more gentle disposition. None of them would follow him as King, but he knew all of them would be leaders of his people in some fashion.

Theofinn responded, "Yes. I do have my reasons. Think back to the prophecy. How was the young man described?"

Teite, ever the student, quickly answered the Master Druid, "He is bold. And well that is, a leader needs boldness."

"Yes my dear. That is true. However, the original prophecy said, 'son of bold'."

"Yes, and that's just a formal way we have of saying he is bold."

King Unaine spoke softly, "The best friend of my youthful days was Brian. He was called by many: The Bold." As he said this, he looked across the table at Skoth, who had taken a deep breath but said nothing.

Teite said, "Well, Da, many a man is called "bold" by his friends. What makes your friend so important? Important enough to be referenced in such a prophecy?"

"Teite, you never knew him. He died when you were but a whelp at your mother's breast. But he was indeed bold. He was the best friend a man, or woman, could have. Loyal beyond all measure. Insightful. Decisive. Fierce, yet compassionate. A great man. If any man deserved the name "bold" it was he. He, more than I, should have been our chief."

"He sounds like he was a great man and a great

friend. But he's not here."

Unaine sighed deeply, hesitated, and then said, "No, he's not. But his son is."

All eyes were on the Chief. He pushed his chair back from the table and stood. Slowly he reached out and gathered into his hand the King Rune, then walked around the table and stood next to Skoth. He placed one hand on Skoth's shoulder and extended his other hand, open and holding the King Rune, and said, "Skoth, son of Brian the Bold, I believe this belongs to you."

Chapter 3 - A Task Given

Almost simultaneously several voices erupted with declarations of astonishment and disbelief, but Unaine quieted them when he went on with a louder, more commanding voice, "It is my belief, and by that I mean as chief of this clan, druid by training, and warrior by fate, that Skoth, son of Brian the Bold, is to be the one to fulfill this prophecy and preserve our future as the people of Eirgalon. I give to him this task. Skoth, come and stand before me."

With that he moved toward the center of the Great Hall to stand within the Sacred Spiral inlaid upon the tile of the floor. It was the traditional Baltic Labyrinth used for centuries in the European homelands of the Viking people and now used here in Eirgalon. As he did so he motioned for the others to come and form a circle around them.

As they rose from the table and moved to the center of the hall, Leesha moved close to her father and whispered, "Are you sure you know what you are doing?"

Leaning close to her he said, "Do any of us ever truly know what we are doing? But, yes, dear daughter, I am sure. That's not all either. I suspect you will have a part to play in this. Now please take your place on the outer circle of the spiral and we'll get on with this."

Sko, tongue-tied now more than ever, walked behind Unaine into the center of the sacred spiral by following him on the long winding inward spiral. His mind was jumping from place to place, from memory to memory, from question to question. He tried to picture his father, but his only mental picture was the description his mother had painted for him with words. They had never told him much about his father. But there was no time for that now. He needed to focus on the moment. The others in the hall were now standing on the outer edge of the circle and he was standing before Unaine who still held in his hand the King Rune.

Skoth moved to kneel, but Unaine stopped him, saying, "Our King kneels to no man." Then he placed the rune into Skoth's hands and held them together with his own and said, "Skoth, son of bold, I name you as the youth to lead us. Tis a kingly role. The task to find the key to preserve our future is yours. I know not how this is to be done, for that is your quest. It is yours to determine. I pledge to you today my support. I will help you as I can. Speaking for the people, I say that we will aid you on your quest." Turning to those on the circle perimeter he said, "May the people present give consent."

The surrounding folk responded with, "So mote it be."

"Well, then. That's done!" said Unaine. "Now, let's sit down again and help young Skoth figure out where to go from here."

A long, tedious, and sometimes heated discussion around the table followed. It lasted through the evening meal that the servants of the Great Hall provided, and well into the waning hours of the evening. Unaine certainly had some ideas about what course of action might be wise, but it quickly became apparent that he wanted to provide information and advice while leaving the decision making to Skoth. After all the discussion, only a few decisions were made actually made. Skoth was determined to proceed by traveling up the mighty River Mahakentuck and he wanted more study and research done on what was meant by the "key" in the prophecy. With plans made to meet on the morrow to continue the discussion, the participants went their separate ways for the evening.

Unaine and Erik were the last ones remaining in the Great Hall after all the others had left for the night. They stood side by side watching them leave. Unaine put a hand on Erik's shoulder and said, "Well, that was a long day. But there is one more word I would have with you."

Erik turned and looked in his friend's eyes, "I know you pretty well, Chief. I have a feeling I know what you want."

Unaine lifted his eyebrows in question, " Oh, really?"

"Aye. You'll be telling me that you want me to tag along with him wherever he goes. Protect him from himself. I'm to be his nursemaid."

"Well. I wasn't exactly going to say it that way. But yes, I want you to go with him wherever he goes. He will need a good man at his side. Someone to cool his youthful temper when it rises too high. Someone to get his blood boiling when he seems too cool. Someone to build him up, but yet to keep him humble. Someone who can give wise and honest counsel. Someone who can watch his back, and protect him when needed. Someone . . . like you."

"Are you sure I am the best man for the job?"

"Erik, if there is anyone alive who can do all those

things, and also provide a strong sword to protect him, it is you. I trust you. Now, let's go get a drink. I think Helga is probably expecting us down at the Wandering Woman."

Erik sighed a long sigh and Unaine grinned as the two of them walked off together in the dusky evening light.

Chapter 4 - Many Gifts

Leesha, Teite, and Enat separated themselves from the young men as they left the meeting and made their way to the room they shared in the fortress. Once in the room, they quickly got down to business. Leesha took charge and they formulated their plan of action.

Leesha said, "Mother told us long ago that she foresaw that we would have an important role in our people's future. I think this is it, and I think that this is why Father, specifically wanted us at that meeting. He always listened to her, even when he pretended not to. So now what do we do?"

Teite spoke up, " Well, I agree with Sko that we need to do more research on the issue of the key. I think that I should stay here at Dunsheelin and work on that."

To which Leesha added, "You'll need Neal here, too. Those old men and druids know a lot, but we need a young man with new insights and a quick mind. Neal is the one for that."

"I won't object to that. We get along well enough."

Enat just looked at Leesha and rolled her eyes, while Leesha said, "Well enough, tis true."

Enat suggested, "I think that Leesha and I should tag along with Sko and Karl. You know, to keep them out of trouble.

Leesha said, "Well most assuredly he is going to plan on taking Karl with him. Those two don't like to go off on any adventure without each other. And they sure do get themselves into enough trouble. They'll need the both of us, just to keep them from making total fools of themselves."

Now it was Teite's turn to roll her eyes, which she did to such great effect that both her sisters were startled.

Leesha recovered and went on, "Those wise men in the hall today think they know it all, but they don't. If those boys don't have the benefit of the advice of some smart women with them they will be like babes in the woods, for sure. I think we should take this to the Women of the Sauna this evening and get some advice from the elder women."

Teite was quick to agree with her but added, "I do wish Mother was still with us, she would certainly have some guidance for us."

Enat sighed and said, "Aye, we miss her even more now, if that is possible. She died far too young. She would have been a wonderful Amma to our children."

Then Teite, the eldest (and some would say the closest in spirit and manner to their deceased mother) said, "Ahh, but she did leave us with something. Certainly the power of the Women of the Sauna is one thing, but there is also this." Then she walked to her dresser and pulled out a small bundle that was neatly tied with a small braided cord. "In that last week, when she lay weak and in pain, she told me she had a premonition that she would die, but that we would need this. She told me about it, but told me not to open it or use it, but to guard it in secret until the time came to search for the key. I didn't know what she meant by that. But I knew enough to believe her. So I set it aside and have said nothing about it until now. This, I judge is the time."

With that said she started untying the neat knots that held the small bundle together. Laying the outer plain undyed homespun wool cloth to the side, she laid before them a small brown leather drawstring pouch, a small folded and tied piece of green-dyed linen, and a thin foot long object wrapped in the same type of homespun wool as the outer wrapping. When she opened the leather pouch she drew out a folded white linen cloth. Peering into the pouch she saw that it was filled with a set of runestones and a small rolled piece of parchment.

Unrolling the parchment, she declared, "It is in Ma's handwriting, most certainly." She looked it over, reading it to herself.

Leesha, her impatience coming forth, said, "Well, out with it! What does she say?"

Teite read the words, "Cast the runes when in need, ask for help from other lands. Follow with care where they lead, for the right and just, be sure to stand."

Now Enat spoke again, "This is a precious gift to be sure. Rune sets are powerful magic. I don't know where this comes from, but if Ma gave it to us, then it must be truly just."

Teite unfolded the white linen cloth that was with the runes knowing it must be the throwing cloth. The cloth was almost as important as the runes for it was onto the cloth the runes were thrown and read. If it was a cloth of power and purity, the runes would be thrown true. If it was a weak or flawed cloth, the runes could well guide the reader to ruination. One side of the cloth was unmarked, but on the other side fine etchings covered it. It was bordered with Celtic knotwork, and in the center was the Sacred Spiral.

"What a thing of beauty," said Leesha. "Teite,

without a doubt. Ma meant for you to have this. You have studied how to read the runes with the Druids and with the Women of the Sauna. You best would know how to use this."

"Perhaps," said Teite, "But let's see what the other items are." With that, she untied the neatly folded green-dyed linen cloth. As she opened it a small object dropped out of it and bounced on the table, landing on the leather rune purse. She picked it up to examine it. It was a small copper pendant, tarnished green with age, which carried an image of the Green Man upon it.

"Look at the cloth," exclaimed Leesha. It was approximately the size of a napkin, and they could see when they had spread it on the table that it bore the same image of the Green Man. A small piece of parchment was pinned to one corner of the green linen. On it were inscribed three words: seek, trust, join.

"This seems a little more cryptic," said Leesha. "Nevertheless, the linen and the pendant must be important in some way."

"No doubt they are," responded Teite. "Since Enat is the one of us who has the green thumb for growing things, these items might be intended for her. Mother knew of her gift for living things and her connection with the world of nature."

"And if that is the case, then whatever is in that final piece of homespun wool would probably be intended for me. I wonder, what might it be?" Lifting it gently off the table, untying the cord, and unwrapping the cloth from around it revealed piece of parchment wrapped around an object. She unrolled the parchment, which revealed a smoothly polished foot long piece of wood inscribed with numerous symbols. It was about the thickness of a man's thumb and embedded into the thicker handle portion of it was a green gem. In addition to the Celtic symbols inscribed upon, written in Old Ogham script, was the word EOSTRE.

They were studying it with awe when Teite's eyes went to the parchment that had been wrapped around it. "Sure enough, there is writing on this parchment too." She picked it up and began reading. "This wand is fashioned from the wood of Yggdrasil - the ash tree which is queen of the forest. I know not all its powers, only that it ties the worlds together. Both male and female are needed for harmony - Oak and Ash. This wand came to me from the hands of a wise woman of the far isles. Use it wisely."

Enat spoke up, "For sure this is intended for you, Leesha. You are the most daring of the three of us. You are a natural leader. I even think that the Women of the Sauna have it in mind that one day you will be one of them."

Teite agreed saying, "She's right, Leesha. You have the natural charisma that a true leader holds, and you are smart about how you use it. Add to that the time you have spent with the Druids and the Women of the Sauna and it only makes sense that you should be the one to be responsible for this wand of power."

"Thank you, sisters mine. I won't deny it is a beautiful piece of work, but even Ma wrote that she didn't know its powers. How am I to even know what it can do?"

Teite smiled a knowing smile at Enat, and then turned to Leesha and said, "I'm sure you'll figure it out. Now, what about the Women of the Sauna? How much of this should we share with them?" She paused in thought, and then said, "Ever since Ma died, and then also old Gretchen and Sweet Maeve, the Women's Sauna hasn't spoken strongly. They might not know what to make of this."

Leesha said, "True enough. But they won't be able to help us at all if we don't share it all. Knowledge is power. If we want them to have the power to help us, we must let them add the knowledge of this situation, and of these gifts, to the wisdom they have."

There wasn't much more to be said after that as the women came to quick agreement to take everything to the Women of the Sauna. They wrapped up the artifacts, each one putting the one that had seemed destined for her, into her own purse and they departed the room to join the Women of the Sauna in their evening ritual.

Chapter 5 - Friend or Foe

When Dakatomi and Tkaden left the meeting, they did not go to the inn where they had a room, but rather walked along the shoreline of the lake. The gathering darkness hid their actions from unobservant folk, but one man who watched from a distance was Theofinn. The aged druid did not follow them on foot, but from the hidden darkness of his upper chambers in a turret of the fortress, Theofinn followed them with his eyes. Theofinn loved the grandson of his sister, however, he wasn't sure he trusted the shaman who walked beside him. He wondered at what plans might be spinning through that calculating mind. The further the two men walked the harder it became for Theofinn to see them in the gloaming light. He could see that the younger man stopped and waited while the older man continued to walk on. He was at the furthest ranges of Theofinn's vision, melting into the distant darkness, when Theofinn could briefly discern a human shape step out from the forest to meet them. Then they all dissolved from sight into the deepening darkness.

The darkness hid his conversation with this shadowy figure, but soon the old shaman and the young man walked back into view and made their way to Bridgett's Inn where they had their lodgings.

Dakatomi gave the innkeeper a hearty welcome when he came in the door and let it be known that they would have no need of a meal since they had eaten while in meeting with the chief. He was thinking to himself that it never did any harm to remind the common folk that you were connected to important people.

The innkeeper replied in a decidedly unimpressed way by asking if they would be wanting any breakfast in the morning, or would they be breaking fast with the "high and mighty chief"? Dakatomi sensed he had overplayed the significance of the event and made light of his effort to impress by responding, "It would be nice to eat his food for free again, but he said he had no need of us till after breakfast. And even more so, you gave us such a feast this past morn, we doubt he could rival you." It never hurts to compliment those who provide for you. That thought was obviously more appreciated by the innkeeper as he promised to match the previous feat on the morrow.

They made their way up the wooden stairs to the second floor where they had their room. When they closed the door, Tkaden said to Dakatomi, "I don't know what to think."

"About what?"

"About everything and anything. To start with, I came with you to Dunsheelin because you convinced me that I was so important to our future. I wasn't so sure. And now, with Skoth proclaimed to be the one, I am even less sure what I am here for."

"It's not wrong to wonder."

"Well, I do wonder. And, you know, for a shaman, you sometimes have an infuriating way of not really providing an answer."

"Do you need an answer for everything?"

"C'mon, Dakatomi, don't play the teacher with me

right now. You put me into this situation. It was your interpretation of Nokomis' visit and her words that landed me in this spot."

"Young friend, I still believe it to be true. You are the true blending of our people Wabanaki and Celt. You are of this land. You are of our traditions. They may look to this young Skoth, but it is you that will lead our people in the way Nokomis has foretold."

"And what of the dark friend you talk with? Do you agree with all he says? Do you wish for conflict with our Celtic friends?"

"It is not something I wish for, but in the generations they have been here, they have grown in size and number while we have not."

"But have we diminished? Could we not grow in peace? Could we not become one people in this land?

Dakatomi hesitated before responding, "That indeed is how they interpret the prophecy of Thorfall, and also the visit of Nokomis. But Malsum's words are not to be ignored. He sees those same prophecies as portending the gradual diminishment of our people until we are so blended with these recent invaders that all of whom we have been will be lost. Is that what you wish to see?"

"No. Of course not. But who is to say he is right.?"

"Exactly! And who is to say he is wrong? He has claimed the gods speak to him. Perhaps he has the greater claim to truth."

Long they discussed in this fashion. Even after taking off their outer clothing and laying down on their beds for the night they continued this discussion, but in the end they came to no conclusion.

Chapter 6 - The Women of the Sauna

It was a gathering of the wise women of the clan that met that evening in the privacy of the women's sauna. The name for the women leaders of the people was no accident, for it was in the evening, after the work of the day had been laid aside, that these women would spend some time in a sauna cleansing their bodies and discussing the affairs of the clan. Some say that the tradition came from Scandinavia far to the east; others say it descended from the sweat house traditions of the Wabanaki. The truth was probably some of both, but what was certain truth was that it was often within the sauna that the real decisions affecting the lives of the people were frequently made.

In the sweat room, made of boards planked from native oak and cleanly overlapped to make good seals that would keep the heat and humidity in, sat the elderly ladies who were called the Women of the Sauna. One of them poured more water over the hot rocks and steam filled the enclosure. They sat naked on the smooth wooden benches, saying little and soaking up the heat while the sweat washed out the grime of a day's work. Finally Auntie Kati questioned out loud, "Well, I'm wondering when those girls of Unaine's will make their appearance. After all that went on in the Great Hall today, I am expecting them to show up soon."

At that moment, there was a quick rapping on the door, a short pause and then the door opened briefly as Teite, Leesha, and Enat hustled in and closed the door. They had, of course removed their clothing in the outer antechamber of the sauna before entering, but with their towels they did carry their satchels that contained their special relics in with them. The four women already in the sauna moved together to make room for the younger women.

"It's about time you showed up," said Auntie Kati. "We've been expecting you."

Teite was the oldest, but it was usually Leesha who took the lead in situations like these. She spoke up, "And greetings to you as well, Auntie. If we had known you were waiting for us, we would have come sooner. I'm so sorry we missed your message inviting us."

"Humph. Well, you are here now. So, you might as well settle in for a few minutes, get relaxed, and then we can discuss the events of the day."

They did, indeed, relax and relish in the steam of the sauna for several minutes, before Gwen, who had a much less prickly nature than Kati, said, "It's time dears. Why don't you go ahead and share what happened today."

The three young women first related the events that have transpired in the Great Hall. There were only a few questions asking for more information or clarification from the older women as the tale unraveled. This surprised Leesha, who was doing most of the talking, until she remembered that Gwen often worked in the kitchen of the Great Hall. No doubt she had her own ways of knowing what happened there and had already shared it with the others.

When the time came to sharing the items from their mother, Teite took over as the narrator, "Then there is this to share with you." She motioned to their satchels. "Each one of us has in our bag something special that Ma left for us. We want to tell you about them and to get your thoughts about them." She started to reach into her bag to take the sack of Runes out.

Gwen held up her hand and said, "There is no need to show us. We have known about them for a long time. Our sister, your mother, Jeni, was entrusted to give them to you when the time was right. Now is certainly the right time for you to have them."

Long into the night they talked. Many thoughts they shared. Many heated rocks were steamed. As they sat together the women of the sauna shared what insights they had into each of the special relics that the younger women carried. They also reaffirmed that Leesha and Enat should stay close to Skoth and give him sound advice, while Teite should use her knowledge and work with Neal and the scholars in the more academic search beginning here at Dunsheelin.

Finally, when all was said that needed to be said, the women filed out of the sauna and into the dressing chamber. They made small talk as they dressed and prepared to go to their separate lodgings. They were saying their good-byes when they heard the commotion.

Chapter 7 - Boat House Bust

The three young men had walked out of the meeting and made their way to a favorite tavern, Brendan's Boat House. It was a typical night at Brendan's. The sun had set, and the establishment had its usual crowd. They were boisterous and loud. It had been a hard day of summer work for most of them, and with good food and ale in their bellies they reveled in an atmosphere of satisfaction. The room was filled with tables of men and women enjoying good conversation and laughter.

When the young men walked into Brendan's they were greeted loudly by several of the folks, and room was made for them at one of the tables. They had no opportunity for privacy or quiet conversations as their group of friends quickly pulled them into the revelry of the evening. Perhaps they should have noticed the table of strangers in the far corner of the room, but with the warm evening, the stout ale, and the merriment of their friends they paid scant attention to such details.

Hearty stories, free-flowing laughter, and robust song carried them through the evening. Skoth, Neal, and Karl engaged in the entertainment of the evening with obvious enjoyment, although there were a few moments when Skoth seemed to slip away and slip inside his thoughts.

It was during the singing of one of the traditional ballads recounting the ancient settling of Eirgalon in the time of Fergus that the unexpected happened. Unaine and Erik were pushing their way through the entrance door (apparently they had had their fill of the Wandering Woman and had decided to come and check out Brendan's Boathouse), and the crowd was beginning the rousing chorus lines of the ballad when a knife came slashing through the air toward Skoth. It was spinning artfully through the air sure to impale itself deeply into Skoth's back, but it never reached the intended victim. As fate would have it, Neal was raising his mug of ale in salutation and that deflected the knife off its course and high into the air. It flipped high in the air and then onto the table in their midst, standing upright as it embedded its tip into the table and quivered to stillness.

Neal's mug clattered to the floor spilling the frothy ale and Neal spilled forth a string of curses as he clutched his bleeding hand. The table in the dark corner of the room erupted into a flurry of action. Men were jumping to their feet with weapons drawn. Chairs and tables were upended, as the occupants of that far table in the dark corner came rushing across the crowded room.

Erik knew something was amiss the moment he pulled the door open. His eyes caught the flash of the spinning knife and it was as if time slowed for the veteran warrior. In one fluid motion he sprang forward drawing his sword. He was running past the table of the young men and slashing into the attacking men before either the young men or the attackers realized what was happening. He had already cut down the two leading assailants before Unaine and then the others joined him in parrying with the other two men and pushing them back into the corner from which they had sprung. They had them cornered.

Erik shouted at them, "Throw down your weapons!"

Normal men would have given up the fight and cast their weapons down, but these were not normal men. They took a final step backward into the corner and then turned toward each other, and as if united in mind and purpose slashed their swords into each other's throats. No confessions would they make as they crumpled to the floor in death.

Bedlam ruled the moment in Brendan's Boathouse. Some patrons went shouting out into the street, others shouted for men to tend to the men Erik had dispatched to the floor, and yet others scrambling to make order of a room filled with the chaos of a bloody fight.

Erik looked around the room. He didn't waste much time looking at the last two fighters. There was not much use in wasting time crying over their spilled blood. Neither of them would ever be speaking of their deeds. But Erik did look for the two men bleeding and moaning on the floor behind him. One was bleeding out from an artery in his leg and would no doubt soon die from loss of blood.

Erik dismissively said, "Looks like that one will soon be making his way to Hel. But before he leaves us you can try to get something from him."

The dying assailant spat at him and feebly tried to reach out for the dagger in his belt, but soon his eyes glazed over and he drifted into oblivion.

The other attacker was being held on the ground by several men, as one of them tied a tourniquet around his arm to temporarily stem the bleeding from where Erik's sword had severed his hand. Erik strode over to him and holding his sword over his chest said to him, "Speak up, you maggot, what are you about?"

The man clenched his mouth tightly shut and Erik was about to drive his sword into the man's heart when Erik felt a pressure on his arm. He looked up and into Unaine's eyes.

"Hold, my friend. Let others work their way with this man. You have done your share this night."

"As you wish, Chief."

"Tis good. Step aside and let them bind this man." Turning to a young man in the crowd, Unaine said, "You, Ralf, run to Theofinn in his tower. Tell him what has happened here, and tell him to expect this prisoner in short order."

With a quick reply, "Yes, Sir!" Ralf was out the door and on his way.

Unaine rapidly scanned the remaining occupants of alehouse's common room and said, "Karl, you escort these men in getting this prisoner over to the tower. Neal, come here and let's have a look at that hand. Perhaps we'll have to send for a healer to bind it."

One of the women, who had been celebrating with the crowd before the commotion began, spoke up, "No need for that, Chief. I'm the best there is. If I can't clean it and fix it up, it can't be done."

"Thanks, Tillie. I didn't notice that you were here. But take care. And no one touch that knife," he said as he pointed to the knife still stuck in the table. "A knife thrown by an assassin could well have something nasty on it."

"I'll be careful," she replied and went to look at Neal's hand.

Skoth, who had said nothing to this point, now said,

"Assassin? Who would he be trying to kill?

Erik, never one to mince words, said, "Who do you think, you idiot! That knife was heading straight for the middle of YOUR back!"

"What? What are you talking about? Why me?"

"Are you daft, boy?"

Unaine interrupted, "Easy Erik. Skoth, son of Bold, is no fool. It will dawn on him soon enough."

The mention of his heritage was enough to ground Skoth's thoughts. His mind thought, "Oh, I wasn't thinking of that," but he said nothing out loud. He just gave a sheepish grin.

"Your life has changed, young man. You no longer belong just to yourself; you belong to all of us now. Your life is not your own. I know something of how you feel. I remember when the realization hit me. It will take some getting used to."

"What am I to do?"

"Well, first, I suggest you come with me to Theofinn's Tower and have a little conversation with our guest."

"Aye, but what about Neal?"

Unaine turned to Tillie who had been working on Neal's hand, "Tillie, what do you make of the wound? Will he live?"

"Aye, my lord," she responded with a laugh, "Tis a right bloody cut, it is, but it should heal up just fine. I've cleaned it well enough, but I can't tell if there was anything vile on the blade to infect it. I'll keep checking when I change the dressing, but I suggest you take that blade with you to Theofinn and have him inspect it to see if there might be something on it."

"That we will! Skoth, Neal - the two of you come with us. Let's go visit our guest."

Erik grabbed a towel from the bar and used it to pull the knife from the table and remarked, "A pretty piece of work this blade is. I'd like to take a closer look at it myself when old Theo is done with it."

With that, they said their farewells and were making their way to the door when in rushed the three sisters. They all started questioning at once, but when Unaine held up his hand with its palm facing them, they surprisingly went silent. With a crook of his finger he beckoned them to follow him. Again, surprisingly, they meekly and quietly followed him.

Chapter 8 - Talk in the Tower

When they arrived at Theofinn's Tower, the assailant had already been strapped to a sturdy chair, which was sitting in the center of the common room in the base of the Tower. His captors had tied him securely to the chair and then withdrawn. There was a tourniquet tightened around his right arm and his stump was wrapped with bloody bandaging. His eyes were slightly glazed as his body was fighting the trauma and shock of the injury. Every few moments he would grimace in agony as nerve endings of his severed arm sent throbs of pain shooting through his body. Theofinn, standing several feet in front of him with his arms crossed, was eyeing him over.

Theofinn looked past the prisoner to the entrance of the room where Unaine and his entourage were entering the room. Their faces were set with grim determination. With a slight motion of his head Theofinn indicated they were to stay behind the prisoner, so Unaine paused and kept his entourage out of sight of the prisoner. Theofinn took a step closer to him, which made the man's eyes lift and focus on him. He groaned in pain, and then feebly spat at the old druid.

"Just kill me and be done with it!"

Theofinn sighed in response, "A most tempting request. But unfortunately, no. Not exactly what I have in mind."

The prisoner again spat at him, only to end up wincing in pain as the action pulled on his bonds and aggravated his injuries to send a new wave of pain pulsing through his body.

The druid muttered, "Poor, poor, soul," and turning, he shuffled with feigned arthritic pain to a cabinet behind him. There he rummaged through the shelves and drawers until he had assembled a small bowl filled with a potpourri of dried plants. With his body shielding his actions from the others in the room, they could see that he made some sort of quick motion with his arm, and suddenly there was smoke. He turned toward them and they could see the mixture in the bowl was smoldering with small flames. They could smell the sweet scent of the mugwort and amaranth leaves as it filled the room. Theofinn slowly made his way toward the center of the room. Many of the others noted his slow progress and wondered what was going on because while he was old and no longer spry, he was certainly no cripple to be hobbling like this.

Then Theofinn muttered, loud enough for the others - and the prisoner - to hear, "You'll pardon the scent of this sweet herb. Folks rouse this aching old body out of bed and it needs some relief. And as for you, my unasked for guest, you will excuse me if I set it behind you - I wouldn't want you to be spitting in it."

With that he placed it directly behind the man, close so that captive would get the full effect of it as it ventilated upward to the air vent in the center of the ceiling, while the perimeter inhabitants of the room would get little effect. Mugwort is, of course, a healing and mild mood-enhancing plant the Celts had brought with them to Eirgalon, but who (other than the master druid himself) knew what it was laced with on this night. Theofinn shuffled again over to side of the room and slowly dragged a chair towards the prisoner. He settled himself onto the chair and then sat in front of him and then let his stare settle on the man for a long time.

Finally Theofinn spoke, "It looks like you are in quite a predicament, young fellow. Do you know who I am?"

The prisoner's eyes focused on Theofinn, and after a short pause he spoke, "You're one of those pale shamans. You have no power over me, old man."

"Ahhh. So you say. Then you have no fear of me," said the druid as he leaned back in his chair and smiled, then he said, "Oh, by the way, are you feeling any pain in that missing hand yet?"

The power of suggestion is an awesome thing, or perhaps it was some other magic that old Theofinn was working, for immediately the prisoner looked down at the stump of his arm and roared in obvious pain.

"Oh, my," said Theofinn, "Did I just do that? Perhaps it would help if you told me your name."

"It feels like it is burning! Make it stop. My name is Saronatom. They call me Tom. Now make it stop."

"Aye, Tom. Relax a bit. The pain will ease." said Theofinn, and then he cupped his hands to his mouth and acted as if he was blowing into them and then opened them downward as if he was releasing something.

The grimace of pain left Tom's face and a look of surprise appeared. He began to believe that the pale shaman was in control of his pain.

It wasn't long before Tom had revealed who he was and what he was doing in Dunsheelin. He named himself one of Malsum's men and described his task as sending the young man Skoth to the land of the dead. When pressed to reveal more about Malsum and the purpose for this deed it became apparent to all present that he knew little beyond the general details. He was not the leader of the assassins, but the most menial of their members, and knew but little of their plans.

Theofinn gave orders for a couple of his apprentices to unbind Tom and tend to his wounds, and then to make sure he was safely locked up and guarded in one of the tower rooms. Leading his group of observers out of the room, he took them to his conference room where they could discuss this situation in more detail.

They quickly settled themselves around the table in Theofinn's conference room. It was much smaller than the Great Hall's conference table, and the chairs were less ornate, but it was large enough for their needs and they all found a place: Theofinn, Unaine, Erik, Skoth, Karl, Neal, Leesha, Enat, and Teite. Once settled, all eyes turned to Unaine, but he said nothing. Instead he turned his eyes to Skoth and waited.

Skoth breathed deeply, and then spoke, "I'm not sure what to make of all this. I never thought when this day started that it would end with a knife hurtling toward my back. Theofinn, I would value your thoughts on what has just happened."

The men who were present, simply nodded, as if this was the most logical and expected comment Skoth could make. Theofinn surprised him with his response, "Well, my young chief, it seems that this Malsum fellow, whoever that may be, either has a strong dislike for you or doesn't want you to succeed on your quest."

Unaine, still Chief of his people even though he had anointed Skoth to the kingly quest, added, "Yes, indeed. It seems you have an adversary in addition to a quest. Your life just got more interesting and more complicated, I would say."

Erik, starting to act a bit protective of his young charge, spoke up, "Now don't be scaring the youngster you old bags of skin. I taught him how to fight. He knows the first step in a fight is to know his opponent. He'll find ways to learn about this Malsum character and what he is up to."

Leesha, who had been holding her tongue for she considered a long time, added, "We can help him with that. He's not alone."

Skoth looked at her and nodded. He knew she was right, but he didn't really want to say that to her. Now Erik asked, "Does that include our Wabanaki friends? Maybe they are in league with this Malsum. Could they be behind this?"

"Good question, Erik," said Unaine, "There is that possibility, though I hope not. I rather like that young Tkaden."

Hours of conversation and conjecture followed. It was late into the night when Skoth said abruptly, "Enough. That's enough for now. We'll hash out more details in the morning, but for now I think we better get some sleep. We'll meet at the Great Hall mid-morning as we had planned. None of you are to speak a word of this night to Tkaden or Dakatomi.

Beyond what they hear on the street, I don't want them knowing about this. I want to see their reaction when they learn of it."

Theofinn smiled and said, "Wise move, young Skoth. Perhaps the old Chief is right about you. May I suggest that you also stay here for the night. I've some guest quarters available. It might be better for you to avoid your own quarters for the night."

Erik added, "He's right about that, you know. And if you don't mind, Theo, I'll bunk here for the night, too." A smirk crept across Unaine's face as he glanced toward Erik, for he knew Erik was already taking his task to heart and that even though he might be loath to admit it, he did care about the boy. When Erik saw Unaine's look, he harrumphed and turned quickly away.

The others nodded their assent, and with assurances that they would be at the Great Hall in the morning, they departed.

Chapter 9 - Breakfast and a New Day

Dakatomi and Tkaden were warmly greeting by the innkeeper's wife when they entered the common room in anticipation of a hearty breakfast. While the meal didn't surprise them, it was as hearty and savory as they expected, the conversation and information did. There was no shortage of folk at the breakfast table that wanted to gossip about the events at Brendan's Boathouse the previously evening. Dakatomi listened attentively, and even asked a few probing, yet innocently framed, questions during the course of the meal. By the end of the meal, and by the time that they had to make their way to the Great Hall for their meeting, they had gained a thorough history of the night's events leading up to the time when the prisoner and others arrived at Theofinn's Tower. Nothing definitive was known about the events that transpired after that.

When they arrived at the Great Hall, Unaine and his girls were just getting up from the table where they had moments before finished their breakfast. Neal and Karl were coming into the hall from the kitchen entrance as Dakatomi and Tkaden came in from the front entrance. No doubt thought Dakatomi, the young men were simply trying to scavenge a bit more food prior to the work of the day. Dakatomi immediately noticed the bandaged hand of Neal, and the tired look in his eyes. From the breakfast conversations, he knew there was a suspicion that the blade of the knife had been poisoned and now he wondered if that is what he was seeing in Neal's eyes.

As they were greeting their hosts, more people (Theofinn, Skoth, and Erik) came in behind them. The staff of the Great Hall scurried about cleaning off the remnants of the breakfast table and making sure the conference table and chairs were arranged for the morning meeting.

In short order they had settled themselves around the large table. As host of the gathering in the Great Hall of Dunsheelin, Unaine called the meeting to order, but without hesitation he looked to Skoth to give the meeting leadership and direction.

Skoth, taking seriously his role as a leader, began by saying, "A bright summer morning it is, but dark and devious plots are at play. The events of last night warn us of the danger surrounding us."

Skoth was carefully watching Dakatomi as he spoke, but Dakatomi gave nothing away by his reaction. He skillfully addressed Skoth, "If I may interrupt. As Tkaden and I broke fast this morning at the guesthouse, we heard much about an altercation at an alehouse. You were the center of it. I'm sure much is just gossip, but how much is true, I know not. Would you be so kind as to share a brief summary of what really happened?"

Unaine recognized the sly way Dakatomi directed the conversation; so that by being told the story, they would know to reveal no more of it - if indeed they were a part of the more of it. He was about to respond when Skoth replied, "If you don't mind, I'll let Theofinn recount the story. I'm sure he will tell you the important details. I might wander off track a bit. I've been a bit distracted lately."

Unaine smiled inwardly, thinking to himself that

Skoth was no one's fool. He might look and act a little foolish at times, but the quick move to let the master druid tell the tale was a wise course of action. Theofinn would give nothing away.

And so Theofinn told the basics of the alehouse attack and Dakatomi learned nothing new. To the intelligent observer, watching the two old wise men converse was like watching a game of Skaktafl (which some folks were starting to call "chess"). Theofinn told the Wabanaki nothing of the injured man's words of Malsum, and Dakatomi gave no hint that he knew more than what was told. The young folk, including Tkaden, were all smart enough to keep their mouths shut and to let the older men carry the conversation.

After the update was given, Skoth said, "Thank you, Master Theofinn, now let's get back to the reason we were to meet this morning. It appears that history has thrust upon us, well, me specifically, but I think it is for all of us, a quest of some importance. I don't know what will happen in the future, but this is what I will do at this point in time. I will be leaving Fada Innis and traveling up the Mahakentuck. With me will go Erik, Karl, Leesha, Enat, and Tkaden. If they consent, that is. I am asking Neal and Teite to stay here and do what they do so well, research. They will, of course, have the wise guidance of Theofinn to aid them."

"And what would you have of me?" asked Unaine.

"Chief, you are still my king. I give you no orders. I ask that you continue to give your support and advice, that you lead our people of Fada Innis, and that you permit your daughters to travel with us."

With a hearty laugh, Unaine said, "Well said. You

shall, of course, have what you ask for."

Leesha could contain herself no longer, "Now wait a minute, your daughters need no such 'permission' to go wherever and whenever we please. We have already decided - on our own - what we will be doing!"

"Oh," said Unaine, "and what is it that you will be doing?"

"Well, going with him," she sputtered, "but it's not because we have your permission! It's because we are deciding to do it!"

"Ah, well. So be it as you say, my daughter. You choose to tag along with him. I just want him to know that HE has my permission to take you with him."

Skoth could see Leesha was annoyed and so said, "It's alright, Leesha. I was just being a bit formal. For the record, you know. Of course, I, better than anyone, know that you have a mind of your own and will do whatever you want. You don't have to get so worked up about it."

"Humph! Well, all right then. You know we'll be going with you. You may not realize it, but I think we will be a help on this quest. Perhaps one day you will appreciate us, rather than consider us to be what Father calls, 'tag-alongs'. But it isn't us you should be asking now. Perhaps it is Tkaden you should be asking. He may not want to take his chances with you."

Tkaden entered the conversation by saying, "I don't want to get involved in any family disputes, but I do want to go with you, Skoth. I think we have an interesting time ahead of us."

Skoth said, "Well, then, it is decided and agreed to."

Erik interrupted, "I'm not trying to tell you what to do, your royal highness, but I personally would like a couple more strong arms with us if we are heading up river. Could I at least take a couple of my men with us? You know, just to do the paddling."

"Erik, please leave off the 'king' business. Just call me by my name. Maybe you could lay off some of the more derogatory names you've used for me over the years, but I'm all right with 'Skoth'. And, no, I don't think we want to take any of your men. At least we don't want to look like we are taking them. After last night, I don't even want people to know we are leaving together. We are going to leave Dunsheelin separately and meet up at Cold Springs. Erik, you can send a couple of men you trust to go there and get some transportation for us to cross the Fadis Innis Sound to the mainland. The rest of us will meet up there in a couple of days."

Dakatomi offered to go with them, since it really wasn't much out of the way for him, but Skoth politely declined. Theofinn jumped into the conversation and asked Dakatomi to stay a few days and to have some conversations with him about the history of the Wabanaki people. Not all the details were worked out at this time, but the basics were set in motion. The Chief's daughters were said to be traveling out of town on some Women's Circle business (which in fact they were), Karl was said to be taking Tkaden on fishing trip, Skoth was said to be going to check out a team of horses he had heard were for sale out on one of the western farms of Fadis Innis, and Erik, well, he often went out of town on the Chief's orders so no one would question his departure.

Chapter 10 - Departures

Two days later, in the hazy fog of early morning on a mid-summer's day Karl and Tkaden walked down the road into the rising sun. They were carrying packs, which to a casual glance appeared to be filled with fishing gear. As they encountered an occasional early riser they would make small talk and banter about who was going to catch the most fish. To all appearances, they were fishing buddies on their way to a favorite fishing spot. But appearances can be deceiving, and as they worked their way east around Lake Ronkonkoma they failed to stop at any traditional fishing spots. They followed the road as it turned north along the eastern shore of the lake, and when they came to the crossroads at the northeastern reach of the lake, they took the western road.

Later that morning, each of the young ladies, Leesha and Enat, filled up a traveling pack with clothing and personals item they could carry on their backs (a typical look for them when they were traveling away from Dunsheelin), and having said their good-byes to their father and sister they climbed aboard a farmer's wagon, whose driver had been patiently waiting for them, and headed down the road that led to the broken lands at the west end of the fair isle of Fadis Innis.

After the noon meal, Erik exited the Great Hall attired in his traveling clothes - which, to be honest, varied little from the way he was normally dressed. At the door he turned and said to the Chief in a formal manner, "Health and prosperity to you and the people," and then in a much less formal way, "Oh, keep yourself out of trouble while I'm not here to look after you." Then, with his sword at his side and his pack, bow, and shield slung over his back, he ambled on down the road heading north along the western shore of Lake Ronkonkoma.

Of the travelling fellowship, Skoth was the last one to leave Dunsheelin. He had spent the early afternoon at Theofinn's tower in private conversation with the old master druid and king's counselor. No doubt many questions were asked, many suggestions given, numerous words of advice shared. Skoth left the tower with a sort of dazed look on his face, not an altogether unusual look for him, as he made his way back to his room to grab his bag for the journey.

He was surprised when he stopped at his room to grab his knapsack and traveling apparel to see Neal and Teite seated on his bed waiting for him. Neal looked a bit more rested and healthy, though his hand was still bandaged, while Teite looked a little more worried than she usually did.

Teite said, " You weren't going to be trying to sneak off and leave without saying goodbye to us, were you?"

"Oh, no. Of course not, I was just coming to pick up my pack, and then I was going to track you down and say good-bye," replied Skoth.

"Well, it would be just like you to run off without thinking of us, but we knew you'd make one last stop here before you go, so we thought we'd wait here. I also wanted to say good-bye in private because I," and with a glance at Neal, she changed that to, "we, want you to cast the runes from this special set I have with me."

"Why?"

"Because they are from my mother, and I think they might have something important to tell us. Maybe it will be something that helps you."

With a sigh, Skoth said, "so be it," and he pulled over the one chair in his room to sit next to them.

She pulled out the small rune bag and cloth from the satchel that she always carried with her and spread the runecloth out neatly on the end of the bed. She asked Skoth to hold the bag in his hands and to think of the journey he had in mind. When he handed it back she asked them to avert their eyes while she pulled the runes out of the bag and laid them face down on the cloth. Then she asked them to turn and watch. She closed her eyes, reached out and touched a rune. Opening her eyes, she turned it over. It was Jara.

She said, "This means that you will draw four runes. I might also add, that this rune symbolizes birth and that seems to fit. This is the 'birth' of a new endeavor for you and for us all."

Skoth said, "Aye, tis that. Just tell me what to do."

"Draw three runes, any of them, and then turn them over. The first will tell us about what the current situation is, the second will suggest a course of action, and the third will foretell the outcome that will result from that action."

Skoth laughed nervously and said, "If you are serious about this, then maybe you should have had me do this before I decided what to do. What if I just made a big mistake? And didn't you say to draw four runes? What about the fourth?"

"Yes, I am serious. And if it were a mistake, wouldn't you want to know now?

"And the fourth?"

"The fourth is a rune of succor. It speaks of what may help you in your quest."

Skoth exhaled loudly and reached out, and in turned picked up and laid down three runes: Tir, Rad, and Ur. He hesitated when it came to the fourth rune, reaching for one, then stopping, then moving his hand back slowly over all of them. Finally he reached down and picked up his final rune, Lagu. He held it briefly, turning it over in his hand before it laid it near the rest.

Teite said, "This looks interesting. Are you ready to hear what the energy of the spirit world is saying?"

"Go ahead."

"The first rune is Tir, and it indicates conflict. It tells us that you are in a great battle. I think we can be assured that this is a true quest you are pursuing and that you have adversaries you must fight. As I read the second, Rad, it suggests a course of action for you to take. It suggests that you must make a journey. Since we are already aware that you are indeed embarking on a journey, it appears to reaffirm your choice to take such action."

Skoth, trying to be gentle, said, "Well, Teite, so far there is nothing new here."

"Maybe, and maybe not. The runes are always open to some interpretation. Sometimes they reflect realities of which we aren't aware of immediately. For example, Rad could be indicating a spiritual, or inner, journey. Unaine and Theofinn are convinced this is a key historical moment for our people, but this is your rune cast, and it may well be that you are to undertake some kind of inner journey. Be aware of that possibility.

"Rest assured. I'm ready. You know more about it than I do."

Teite smiled and said, "Well, thank you. That is one of the smartest comments you have made in quite a while."

Neal, who had been sitting silently, just groaned and said, "C'mon, Teite. Don't go acting like Leesha now. Explain the third rune. What does Ur indicate the outcome of this quest will be?"

"This is a little bit harder to interpret. Generally speaking Ur indicates that a large challenge lies ahead. It is a challenge that you should meet with determination. If you have stamina, you will be successful. I stress that this is your rune cast. Ur tells us it is something you must do for yourself."

Skoth looked puzzled and asked, "Then why the fourth rune. If it is something I must do for myself, then why a rune for help."

"Accepting help, does not negate the fact that you are accomplishing something. It simply means you are finding ways and people that help you achieve it. You must still take action. You have the responsibility, you have the consequence."

"Yeah, you're right. So, what does the fourth rune say?"

"It is Lagu. It is not what I expected. It has elements of listening to your inner voice, that I did expect. But the manner in which you drew and laid it indicate that it is not your inner voice, but a female one that will help you."

"Why is that unexpected? I have you three sisters all

helping me?"

"True, but this is someone yet unknown."

In a somewhat sarcastic manner, Skoth said, "Great. Just what I need. Another female that wants to boss me around."

Teite laughed softly, but said, "I don't know about bossing you around, but helping you in some way . . . of that I am sure."

Karl spoke up, "It is time for you to be off, isn't it?"

Skoth said, "Right you are. I should be going. I'll grab my gear and go," and smiling, added, "You two, keep an eye on events for me here. Send me word if you find out something important that I need to know before I return."

They said their brief farewells and then Skoth shouldered his pack and sword, and he was off on his journey.

Chapter 11 - Surprise Encounter

A few light cumulus clouds drifted through the bright afternoon sky as Skoth sauntered down the western road heading out of Dunsheelin. He had tried to put on a happy and carefree face and whistled a bit as he walked. To all appearances he was simply on one of his frequent jaunts to the western end of Fadis Innis. As he passed travelers on the road and crofters in their fields and by their cottages, he gave them his normal waves and greetings. Nothing about him or the countryside seemed unusual or out of place. That is, not until he came of the grove of trees where the road passed under the branches of some tall oaks.

There he saw the old Wabanaki shaman, Dakatomi, sitting against the trunk of one of the huge oak trees calmly puffing on a long-stemmed pipe - and it was good tabac from the smell of it! As Skoth approached, the old man motioned for him to come and sit beside him, but said nothing.

Skoth said, "I didn't expect to see you here."

"No, I imagine you didn't."

"Well, it is a nice place to relax on a summer day and have a smoke. I suppose you didn't have anything better to do."

Dakatomi smirked at that. There was something about the young man that amused him. He said, "Not at all. Nothing better to do. I was spending a couple of days visiting with old Theofinn, but something came up, and he didn't have any time for me this afternoon. Please, sit with me for a few minutes."

Skoth was never one to be rude (well, not

intentionally at least) so he shrugged off his pack and sat down next to him. He thought about pulling out his pipe and asking for some of that fine tabac Dakatomi obviously had, but held his tongue. The old man seemed to read his mind and held out his pipe, offering it to Skoth to take a few puffs - which Skoth obligingly (and appreciatively) did.

After exhaling it and handing the pipe back, he said, "I have to admit, you Wabanaki sure do know your tabac."

"Indeed. There is quite a bit we do know. I'm glad to hear one of the younger Celtic generation acknowledge it." He replied with a smile.

With a chuckle Skoth said, "You have a point. Sometimes we young folks think we know it all." He hesitated and then went on. "You didn't really come out here this afternoon just to take a walk and have a smoke beneath this old oak tree, did you? You figured I'd be going this way and you wanted a few words with me, right?"

"You do have some insight, young man. I have come to see that. No, I didn't take this walk for pleasure. I did, in fact, want to see you. Are you curious as to why?"

"Certainly."

"But you aren't going to ask?"

"Ask too many questions of a wise man and you get made a fool of. At least that's one lesson I learned from Theofinn. I figure you're the kind of man that will tell me what you want to, when you want to, as much as you want to. But not much more."

At that Dakatomi had to laugh, "You have a point."

"Thank you."

"Let me be blunt. We both know that I am not sure

you are the one to be the High King of Eirgalon."

Skoth nodded and said, "Yes, you made that clear at the meetings."

"You will have to prove yourself. There are other possibilities."

"Sure, I know you think Tkaden is the one."

"Perhaps he is. But there are also other possibilities before us."

"Like…?"

"As I said, you will have to prove yourself. Finding and dealing with such will show your mettle. You may be up to the challenge, but you may not."

"So, are you encouraging me, or warning me?"

Dakatomi gave a wry smile, "Now that is a good question. What do you think?"

"I think that, as the chief would say, the ship hasn't come in on that one."

"As you say. Perhaps it is not even on the horizon yet."

Skoth breathed a long sigh and said, "Well, thank you Master Shaman for the words, but I really must be going. I suspect you must too."

"Yes, without a doubt the honorable Theofinn is trying to find me. He has spent the last couple of days trying to keep his eyes on me. My disappearing this afternoon must have him a bit concerned."

Skoth was reaching to pick up his pack, when Dakatomi said, "Wait. One more thing."

Dakatomi then reached into his pocket and pulled out his tabac pouch. It was a fine deer leather pouch tooled with native beadwork and had a small trinket of metal attached to it. As Dakatomi reached out to hand it to him, Skoth had a sense of something move in the woods behind the shaman.

Dakatomi said, "I'd like you to have this little gift from me. Keep it with you. And remember my people when you have a smoke."

Surprised, but not one to turn down a gift, Skoth took it from him and placed it in his knapsack. The sensation of movement in the woods bothered him, but he said nothing about it. He did thank Dakatomi for the gift and promised to keep it and to remember. With farewells being said Dakatomi began walking back toward Dunsheelin. Skoth stood and watched him for a few moments and then turned his back to him and started to head back down the western road.

Chapter 12 - Through the Woods

The next several miles were filled with a couple hours of furtive glances by Skoth to the sides of the road. The woods along the road were broken by the numerous fields and homesteads of the small crofters that lived along the road. But there was always enough of the heavy summer foliage that made it impossible to see into the woods, and Skoth just couldn't shake the feeling that something was there. The sun was nearing the horizon by the time he came to the junction of the roads where one road continued west to the broken lands, and the other went north to village of Cold Springs. Skoth knew it would take nearly another hour of fast walking to make it to the village where he was to meet the rest of the group. It would be dark before he arrived. Without hesitation, but with a glance to all directions to make sure no one saw him take the Cold Spring road, he quickly made his way.

The woods seemed to close in about him as the sun set and the light diminished. He thought perhaps he should stop and visit overnight at one of the crofter's homes, but he wanted to get to his friends at Cold Springs. It was a bustling harbor village and no one would think twice of seeing him there.

He was approaching the stone formation named the Rock Pile. It was called that because it was a pile of jumbled rocks raising about thirty feet above the surrounding terrain. The snapping of a branch in the woods to his right brought his senses to full awareness. Turning his head in that direction, he saw a huge stag plunging out of the woods with its monstrous antlers lowered and charging at him. He was reaching for his sword, but it was doubtful he could have drawn it in time, when he heard an arrow go whistling by him and thump into the chest of the charging beast. The momentary stagger of the beast was enough to enable him to draw his sword and slash at the stag's head, just as another arrow found its mark, plunging into the deer's heart. With a gasp, the stag dropped to the ground in front of Skoth.

Skoth stepped back from it. He kept one eye on it while he turned slightly to the side to see who the archer might be. Even in the gloaming light he could make out Erik scrambling down the Rock Pile.

"Ho, there, my young friend. Looks like we've got meat for our supper tonight!"

Skoth stammered, "What? Erik, what are you doing here?"

"Gads, man! Is that any way to greet the guy who just saved you from being gored by that big fella there? And might I suggest you step up and slit his throat. Just to make sure he's really dead. He might just jump up and try to poke you again. Were you just trying to see how close he could get before you drew your sword? What were you daydreaming about? Perhaps some young lassie or something?"

By that time Erik had reached Skoth, unsheathed his hunting knife and stepped forward to begin the task of bleeding and dressing the deer.

"C'mon," he said, "we'll have time to talk about this later. Help me gut him and drag him back to our campsite over on the other side of the Rock Pile.

Skoth grunted an aye, they said a brief prayer of thanks to the deer for its life, and then they got to work on it. In short order they had gutted the beast, tied a cord around it and dragged it back to the campsite. Sko noticed that Erik had set up camp in a niche in the Rock Pile, on the northwestern exposure, which could not be seen from the road, and had a small fire already burning. Erik grabbed a couple of more pieces of wood that he had stacked near the fire and tossed them on to it.

Erik said, "If we're going to have some of this fresh venison tonight, we going to have to get this fire a bit hotter. Why don't you set your gear over there by mine and we'll set up a nice spit to roast a haunch of it, and then while it is cooking we can talk."

The men went about stoking the fire and building the spit, cutting and skinning the stag, and then starting some meat to roast over the fire. Some of the choicest cuts of the meat they wrapped in the deer hide and then hoisted it on a rope into a tree, so that any roving animals wouldn't get into it during the night. Finally, when they had finished their tasks, they sat by the fire and as the venison roasted on the spit, they were ready to talk.

Skoth waited silently for Erik. Erik, testing the young man's patience, said nothing for several minutes. They just watched the fire.

Finally Erik broke the silence, "Well then, Sko. It seems you did something to annoy that stag. Any idea about what it was?"

"No, but it was a strange afternoon. Ever since I left Dakatomi on the road I felt that there was something following me in the woods."

Erik raised an eyebrow at the mention of Dakatomi, but said nothing and let the young man continue.

"We talked by the grove of old oak trees just west of Dunsheelin and at the end I thought I saw some movement in the woods there, but I couldn't make anything out. Ever since then I had this sort of crawly feeling, as if someone was watching me."

Erik grunted, "Humph. Anything else strange?"

"Well, that crazed deer . . . and you being here. Both of those are strange."

"As for me, I thought it would be a good idea to meet you out here, so you being in Cold Springs with your friends wouldn't seem so noticeable. That deer, however, that was strange. Something sent it your way. I doubt it would have killed you, even taking you by surprise as it did. But it might have slowed you down a bit."

"What would have caused it charge me like that? I didn't do anything to it."

"There are, at times, strange occurrences that happen in this world, and powers that we don't always understand. I'm not sure exactly what, but some power attacked you through that stag. Oh, it was an ordinary enough deer, big brute that it was, but sure enough there was some malevolence behind it." He hesitated, then when on, "Well, at least we got some fine meat out of it! Let's eat!"

Their conversation dwindled into small matters as they set about enjoying the roast venison. Soon they arranged their bedding near the fire. They agreed to alternate taking watches during the night, with Erik taking the first watch.

Chapter 13 - Cold Springs

Skoth's sleep was punctuated by dreams of the stag charging him, and when dawn touched the sky with her fingertips of rose, Skoth was already up and putting his small cooking pot on the fire to brew a few cupfuls of spruce tea. There was nothing like the slightly sour, yet mildly bitter, taste of the spruce tea to bring flavor to the new day. Erik strode back into the campsite from the direction of the road and leaned over the brewing tea and inhaled deeply.

As he exhaled, he exclaimed a satisfied, "Aaahhh," and went on to say, "Well now, Sko, there are a few tasks you do right. How about a cuppa that tea for me?"

Skoth laughed and poured a cup for Erik and then one for himself. As they savored their morning drink they made plans for the day. Erik suggested that Skoth go directly to the docks and find the boat that Erik's men had waiting for them to take them across Fadis Innis Sound to the mainland, while he would go into the town and let the others know to head there as well. It seemed wise not to tarry long, but to move quickly away from people who might recognize them and ask too many questions. Skoth agreed to that course of action but let Erik know that first he intended to stop at the sacred spring, for which the town was named, and offer a few prayers. Erik agree to that for the pool was beyond the outskirts of the town, which actually was built on the shoreline but which drew its drinking water from the stream that ran through the woods for a half a mile from its source.

They cleaned up their campsite and then started

walking the road to Cold Springs. In addition to his normal pack, Erik shouldered the venison wrapped in the deer hide. Skoth looked at the old warrior and marveled at his strength.

Skoth asked, "Hey, Erik - what did you do with the rack from that stag?"

Erik grinned and said, "It seemed to me that it was appropriate to leave it here, so I took the head and antlers to the top of the Rock Pile and mounted it on a spruce pike that I wedged between some rocks. Tis a right fine lookout now. Maybe you'll see him before him before he sees you next time, should you come back this way." With that he chuckled and walked on.

In short order they approached the forested glen that surrounded the Cold Spring pool. There they parted, with Erik going down the road to the town and Skoth entering the secluded space of the sacred glen. He could feel distinctive aura about the place as he walked forward. It had the feeling of a sanctuary as the branches of the surrounding ash trees provided a vaulted ceiling and the sound of splashing water echoed through the glen. In front of him was a pool of crystal clear water. Out of the rocky shore on the far side of the pool tumbled an artesian spring. Opposite to the spring, the water spilled out of the pool and ran in a small stream out of the grave and down to the shore of Cold Spring Harbor. The ground nearest the pool was pebbled with small stones, which then gave way to woodland ferns and grasses as one moved away from the pool. He followed a path to the pool, where someone had obviously placed a few flat stones to kneel at the water's edge and a couple of larger boulders to be used as sitting stones.

He paused, then took off his pack and knelt down at the water's edge. He touched his forehead, then his lips, then his breast, (symbolically indicating the prayer that his thoughts and words would be true to his heart) and spoke an invocation, "Spirit of this place, face of the Divine. Keep protection near and danger far away. Keep hope within and doubt without. Keep light near and darkness far away. Keep peace within and keep evil out."

The he cupped his hands in the water and lifted a handful of water. He opened his hands and let the water splash back into the pool. A second time reached in and lifted his hands full of water. A second time he opened his hands and let it splash into the pool. A third time he cupped his hands, filling them with water, but this time he lifted them to his lips and drank the cold, sweet water.

At that moment a beam of sunlight seemed to pierce through the canopy of leaves and strike the bubbling spring. A small creature, a water sprite with the size and speed of a hummingbird, flew out from the waters of the spring. For a moment it hovered above the splashing waters, iridescent in the dappled sunlight. Then it flew straight at Skoth, striking him in the chest where he wore the King Rune on a cord around his neck. He felt a sharp and intense heat. He grabbed at the sprite, but by the time his hand reached his chest, both the pain and the sprite were gone. He opened his shirt to pull the necklace from beneath his clothes. The rune, which had been a polished grey stone with the rune etched in black upon it, was now a burnt amber. Even more to his amazement was the fact that when he looked upon the skin of his chest he saw that same rune was branded there.

He placed the rune back inside his shirt and fastened it, and then he bowed his head and remained kneeling in silent meditation for a few minutes. After a final fingertip touch to the waters of the sacred pool, he stood up, shouldered his pack, and walked down the path leaving the pool. He left with a smile on his face, peace in his soul, and determination in his heart.

While Cold Springs was a bustling harbor village, it wasn't difficult to find the way to the docks. The main road ran directly to the shoreline where there were several docks extending out into the water where several larger ships were moored. There were also several smaller boats that were pulled up on to the sandy beach.

Skoth could see Rolf, one of Erik's men, standing at the centermost dock. Tethered there was medium size karve preparing to sail. It was a single masted cargo vessel of about fifty feet in length and a beam of about twelve feet, which looked to be almost fully loaded with bundles of trade goods. It looked like it could handle five oars to a side, and Skoth could see several crewmen hefting a few more bundles into its hold. Rolf spotted Skoth and waved at him to come over.

Skoth made his way through the dockside activity. He made small talk with Rolf about the weather, and had begun listening to Rolf's commentary about the local taverns when Erik arrived with the other four members of the traveling party.

With a hearty voice Erik called out, "Ho there, Captain Svenson! Your passengers have arrived, we're ready to board and depart harbor at your pleasure!"

Captain Svenson, who had been fastening some items

near the rudder, stood up and replied, "Well and good that is. These are the final bundles. Then we'll be off. It looks like we'll be picking up a nice westerly breeze today. We may not have to do much oar-work to carry ourselves across the sound. Have your womenfolk sit in the center, on those bundles, and place your men on the rowing benches, three on each side, where they can be used if we need them."

Quickly they clambered aboard. Leesha and Enat sat on the bundles as directed. Erik, Rolf, and Jake settled in on one side of the ship, and Skoth, Karl, and Tkaden on the other. In short order, Captain Svenson and his crew of four, had the boat cast off and under sail for New Caledonia one of the largest of the Celtic cities on the coast of Eirgalon.

The winds, being favorable, meant no oars were needed as the karve crossed the sound, and by early afternoon the vessel had the coastline in sight. There was no conversation about the quest, only casual conversation, because they wanted no idle words to be passed on by the crewmen, who could all too easily overhear them. By mid-afternoon they were rounding the point and entering the river Oustona. New Caledonia lay on the western bank of the river. The captain had them using oars now and steered them into a dock near the southern end of the harbor. Soon they were docked and ready to depart the ship.

Chapter 14 - Arrival in New Caledonia

Their destination, New Caledonia, was larger than Dunsheelin but with a more diverse population. It was a Celtic community with a majority of its residents being descendents of the Norse-Celtic people who had migrated from Europe generations ago, but there were a considerable number of the Wabanaki people who lived amongst them, and with whom there had been frequent intermarriage throughout the generations. Both cultures did have historical tendencies of conflict and warfare, but also had strong family values and loyalty to their community. There might well have been serious conflicts and warfare in the early years of the Celtic migration and settlement if not for the fact that diseases had decimated the Wabanaki population. While the land had been heavily populated before the migration, the loss of population by the Wabanaki opened many lands for the new inhabitants. The Wabanaki had welcomed these new people and had even developed a largely peaceful co-existence with them, even to the extent of developing a blended culture of European and Wabanaki roots. The areas along the coasts tended to be more heavily populated by the Celts and mixed bloods, while the areas inland had populations that were a mixture of communities, some being mostly Celtic and some being mostly (if not entirely) Wabanaki.

Once the ship was securely moored, the passengers

climbed onto the dock. Erik handed a small pouch and whispered a few private words to his men, Rolf and Jake, and the two of them quickly walked off.

Erik turned to Skoth and said, "I know of a good inn not far from here where we could get lodging for the night, or for as long as you plan on staying here. Should we head that way? Or do you have other plans?"

Nodding his head, Skoth responded, "That sounds like a good idea. It's been a long day. A good meal, a nice bed, chance to hear the local news. That sounds good. Lead the way."

A few minutes later they were in front of the establishment called Tante's Inn and Table. It was a two storied building with a large kitchen and common room downstairs, and rooms for boarders up stairs. Erik said, "If you don't mind, I know the lovely lass that runs this establishment, so I'll just go ahead and get rooms for us. How long should I tell her we are planning on staying?"

Skoth smiled to himself when Erik made the comment about knowing the woman, but ignored the chance to comment on that and he said, "For sure, go ahead. See what you can get for us. I don't anticipate staying here for more than a couple of days, but can you see how flexible she is?"

Erik grinned and chuckled, "Aye, flexible. That be a good description of Susie. I'll see what I can do."

With that he led them into the inn. It had a welcoming air to it, with a nice homey feeling. The common room had several tables and there were already several townsfolk present who had completed their work for the day and were stopping in to eat at Tante's Table and to share a few mugs of ale. Erik went to talk to the woman behind the bar while the rest of them pulled up chairs and sat down around a table.

Within a minute a tall, and well-endowed woman of about forty years was at their table. Her bright blonde hair was tied in a thick braid and her smile was infectious. Skoth didn't even have time to stand up from the table before she had pulled him up and wrapped her arms around him in a bear hug. Skoth's eyes were bulging in surprise as he made eye contact with Erik who was following the woman and obviously enjoying himself as he saw Skoth's reaction.

The woman slowly released Skoth from the bear hug, but kept one hand on his arm, as she exclaimed, "Well, well, now. So this be Brian's boy. Ach, if you don't look just like him. The eyes, be a bit different, tis more green to be seen in yours, but you're his whelp. Sure enough, you are."

She looked past him to the young folks sitting around the table. Their mouths agape and their voices silent. Dumbstruck.

With nary a pause, she went on, "And you two young ladies. All grown up are you now, and such beauties! Unaine must be beating the young men away from you with a stick!"

Karl blushed and Leesha was the first of the young folk to find her tongue, "I'm sorry but I don't recognize you. And you would be?"

"Why I'd be Susie. And I'd be the owner of this fine establishment. I'd also be a friend of your fathers. I knew those two and Erik when they were no older than you are now. Those were the days. What interesting times we had."

Leesha said, "Tis a pleasure to meet you. So you're

the Tante this place is named after?"

"Oh no. The original Tante was my mother's auntie. Now there was a woman! But that is a story for another time. Before we get to the telling of tales, let's get you settled into some rooms and let you freshen up from your travel. Then you can come down and join us for the evening meal, such as it is."

She then led them up the stairs and showed them the rooms she had for them. Leesha and Enat she put in a comfortable room at the top of the stairs. It was typical room you might find in any inn and had two small single beds in it. There was a small window that looked out over the street to the front of the inn. Leesha and Enat stay in the room to get settled and Susie showed the young men to a room across the hallway. It was what she called the bunkroom. She explained that since they often had groups of travelers stopping in she had arranged one room of her inn with two bunk beds, so that four men could stay in the one room.

She turned to Erik and said, "Now, you can well enough stay with these young men, there's beds enough in here for all of you, but I do have this small room downstairs at the foot of the stairs and near the back door. I don't have anyone in there tonight, and you are welcome to use it. Free of charge of course."

Erik stroking his beard in a thoughtful manner, "Hmmmm, you say no charge. I might enjoy having a room to myself here. It might come in convenient. Sure, I'll do that."

Susie winked at him and said, "I thought you might." He winked back, "I figured you'd think so."

Skoth and Karl rolled their eyes at each other, and Tkaden, watching them, allowed a slight smirk to creep across his face.

Erik turned back to the young men and said, "There'll be times enough when we have to share sleeping quarters or campfires, I'll enjoy the bit of privacy while I can get it. Besides, I'm thinking it might be a good idea for you two, who have gotten into your share of trouble together over the years, to spend a little private time getting to know Tkaden a wee bit better."

Susie said, "We'll be starting to serve supper in about half an hour. See you then." With that said she looked them over again, smiled, and walked out of the room with Erik.

He turned around at the doorway and said to them, "Get settled in. See you down in the great room in half an hour, and bring the girls with you." And off he sauntered down the hallway following Susie.

Karl went over and shut the door, turned back toward them and said, "Let them go have their fun. I wanted to hear about what happened on your walk to Cold Spring. When Erik showed up at the inn to bring us to the ship he was carrying a hide of venison. He said something about the stag just jumped right into your path. So give us some details."

Skoth had no time to even begin an answer before there was a knock at the door and it came flying open with Leesha and Enat hurrying into the room and hastily shutting the door behind them.

"Finally! We're alone with no ears to overhear us. Now tell us all the details!" Leesha blurted out.

Enat added, "And don't skip any of the good stuff."

So Skoth related the events of the journey, but contrary to their request he did avoid mentioning certain items. He did not relate his conversations with Theofinn or all of the words of Dakatomi. He did however show them the tabac pouch Dakatomi had given him.

Tkaden turned it over in his hands and said, "This is beautiful beadwork and the smell of the tabac is pleasing, but I have to tell you: I have never seen Shaman Tomi use this pouch before. Even on our journey to Dunsheelin, he used a different pouch."

With a puzzled expression, Skoth said, "Hmm, he seemed to value it. And he referred to it as 'his'."

"Well, it is valuable, and maybe it is his, but I have never seen it before. Do you know what the little medallion on it means?"

"It looks like a raccoon to me."

"Azeban."

"What?"

Tkaden explained, "It looks like a image of Azeban, the trickster in the beliefs of our people."

"Trickster? So what was he trying to tell me?"

"Good question. I wish I could tell you what is behind this but I don't know. Shaman Tomi is a great one for posing problems, not for giving answers."

Leesha looked at it and said, "I don't know, Sko. I'm suspicious of the old man and suspicious of any gift he may give you. I'd be careful with that. I might not even keep it. What if he placed some sort of hex on it?"

Karl said, "Ah, Leesh, you're just worried about nothing. It's a fine pouch, with great tabac in it. Nothing to worry about!"

Skoth took the pouch back from Tkaden and said, "The elders always used to say not to look a gift horse in the mouth, but perhaps I'll be a bit watchful with this gift."

About the action of the water sprite he hesitated to tell them. He was still unsure of Tkaden, especially after the girls had so strongly voiced their concerns about Dakatomi. But in any case, there was no time to get into the telling of it now. They were expected downstairs. It was time for dinner.

Chapter 15 - Evening at Tante's

Supper in the common room of Tante's was a solid meal, almost as good as home cooking. The atmosphere was friendly amongst the lodgers and the locals who had come into enjoy the meal and ale. Conversations around the room revealed mostly local gossip, but there were questions about events on Fadis Innis, and there were occasional references to events across the sea where there were some hints of conflicts brewing between Celtic-Viking rulers of the Anglish Isles and the German kingdoms of the mainland. New Caledonia was a major seaport of the Celtic civilization that was spread across the Northern Atlantic and included the isle of Eire and the rest of the Anglish Isles so news of far events was to be expected. There were also a few negative comments voiced about the Haudenoshonee out in the western lands. Skoth determined he wanted to ask Tkaden about these comments privately.

When the last of the meal had been cleaned away, the traveling party retired to the bunkroom upstairs to make their plans for the morrow. There Skoth surprised them and said that they would be going up the Oustona River rather than crossing overland and going up the Mahakentuck. They made plans to acquire a couple of river canoes and supplies the next day and then they retired to their separate rooms with plans to join for breakfast in the morning.

Leesha and Enat went to their room, but after a few moments they opened their door just a crack to see if there was anyone in the hallway. When they saw it was all clear they slowly opened it and made their way stealthily down the stairs. There were still a few customers in the common room sharing conversation and drinks. Susie was sweeping the floor behind the bar and saw them when they came down the stairs. She set the broom aside and went toward the kitchen motioning for them to follow. Her kitchen help had finished up for the night and had already left so they had the room to themselves. Susie pulled some chairs over to the worktable and invited them to sit.

Susie looked them over for several moments before speaking, then she settled her gaze on Enat and spoke, "Enat, my dear, lovely as your mother you are. Tis a pleasure to finally meet you. I have heard reports of the three of you. I wondered when Unaine would finally let you lassies venture off that fair isle."

"We've been off before. Last summer we made a trip with him up the coast to Marte's Cove. But we've never been to New Caledonia before."

"But now here you are. And on some grand adventure if I am to be the judge of it."

Enat and Leesha looked at each other, but said nothing.

Susie continued, "Don't worry, I'll not be telling any tales about the two of you, or should I say the six of you. Erik may not say a lot, but I know him. And what he doesn't say is sometimes more telling than what he does. You don't need to tell me anything, but I think there is something I need to tell you."

Again the two young ladies looked at each other, said nothing, and then looked back at Susie.

Susie went on, "Enat, my girl, I noticed the medallion you are wearing, the Green Man. May I look at it a mite closer?"

Enat leaned forward and held the necklace out from herself. Susie reached forward and held it in her fingertips to look at it closely. She allowed it to fall back to Enat's chest and she leaned back in her chair with a thoughtful expression on her face.

"I'd not be the one to tell you what to do, but I'd give you some advice if you'd be willing to hear it," she said, "but certainly the following of it would be up to you."

Enat glanced at Leesha and said, "We're interested. What is it you have to say?"

"Aye then, here it is. It may be dangerous. I can't promise you it isn't. But I think you have to travel to the north, beyond the Celtic village of Glenoak, which is in the highlands between the headwaters of the Oustona and the Necticut Rivers. There you should search out a old man who goes by the name of Fearglas."

Susie sat in silence.

Leesha, not one to enjoy silence or long pauses, spoke up, "That's it? Go find this Fergus fellow? What then? Isn't there more?"

"Dear, dear, dear," tutted Susie, "first of all, he is called 'Fearglas' not 'Fergus' and he is called that for a reason. Tis a name which means the same as that medallion your sister is wearing. It means 'green man' and, if I have any wits to me at all, your ma would have gotten that medallion from Fearglas himself. If you want his help, then take it to him."

91

Leesha, still impatient, said, "And what kind of help will that be? And why should we want it?"

"That, my girl, I don't know."

"How do we know you're not leading us on some kind of wild goose chase to distract us from helping Skoth?"

Susie smiled, "So helping Skoth you are. Well, you don't know for sure. You'll just have to trust me. Think of it as Women's Circle business. We do have a Women's Circle in this little hamlet, after all."

Enat jumped back into the conversation, "But of course you do. Listening to you, I can tell you are a part of it." and then turning to Leesha, she said, "And sister dear, remember the words 'seek, trust, join'? I think that now is the time for a little of the trust."

Leesha responded, "Oh, of course. Susie's words ring true."

Susie grinned and said, "And to think you two were planning on sneaking out of here in wee hours of the evening in an attempt to find the Women's Circle, when I was right here. Under ye noses, so to speak."

Surprised and slightly embarrassed, Enat responded with stammers, "We didn't know. I mean, you're Susie. I mean, we saw the way Erik leered at you. I mean, oh, you know what I mean."

"Surely I do. So Erik was leering at me, was he? Well, I'll just have to do something about that," she said with a twinkle in her eye, "now off with the two of you. Up to bed and get your beauty sleep! And if you're lucky, maybe some of your young men will be leering at you!"

Quickly the two made their way up the stairs. Susie

stood there with hands on hips watching them go and thinking that it was time to chase out the last of her customers, and do something about Erik! She smiled.

Chapter 16 - A Day in New Caledonia

The sun rises early and the summer daylight hours are long in the land of Eirgalon. It was before dawn, when the sky was beginning to brighten, that Tkaden quietly crawled out of his bunk, pulled on his clothes, and slipped out of the room. He made his way down the back stairway and then out the back door of the inn. There was someone rustling about in the kitchen, but he didn't think anyone had noticed him. He wasn't gone long, perhaps only a quarter hour, when he slowly entered by the back door. He closed it gently making sure it wouldn't make a loud noise and was startled when a voice sounded from the open door to Erik's room.

It was Erik who softly questioned, "Have a nice walk?"

Tkaden was startled by the question and turning to the open door saw Erik sitting on a chair and sharpening his knife with a whetstone. He stepped into the doorway of the room and answered, "Actually, I did. You are up early, Master Erik."

"No need of using that polite bullshit with me, young man. I ain't nobody's master. I might be up early, but it looks like you are too. I reckon you just needed a bit of fresh air after sleeping with those two. Ha."

Erik's manner put Tkaden at ease and he replied with a chuckle, "I know what you mean, but really I was just going out to greet the sun."

"Greet the sun?"

"Yeah, it's something my father taught me. Do you

want me to explain?"

"Sure. Give it a try."

"Well, every day, or at least when it is possible, when I wake up I get dressed and step out into the natural world. I find a place facing east where I can see the rising sun, and then I say a three-step prayer. I take a step and say a prayer of gratitude for the day. I take a second step and acknowledge my talents and abilities, and I ask for wisdom and guidance in using them. Then I take a third step and ask for my eyes and heart to see and appreciate the wonder and mystery of this world."

Erik steadied a long look at the young man and then said, "There is more to you than meets the eye, young man. You best be heading back upstairs and rousting those sluggards outta bed so they can get breakfast. Time to get a start on this day. We have lots to do."

Tkaden turned and climbed the back stairwell to the bedrooms while Erik sat for several moments with a thoughtful expression on his face. Then giving a small shrug and he got up and went across the entranceway and into the kitchen.

The women were the first to come downstairs, but the three young men weren't far behind. They settled themselves at one of the long tables. Susie's girls brought out a steaming pot of spruce tea, a huge platter of bread with tubs of butter and jam, fresh apples, and a cauldron that had the remnants of last night's leftover stew.

At the end of the meal, Susie came over to the table and offered to take Leesha and Enat to gather a few supplies for their journey upriver, which was much appreciated since they had never undertaken such a task before and Susie certainly had contacts throughout the town that would be of benefit to them. She took them with her into the kitchen and a few minutes later left with them through the back door.

Erik, Skoth, Tkaden, and Karl left to go down to the docks to see what kind of passage they could secure for their journey upriver. The air hung heavy around them and it felt as if a storm was coming in. The streets were bustling on this cloudy summer morning. It was as if everyone felt they had to get their work finished before the rain started.

Skoth had this prickly sensation on the hairs of his neck as they walked down the street away from Tante's Table. He couldn't shake the feeling that he was being watched, and although he made a point to scan the street in both directions, he didn't notice anything that was amiss.

They had walked the several blocks to the riverfront and had just stepped onto the riverfront road that ran along the shoreline and docks, when a wagon filled with barrels and pulled by two large brown and white draft horses drew even with them. Suddenly the top-most barrels tumbled off the wagon toward them. The men jumped to the side in an attempt to dodge the falling barrels, however Karl who had been nearest the wagon was hurt when one of them fell on his foot. He could feel a bone snap as a pain went shooting up his leg. The other barrels crashed to the ground with a couple of them splitting open and spilling their contents of oats onto the street. The driver stopped the team and he and his partner jumped off the wagon shouting curses.

In the midst of this mayhem, a slight and frail looking old woman in grey clothing stepped out from the buildings toward Skoth. From the sleeve of her tunic she drew a knife. Skoth turned in time to see the blade coming at him and Erik's leg kicking the hand that thrust the knife. The old woman spun away from them and tumbled to the street from the force of Erik's kick, but to their amazement she leapt upright out of her tumble and sprinted around a corner into an alley. Erik gave chase, but as soon as he reached the alley he stopped. He turned back toward Skoth and with a shrug of his arms he said in puzzlement, "She's gone!"

It took a few minutes to calm the teamsters and to sort through the mess. It also became apparent that Karl had indeed broken his leg. They were preparing to move him when two burly men, looking as much the warrior as Erik did, approached them and demanded they come with them to the see the waterfront sheriff. Erik tried to protest, but they would hear none of it. They insisted that they accompany them, and so, to avoid drawing yet more attention to themselves, they went with the men to the local Hall of Justice, which was only a hundred yards down the road on the waterfront.

When they escorted them in, Erik immediately recognized the man sitting on the magistrate's chair. It was Olaf Sigurdson, and he looked askance at Erik and his young companions.

Olaf cleared his throat and spoke, "I might have known. I'm told that some strangers are making a ruckus down by the docks and who should it be? None other than that old troublemaker from Fadis Innis, Erik the Wild! So the long island wasn't big enough for you, you had to come make trouble over here?"

Erik tried to protest, "No trouble was of my doing. We were just going to the docks on business, when there was this accident . . ."

Olaf cut him off, saying sarcastically, "Sure, an accident. Nothing of your doing, I'm sure. You show up and things just happen. What about these young men with you? What kind of trouble are you getting them into? Just what is this business that you say the four of you are about?"

"Well, who died and made you king?"

"Listen, you old trouble-maker, I am the Sheriff here now! You'll be answering to me!"

Erik snorted in derision, "Bah, I don't need to answer to any second-rate, sellsword, tag-a-long, weak-kneed, horse-thieving, son-of-a-bitch…"

Olaf yelled, "That will be enough from you!"

At that moment the doors opened and a crowd of a dozen or so people, including the drivers of the wagon and several dockworkers, spilled into the room. Everyone in the rabble seemed to be talking. All order was gone and chaos reigned. Even Olaf's bellowing for everyone to shut-up had no effect, but only seemed to make matters worse.

Skoth, took in the melee of chaos, then put his hand to his mouth and blew a loud, screeching two-fingered whistle. Everyone went silent and looked at him. He gave an embarrassed sort of smile, and then said, "Well, you folks were making so much noise. Who could make sense of any of it?" He pointed at the driver of the wagon, "You there, driver, why don't you start."

Before the driver could say anything, a blustering Olaf sputtered out, "Yeah. Good thing you folks quieted down. I was just about to let you have it! And yeah, you, driver, you tell me what is going on here."

It took a few minutes of explaining, with a few interruptions by the involved parties to learn that the drivers of the wagon delivering the barrels to a ship wanted to be paid full price for the load, but the ship's master refused to pay full price because a couple of barrels had been broken in the accident. The driver insisted they had all the grain, and that it was the grain they were paying for not the barrels, and that they could just make do with the cracked barrels.

Olaf tried to pronounce a judgment that the shipmaster would pay only a partial amount, since the goods were damaged and the hall erupted again in loud arguing by all the parties, including Olaf.

Again Skoth his fingers to his lips and gave the piercing whistle. Again the room went silent. The folks turn to Skoth and waited.

He spoke, "Let's settle this now, so I can get my friend here to a healer. Shipmaster, two barrels are cracked and one was totally broken. If you pay full price to our driver here, I will pay you the cost of three new barrels. Not the cost of the grain, mind you, but the cost of the barrels themselves to put the grain in. Does that sound fair to the both of you?"

First the driver, and then the shipmaster nodded in agreement. Skoth reached into his tunic and pulled out a small bag of coins. Opening in the pouch, he pulled out a couple of coins and said, "This is what I would consider the fair price for the three barrels. Any objection?"

"None from me," said the shipmaster with a nod.

"And none from me, chief," said the driver.

99

Skoth grinned at them and said, "Well then, there looks to be a storm brewing. What are you standing in here for? Hadn't you better get out of here and get your work done before it hits?"

With murmurings of assent the men quickly filed out of the hall of justice. As they did, Skoth turned to Olaf and said, "Now can we see someone about a healer for my friend? His foot got smashed up pretty bad out there and he is in a fair amount of pain."

Olaf stood there with mouth agape, but one of his men strode to the door and said, "Follow me, I'll take you to Claire, she's a good healer and she's just down the street."

Karl wrapped one arm around Skoth's shoulders and the other around Tkaden's and they followed him out the door. Erik followed close behind. He gave no acknowledgement to Olaf, but as he exited the hall he cleared his throat and spat. His disdain was obvious. The door slammed shut behind him.

The visit to the healer confirmed that Karl had indeed broken his foot. She wrapped it and gave directions for his care and asked where they were staying. When then told them Tante's Table she smiled and said she'd stop in on the morrow and check on him. The rain started as they were leaving Claire's and it had turned into a downpour by the time they arrived at Tante's. The women had returned only minutes before from their shopping expedition. Susie immediately took charge. She determined that Karl would stay in the back room where Erik had slept so he wouldn't have to trouble with climbing the stairs, and she insisted that he would remain there for several days, or even weeks, while his foot healed.

Chapter 17 - A Change of Plans

The group of travelers had their private conversation in the kitchen that evening so Karl could be a part of it. There had been fewer guests for supper that evening. The driving rain must have kept them away. What guests there were had either departed right after supper, or gone upstairs to their rooms. Susie had bolted the front door so no one else would come in, the kitchen help had left for the night, and now the seven of them sat around the kitchen table: the six travelers and Susie. Leesha and Enat were anxious to hear all the details of what had happened at the riverfront and were anxious to tell their own tale. After hearing of the events of the day from the men, the women told their story.

Leesha began, "Our first errand was for Susie to take us over to the general store and get a few weeks supplies of basic equipment and foodstuffs for a couple of weeks journey, which we had their helper deliver back here to the inn. The shopping was interesting. We learned about what basic equipment we will need as we travel."

Erik interjected, "Well, I hope you didn't overdo it. We still have to travel light, and fast if the need arises. We can't be burdened with a lot of extra baggage. And I hope you didn't tell anyone what our plans are."

"Oh, no, Susie made sure we only got necessities. But this is the strange part. Even though Susie assures us that nothing we got indicates that we are travelling by river rather than by land, the proprietor commented that he hoped we enjoyed our trip up the river. How could he have known that?"

Erik glanced at Tkaden and saw a brief look of dismay cross his face. Erik was going to question him but before he could, Tkaden spoke, "Maybe it was me. When we arrived yesterday, I saw one of my kinsmen on the riverfront. I asked him to pass the word back to my family that I was back on the mainland and that maybe I'd have a chance to see them when we travelled up the river."

Erik cussed, "Well, Thor's hammer, don't any of you young folk know how to keep a secret?"

Tkaden was apologetic, "I really am sorry. I didn't think there would be any problem."

Leesha interrupted his apology by saying, "Don't be so quick to apologize. There's no proof that the words you shared with a kinsman caused either Karl's accident, or the shopkeeper's comment.

With a bit of sarcasm in his voice Erik muttered, "And there's no proof to this point that it didn't. So where does that leave us?"

Skoth said, "It leaves us not knowing and open to possibilities. Leesha, why don't you go on telling us about what happened after the general store."

So Leesha continued, "When we left the store we went round to meet up with some of the ladies of the Women's Circle here. One of the ladies warned us to watch out for the Grey Hag."

Skoth asked, "And who might this "Grey Hag" be?"

Susie responded to his question, "Some people say she is only a superstitious old wives tale, but others say she is real. Legend has it that one of the early settlers here was kidnapped by some of the local Skraelings that we were warring with at the time, and that since no one tried to rescue her, she became one of them and vowed revenge on what had been her Celtic people. She occasionally shows up and then unexplainable trouble happens."

"So you think that Grey Hag may be the old woman in grey that tried to knife me this morning? Why would she do that?"

Tkaden looked thoughtful and ventured an answer, "This is only a thought, but there might be a connection. If the legends of the Grey Hag carry truth about the connection to the Skraelings, then maybe there is some link to the current principal chief of the Skraelings, Malsum. He is dangerous and is said to control strange powers. It is also known that he carries no love for the Celts of the sunrise lands."

"That's not a pleasant thought, because then somehow he knows where we are. That's not something I want."

As the wind grew to a howl and the rain flying in sheets battered the walls of the inn, the plans, which had been made, were now changed. First of all, Karl was in no shape to travel. That meant that if they were traveling by canoe there would be one less paddle in the water. Second, the river was only one highway by which to travel. Many were the paths and roads that wound their way through the fields and forests of Eirgalon. There was no reason they had to travel the river. Third, Skoth thought it might be wise to try to throw Malsum off their scent, if indeed he was on it. And fourth, although she wouldn't explain why, Enat felt that it was important for them to go north to Glenoak. In the end it was decided that Karl would recuperate in New Caledonia under the care of Susie and that the five of them would travel by land, and that they would, indeed, head north in the general direction of Glenoak.

Skoth asked Erik to go out in the morning and to see if he could purchase some horses for their journey by land, discreetly of course, with the hope that they could arrange to quietly leave on the following morning.

Chapter 18 - On the Road

For two days the rains continued, but the third morning saw skies clear and the five travelers on the road heading north. It was the road that roughly followed the course of the river. The horses Erik had secured for them were nondescript and seemed up to their task, but none of them were going to win any races. Erik and Tkaden were in the lead and they were alertly scanning the road and countryside as they progressed up the road. Many were the crofters home and fields they passed and often were the patches of woodlands they traveled through. The road curved around many a hill and often they splashed through small streams with sand and gravel streambeds. The larger streams had stout bridges. It was a well-used road and frequently they encountered farmers taking their goods to market. The young ladies riding in tandem and chattering to each other followed them. Skoth brought up the rear and soon became lost in contemplation as his horse plodded forward. They had no intentions of hurry. They had no desire to do anything to draw attention to themselves.

In fact, they didn't even truly know what they were searching for. This is what had started eating at Skoth. He wondered what he had gotten himself into. He had agreed to the quest: he was to "find the key to their future," but he was beginning to wonder about how foolish that might all be. How was he to figure out what the key might be? How was he to find where the key was? Was he just blinded by the "king" idea? Who was it that was out to kill him? And why?

Was he crazy to set out on a journey without really knowing where he was going?

He chuckled to himself, but loud enough so the girls in front of him turned to look at him with quizzical expressions. He was remembering what his old grandmother, who he called "Momo," had told him as a young boy when he tried to give her a non-specific answer to her question of where he was off to, "If you don't know where you're going, how will you know when you get there?"

He thought to himself, "Well, Momo, you're probably laughing at me now. I sure enough don't know where I'm going, and I sure enough am wondering how I'll know when I get there." He smiled at the memory and his reaction to it. Leesha and Enat thought that he smiled at them and then smirked at each other and turned back to their own conversation.

The rains of the last few days had refreshed the summer landscape and as the sun heated the moistened earth the day became sultry. Erik suggested they make camp early so that "the girls," as he called them, could get used to a camp routine. They wouldn't be staying at inns every day and they needed to know how to set up camp in less than perfect conditions. An early stop and practice at camp duties would help prepare them. They were passing through a wooded area when they spotted a clearing in a wooded area where it looked as if previous travelers had camped. The others hadn't noticed it, but Erik had been watching for a small rune that was lightly and recently scratched into the bark of a maple tree along the edge of the road. It symbolized safety and let Erik know his men had been here.

They hobbled the horses and watered them from a small stream that ran through the woods several paces from the road, made a small cook fire and set some water to boil in a small pot they had brought. Erik showed them how he made a stew with some of their supplies and a rabbit that Tkaden had shot along the way. Erik was impressed by the archery skills of the young man, for when he had pointed out the rabbit while they were riding earlier and had commented on how it would make a fine addition for the evening meal, Tkaden had almost instantly and smoothly drawn an arrow to his bow and released it. The rabbit never had a chance.

Erik taught them his method of making a travelling stew with the rabbit, adding a few edible roots that were found near their campsite, and a few of the dried veggies and spices they had brought with them in their supplies. To the astonishment of the ladies, it was quite good. After cleaning up from the meal, arranging their sleeping rolls, and setting up their watch rotation for the night (which Erik insisted they do), they lay down and passed a peaceful night.

Travel wasn't difficult and they didn't press the horses for speed. Late afternoon brought them to the town on the banks of the Oustona where the river bends to the west and the tide loses its power. Beyond the bend stood a bridge of stone and heavy timbers that led to the northern lands. Rather than looking for lodging they stopped at the farmer's market near the bridge briefly to purchase some meat and fresh vegetables for their cook pot, as well as some fresh bread for the morning. Erik left them for a few moments while they shopped, saying he had to leave a message with a friend, which would be carried back to Unaine reporting on their safety and progress. He soon returned and they remounted and crossed the river and passing through the smaller village on the northern side. They rode on for a couple of miles and as the sun was moving toward the western horizon they found another good spot to camp for the night.

As they sat around the campfire that evening enjoying their meal they talked. Erik was no stranger to this part of the country, and he reveled them with a few stories of when he was younger detailing some of the escapades and adventures he had when he had served as a warrior chasing the last of the Skraelings from this side of the Mahakentuck. They also found that Tkaden had traveled in these lands, though his home lay further to the east and north. For the others, this was the farthest north any of them had been.

The days of travel continued and they wound their way northward through fields and forests of Eirgalon. They could sense the waning of the summer days. The terrain changed slightly to a landscape with more hills and dales and the settlements changed from being predominantly Celtic to a more varied mixture of Wabanaki and Celtic. There was also the occasional area that was predominantly Wabanaki, and for the first time the Skoth, Leesha, and Enat felt what is was like to be in a land where they were the minority. No great insights came to Skoth during this time, and no surprising occurrences happened. He wondered if that would change when they arrived at the only destination he had in mind, Glenoak - the last Celtic settlement. To be sure, there were Celts who lived beyond Glenoak, but this was, so to speak, the end of the road.

One observation Skoth has was that Leesha and Tkaden began spending more time with each other as the days went on. Often when Enat rode next to him and talked with him, Tkaden would be riding next to Leesha, and around the camp in the evening the two of them frequently shared laughter. Skoth wasn't exactly jealous and he didn't exactly have romantic feelings toward her, she was the childhood friend he had enjoyed growing up with, but it did give him an occasional little pang in his heart when he noticed her attention was directed elsewhere.

Chapter 19 – Glenoak

It was early in the afternoon on a cloudy day when they rode into Glenoak and the wind had a little chill to it. They easily found the village inn; aptly named The Village Inn for it was the only inn in the village. It was a solid two-story wood structure, slightly larger than Tante's had been, and there was a stable next to it. They secured two rooms for the night in the inn, one for the women and one for the men, and stalls for their mounts in the stable and then they split up to walk around the village. Leesha and Enat went off on their own, Skoth and Tkaden went a different direction, and Erik went back to the stable to visit with the men working there.

A few minutes later, Erik had re-mounted his horse and was riding out of town on the path that led to the west. He went for several hundred yards and then turned left and followed a narrow path that lead through a ravine. A few dozen yards and the ravine widen into a sizeable clearing. A small fire was burning in front of a small lean-to, and two horses were hobbled and grazing at the upper end of the ravine. From opposite sides of the clearing two men emerged, Rolf and Jake.

Rolf called out, "Erik, you finally made it! Took you sluggards long enough to get here."

Erik swung his hefty body of the horse and onto the ground, "Well, made it we did, and without any more problems. We'll be staying at the inn in town, so stay out of sight. I don't want the young-uns to know you're here."

"Don't you worry, boss. Sly and silent as foxes we are. Just let us know if you need us."

"Keep checking with the stable manager. If I can't get word to you myself, I'll leave a message with him."

With that he led his horse back through the narrow path to the road, mounted it and went back into town and to the stable. He had a few more words with the stable hands and then sauntered down the street and entered an establishment by the name of Finnegan's Rest.

A few blocks away Leesha and come across a weaver's house, known by the symbol of a loom on its front door. They also noticed that hanging in the window was dreamcatcher with blue and yellow feathers tied to it. For those with knowledge of such matters, it was a sign of the Women's Circle. Whoever had put it in the window for people to see was letting it be known that a member of the local Women's Circle either resided her, or knew how to contact a member of it. They walked up to the door and Leesha knocked on it. A voice responded with, "Come in."

When they entered they saw that it was a typical shop of that type with the workroom in the front and a doorway leading to private quarters in the rear. There were two looms inside, near the front windows. At each worked a woman, one was a middle-aged woman with flame red hair tied up and to the back with a kerchief to stay out of her way, and the other was a younger version of her in her middle teens with the same flame red hair, but braided and wound up in a coil.

The older woman spoke, "Well, my lassies, strangers are you and welcome to my humble shop. What is it that I can do for you?"

Leesha started her comments by complementing the woven fabrics of the weaver, "My what fine woolens you make here."

They made small talk and shoptalk for a few minutes and then Leesha commented that she had noticed the dream catcher in the window.

The shopkeeper asked her daughter to mind the front of the shop and motioned for the two women to come with her to the back. When she got to the kitchen she invited them to be seated and said, "Now let me get you a cuppa tea, and we can sit a spell and you can tell me your need."

Again they made small talk until the tea was poured and all three were at the table. Then the woman said, "Time for Circle business it is. What have ye to say?"

Leesha explained, "Well there is a lot to our tale, more than we can rightly tell you, but what we can say is that the Women's Circle of New Caledonia suggested we search for Fearglas in the area of Glenoak. We've made our way to Glenoak, and we're of the thought that if anyone here might help us know how to find Fearglas it would be the Women's Circle here."

"Poor lassies, I fear it isn't so. No one can find him, unless he wishes to be found. In that case, he'll be the one to find you. Not much help have I to give ye, but tis said he lives deep in the highland forests in a hidden glen by a sacred pool. But as the name so says, hidden it is."

Enat pulled the necklace with the Green Man medallion out of the bodice of her dress. She looked at it for a moment and rubbed it gently. She said, "Well then, we hope he will find us. We feel our need is great."

"I canna speak for him. But I've heard it said he feels the need of those with pure hearts. Perhaps it will be so for you. I cannot say."

"What then shall we do?"

She shook her head, "I canna tell ye. Other than be ready should he show himself. I'll talk to the other women of the Circle. Mayhap others may know more, but I canna promise ye more than that. Be ye staying at the Village Inn?"

"Yes. At least for a few days."

"If I know more, I contact ye there."

They finished their spruce tea and went back to the front room of the shop. They said their thank yous and goodbyes and left promising to come back and perhaps purchase some warm woolens for the cooler months to come.

Skoth and Tkaden just walked the streets for a while. Skoth noticed that many of the crops were in and the people were already preparing for the winter months to come. The trees were starting to turn color and the people were getting that "enjoy the final good days of warm weather because it won't last long" feeling.

Of course people noticed them as strangers in town, but no one said anything other than to give them friendly greetings. That changed when they came to the leatherworker's shop. They noticed it as they walked down the street, and Tkaden commented that maybe they should stop in and see what goods they had, since they might need heavier cloaks to deal with the colder weather that was certainly coming.

When they stepped inside the door they heard a voice snarl at them, "Bah, looks like we have some coaster bossmen come poking their noses up north. We don't need your type here. Go on. Get out of my shop."

They quickly backed up and went out the door.

Once again on the street, Tkaden turned to Skoth and said, "What was that about?"

Skoth replied, "I sure don't know, but there's no reason to stay where you aren't wanted. Still, I do wonder. He didn't even hardly look at us before he tore into us. And what did he mean by that southern bossmen comment?"

Tkaden explained, "There are folks here in the inland, away from the coast, and this includes both Celt and Wabanaki folk, who sometimes feel like the chiefs and folk of the coastland think they are better than they are. And that they try to boss the inland clans around."

"But we don't. Do we?"

"Well, since you asked, yes, it could appear that way at times."

That observation left Skoth silent for a few moments causing him to think about what the future of the land of Eirgalon might be. If they were to continue and grow as one people, then they couldn't be feeling like some were superior to others. He remembered a few times in his youthful days when he felt left out because he was an orphan and that others had acted as though they were somehow better than he because of it. That was never a good feeling. Feelings of inequality breed trouble. They decided to head back to the inn and meet up with the others for their evening meal. Both of them were looking forward to a good inn-cooked meal and a nice bed to sleep in.

Chapter 20 - Forest Excursions

The five of them sat at a sturdy oaken table along one of the walls for supper that night, and while they ate they shared some of their observations of the town. Of course, Erik told them nothing of Rolf and Jake. The room had a large hearth on the back wall, which also opened to the kitchen behind it. Several other tables were scattered throughout the room and most had people seated enjoying the meal and some ale. The Inn also appeared to be serving as a local tavern since after the meal people stayed for drink and conversation and others came in to join them. Many of their customers' conversations centered around the upcoming ingathering festival, which they observed at the autumnal equinox and called "Fallfest." The noise of the room was loud enough so that it was close to impossible to hear and follow anyone's conversation beyond the people seated next to you. There were a couple of times that Skoth thought he heard the name "Malsum" mentioned, but maybe that was just his imagination. It was too loud in the room to make out who it might have been who said it.

The noise level in the room diminished and died to a few whispers when a young man pulled out his pan flutes, which consisted of a series of bone flutes tied together, and began playing a tune. Soon a young woman playing a lyre joined him. A few moments later she began singing a ballad of the emerald isle. This got the crowd smiling and even joining in on the refrain, for although few, if any, of the crowd had ever been to old Eire, the evoking of the ancestral home pulled on their heartstrings. The mood in the room was pleasant and upbeat.

The duo had just started their second song, one about old John Barleycorn in honor of the fallfest to come, when the door crashed open. The man that Skoth recognized as the tanner who chased them from the leather shop came in followed by two rough looking men. The tanner scanned the room and then pointed at Skoth, "There he is. Let's get him."

A large burly-armed man, the local blacksmith by the look of it, was seated at the table between the door and Skoth's table. He glanced at Skoth and then pushed his chair back and stood up. In a calm, deep voice he said, "Whoa, there now, Angus. You just stop right there."

That gave the tanner and the henchmen hesitation. They stopped, and as they did the two young men at the blacksmith's table stood up. By the look of them, they were probably his sons. Eric, Skoth, and Tkaden also stood, prepared for action.

The blacksmith went on, "There'll be no trouble from you in here tonight."

Angus, the tanner, glared and spat out, "They're coasters! You know what Malsum says about their ilk!"

"Aye, I do! But Malsum isn't here and these are guests in our village's inn. The laws of hospitality are at play here. No harm is to come to them. No matter what you think. So just take your men and leave. No blood, no harm done."

"Bah! You'll be sorry!" he said has he turned and moved to the door. At the door he stopped and turned around looking again at Skoth, and said, "As for you - we'll be watching for you!" With that he followed his men out of the door, slamming it behind himself.

Before sitting down, he turned and said to Skoth and the others, "I bear no love for coasters, myself, but this isn't the time, or place, for violence. If I was you, I'd be careful travelling about these parts."

Skoth said, "Thank you, sir. I appreciate what you did. It is something you didn't have to do. Would it be all right with you, if I stopped by your smithy tomorrow? I have a small piece of iron work I'd like for you to do."

"Sure, young fella, I'm not one to turn down work. My smithy is on the edge of town on the road heading east. Enjoy the rest of your evening."

The musicians started playing again, picking up the John Barleycorn song from the beginning, and the crowd seemed to forget the altercation and soon got back into the mood of the evening. Skoth and his table of travelers kept a watchful eye for any more surprises, but nothing else untoward happened. After a couple of hours of enjoying the music with the local folk, they went upstairs to have a private conversation before trying to sleep. Skoth let it be known that he was going to pay a visit to the blacksmith in the morning, and the ladies let it be known that they wanted to go for a ride out in the countryside west of Glenoak. They agreed that Erik would go with Skoth and that Tkaden would escort the women.

Chapter 21 - Iron

The remainder of the night was uneventful, although Skoth did have trouble sleeping. His thoughts kept returning to images of the tanner and the warnings he had given. The name of Malsum kept bouncing through his dreams.

For breakfast, the innkeeper served a simple, but satisfying breakfast of oatmeal, cranberry tea, bread, butter, and jams. Without fanfare Leesha, Enat, and Tkaden went to the stable and saddled their horses. Erik and Skoth saw them ride off down the road to the west, and then they turned and walked down the street toward the east.

Fortunately, they did not have to walk by the tanner's shop but they still keep their eyes open and were ready in case anything might happen. When they arrived at the smithy, the forge was already hot and the blacksmith was hard at work. They waited patiently for him to finish what he was working on. When he could take a break from his work, he set down his tools and walked over to them.

Skoth started the conversation, "Thank you, master smith, for what you did last night."

The smith responded, "Welcome you are. I'm no lover of coasters, but everyone deserves to be respected, and no one messes with my friend's inn. They'd have made a royal mess there, and I have no doubt you'd have added to it. Now, about that project you have for me - oh, and by the way, my name is Duncan."

"Well," said Skoth and hesitated, "there is something I feel I need, but I also trust you to keep it confidential. I really don't want word of this spread around, but I need this certain item made. I'm asking you, because of what you did last night; I can see that you are an honorable man, Duncan."

"You flatter me, young fella. Sure, I'll keep still about it, iffen I can make it that is. Tell me what it is that you want."

Skoth reached into his tunic and pulled out the king rune and lifted the cord over his neck. Handing it to Duncan he said, "I need you to fashion the symbol on this rune into a iron pendant of similar size. Can you do it?"

Surprise flickered across the smith's face, he paused and then asked, "Aye, the doing is in my power, but do you know what this is?"

"Oh, all too well I'm learning what it is."

"Ahh. Well then, I'll make it for you. Tis not the totem that gives it the power, tis the owner of it. If this rune be true, then its power will come from you, good sir."

He handed the runestone back to Skoth who lifted it back over his head, settled it around his neck, and tucked it back into his tunic. They agreed that Skoth would return in a couple of hours and Duncan would have the iron medallion ready for him.

As they left, Erik indicated he wanted to walk down the eastern road for a bit heading away from town. As they were walking, the serious side of Erik's nature emerged.

"Sometimes you puzzle me, Skoth. One moment I see the naive, troublesome, inexperienced boy I've known since he was a babe, and then the next moment I'm wondering who the heck you are? And I admit I don't always understand what you are doing. Could you explain to me why you want the king rune in an iron medallion?"

Skoth smiled at the reference to his boyhood and then smiled more at the obvious care for him that Erik showed. "You know how the Chief always insisted that I do my lessons at the Academy, and how he forced me to spend time studying with old Theofinn."

Erik nodded and said, "Aye, and many was the time that you tried to skip out and be off on one of your merry larks!"

"But you or one of the other adults would always find me and . . . well, the point is that I did learn a few things, and one of the lessons that came to my mind last night after the blacksmith intervened was what Theofinn once taught me about the power of metals. I can almost hear his exact words - Iron is the most abundant of metals. Iron carries the male energy. The wearing of iron gives confidence, strength, and stamina. But also lust. You must beware the lust. It also protects you from the malevolent spirits of the world beyond, for it is a human metal - word for word, I swear that's how he said it."

"Ahh, so you were perhaps thinking that your kingly quest could use a little protection from Malsum, should he be sending problems your way. By all accounts he sounds malevolent enough."

Skoth grinned a little sheepishly, "Yeah, I figured it couldn't hurt, and it might help down the road."

Erik nodded his head in agreement and said, "Skoth, my boy, never be afraid to use help when it is available. Theofinn's teachings are never to be scoffed at. I think you just acted wisely, for not only will you have that medallion, but also you have treated Duncan honorably. He won't forget that. Now, let's do a little exploring and then go pick up that fancy piece of iron you commissioned."

A couple hours later they were back at the smithy. Duncan saw them coming, put down his tools, walked over to a shelf on the side of the building and picked up a folded piece of leather.

As if embarrassed slightly, Duncan hemmed and hawed a bit, and almost apologetically said, "Now, it isn't the finest piece of my work. It was a rush job, after all, and it is hammered, not cast, but I hope it will do for ye." With that he handed the folded leather to Skoth and continued, "Ye'll notice I also made a loop in it and ran a leather cord through it so that ye can wear it around ye neck, if ye choose."

Skoth looked it over, "Tis a fine piece of work. It is exactly what I wanted! How much do I owe you for it?"

Duncan smiled and responded, "No charge. If the meaning of the rune be true, and something in me says it is, then the honor making it for you is payment enough."

Erik stood there, with his mouth hanging open. No doubt he was thinking that this was a first. Never in his life had he seen a blacksmith do something for free. Hard-working they were known to be, and hard charging as well!

Skoth thought for a moment, then reached to the inside pocket of his tunic and drew out the tabac pouch that Dakatomi had given him. Unnoticed by any of them, the small token of the trickster that had been attached to it fell away from it and to the floor.

Skoth said, "Well, then please accept this gift of tabac. It is small token of my thanks."

Smiling, the smith said, "Tis a fine pouch."

"It's no longer full, but what is left is some of the finest tabac in the land. "

"I'm not one to be turning down a gift. Tis not a payment mind ye. Has a fine smell to it, it does. I thank ye. And when that time should come when ye want a fine torc of that rune to be hammered and forged. I'd be honored if ye come to me."

Before they left, Skoth took the iron rune from the leather and placed the cord round his neck, tucking it into his tunic. He felt wee bit more confident and hopeful as they stepped back into the street and headed back into town.

Chapter 22 - Problems in the Forest

The dew was still wet on the leaves when Leesha, Enat, and Tkaden, left Glenoak on their horses heading west. They took a leisurely pace. The road went gradually uphill as it followed alongside a creek of tumbling waters. They took pleasure in the soft bubbling sounds it made as it frequently traversed small rocky rapids. They soon left the area of many farms and fields, and entered into an area which was mostly woodlands broken by rocky patches of ground. They traveled at a walking pace for most of the morning and decided to stop and have the light lunch they had packed in their bags. The stop was at a pleasant looking spot at the western end of a rocky clearing where the creek was tumbling through the rocks. They tethered their horses under the trees that shaded the western end of the large clearing that was several dozen paces across, and then they took their lunch out of the saddlebags and out onto the rocks to sit by the stream and enjoy the peaceful calm of the place.

If it had not been for the sounds of the stream, perhaps they would have noticed their visitors sooner. Tkaden was the first to notice movement in the shadows of the trees when he glanced back toward the horses to check on them because they made a whickering sound. He let out a slight gasp, which caused the others to look up and follow his gaze. They were startled to see a couple of men step out of the trees by the horses. With their peripheral vision, they caught movement to the sides as well where they saw other men. They were surrounded.

Leesha said, "I don't like this, but let's go over toward our horses and see what this is about."

Tkaden whispered to the others, not wanting any others to hear, "Those are not my people. Those are Haudenoshonee."

Leesha whispered back, "Skraelings? Here?"

Tkaden shushed her, "Shhh. Don't call them that. That is an insult to them. Let me do the talking."

They tried to walk with confidence and to project an aura of self-assurance, but on the inside they were nervous and troubled. They slowly walked toward the men who stood near their horses, the men on the far side of the clear warily stepped into the clearing and followed them. The men stood silently between them and their horses. When they got within several paces, Tkaden started the conversation by greeting the men in his native Wabanaki tongue. The eldest one, a short and muscular middle-aged man, answered him in back Wabanaki, not Haudenoshonee, asking him in an insulting manner what he was doing out in the woods with two Coaster women.

Tkaden glanced at the two women to see if they had any reaction to the insult. He had never asked them if they could speak or understand Haudenoshonee, though he knew they understood and spoke a bit of Wabanaki. He decided to ignore the insult and to respond in a polite manner. He explained that they were staying in Glenoak and had just taken a ride out into the countryside to enjoy a fine summer day. While they were talking the other men came up behind them. There were a total of six of them. Far too many to fight, and any opportunity to flee would be in vain unless they could get to their horses.

Tkaden didn't want to antagonize them, by saying too much to them, but when he tried to let them know that the women and he were finished with their lunch now and that they now would be riding back to Glenoak he was answered by the man spitting on the ground and uttering a curse in Haudenoshonee. He motioned for them to sit on the ground, which they did. One of the men left, and returned in a short period of time, leading the men's horses.

In Wabanaki, the leader told Tkaden not to worry, and not to put up any resistance or they would regret it. He said that they had instructions from Malsum that if any Coasters were found sneaking around here, there were to be brought back to him, unharmed, if possible, but brought to him in any case. The leader said as a precaution they would tie their hands in front of them and that their horses would be lead by his men.

Tkaden knew that there was nothing he could do at this point but to go along with them and wait for an opportunity to escape. In the ladies' Eirgalon dialect of Celtic (a mixture of old Celtic, Norse, and Wabanaki) he explained to them what the man had said. Although the man had only spoken Wabanaki, and cursed in Haudenoshonee, Tkaden didn't know whether he, or any of his men, could understand Celtic so he didn't add anything else.

The leader then instructed his men to tie their hands and get them on their horses. In short order the prisoners were being lead down the road to the west. One man would ride far ahead and signal the group if anyone was approaching from the opposite direction and then they would quickly leave the road and hide in the woods. Next rode the group leader, followed by the three Haudenoshonee, each leading one of the horses of a prisoner. Then came the last of the captors, riding as a rearguard. They pushed their horses hard that afternoon, seldom having to leave the road but briefly to avoid other travelers heading to Glenoak.

About an hour before sunset, they turned off on a smaller path to the right. Rather than going mostly west, this path angled off to the northwest. They travelled until after the sun had set, and then made a camp near a small stream. The captives were allowed to walk around the camp freely, but they were kept away from the horses, and away from any weapon. The Haudenoshonee men shared a small portion of their travel food with the captives, and allowed them as much of the stream water as they wished, then told them to wrap themselves in their travel cloaks and sleep. A watch was set. There was no chance for escape and they spent a cool and uncomfortable night in the woods.

Chapter 23 - The Chase

The people of the small Celtic outpost on the northern edge of Celtic civilization were busy with the late summer harvest, and had little to say or do with the two men, so it was but late afternoon, when Skoth and Erik arrived back at the Village Inn.

They were troubled a little bit when they found out the others had not returned, but when the sun came to within an hour of setting, they felt something was amiss. Checking in at the stable, they were told by the stableman that he had not seen them since this morning and that they should have been back long ago.

Erik told the stable hand to saddle their horses, and then the two men quickly got their travel packs and some travel food from the kitchen. Before they mounted, Erik whispered to the stableman, "Get word to my friends that we took the western road, there might be trouble and they are to follow as fast as they can."

They trotted out of town on their horses, and after leaving sight of town they made as much speed as they could while they still had light. There was no conversation between them; there was only hard riding. Occasionally they slowed to give the horses a breather, and when they did the men carefully scanned the roadway. In all actuality, it wasn't much more than a dirt path through the woods. At first the woods were punctuated by the occasionally field, but soon it gave way to woodland, broken by rocky outcroppings. Erik could read the signs of their friends' horses going west, but nothing of their return. The sun had set and the light was growing dim when they came to the large clearing.

Erik held up his hand to signal Skoth to stop. They dismounted and led their horses by their reins as they walked forward peering as carefully as possible at the turf, the trees, and the rocks around them.

Within moments Eric had spotted the place where the horses had been tethered and the other horses had joined them. Skoth was walking along the stream and found the remnants of his friends' lunch scattered by the scavengers that had picked over the pieces during the afternoon. Sharing their discoveries they determined that their friends must have been taken by surprise as they lunched. There was no sign of any violent action and the tracks of all the horses headed west, so they were either taken captive or had been persuaded to accompany the others. Erik suggested they rest, and try to sleep for a couple of hours. By then the moon would be rising and he could follow the track easier in the moonlight.

They put their horses on long tethers by the stream so they could take advantage of the water and yet graze on the patches of grass scattered between the rocks. They spread their blanket rolls on the ground and within minutes, Erik was sleeping. Skoth wondered how the man did it. How could he shut down his thoughts and body so fast like that? Skoth was thinking that he'd have to get Erik to teach him that trick, and as he thought about that his thoughts drifted away from his friends. Before he knew what was happening, Erik was shaking him awake and he opened his eyes to see the half moon rising in the east.

Within minutes they had taken a few drinks of water

and wolfed downed a couple morsels of bread. They mounted the horses and were off.

Further on down the road, on the pathway to the northwest, the Haudenoshonee roused the captives when the first light of the sun started brightening the horizon. They allowed them but little time to freshen up before they were mounted and ready to ride again. The leader had again had his men tie the captives' hands and they were leading their horses. What they didn't know is that during the night, while supposedly resting, Enat had carefully pulled the cloth of the Green Man from her bag and tied it around her left wrist. She was unsure of her plan, but she was silently invoking a prayer for the aid of the Green Man. If he lived in these highlands as she had been told, then perhaps he would be close enough to feel her need and hear her supplications.

They pressed on a steady pace, going in single file with the captives' horses being led as the previous day. The leader of the captors took the lead today and sent the man who had been scout to ride at the rear of the line. He must have felt there was little need for a scout since he spaced the riders much closer. They took a short break for lunch and then were on their way again. In and out they wove from forest to rocky glen. Though often it was more open glen than forest.

It was the middle of the afternoon when they crossed a place of high open ground and began descending into a larger forested valley of mixed hardwoods and conifers. The path wound through them and was lined with heavy undergrowth to the sides. It was mid-September and a few of the hardwood trees were starting to show shades of turning their fall colors. Clouds had filled the sky and the wind was picking up. Some strong gusts sent a few early fallen leaves skittering across the path. They were gradually winding their way down the valley and had just rounded a sharp corner in the path, when the leader came to an abrupt stop. Only he, the next warrior, and Enat, could see what had caused the stop. The others were still around the bend.

A large pine tree had fallen across the path. Suddenly there was a commotion from the back of the line. Apparently the wind had toppled another of the large pines, sending it crashing into the last horse and rider. The other horses frantically tried to push forward, but they were bunched up against those who had stopped because of the blocked path in front. From a distance there came a loud wailing sound, which spooked the horses even more. Tkaden leapt from his horse and yelled at Leesha to jump off her horse and get in the woods. They scramble up the hillside the path was bending around. Enat, around the bend, couldn't see what was happening, but she heard the banshee scream and Tkaden's voice, and threw herself off the horse rolling into the woods, tumbling down the hillside opposite the direction of Leesha and Tkaden.

The Haudenoshonee men furiously tried to calm the horses, but with the three of them riderless and the one that had been struck by the tree thrashing and screaming in pain, they were almost uncontrollable. Then they became utterly uncontrollable, for one of the largest bears any of these men had seen roared as it started climbing over the fallen tree in front of the troop. Horses have a great fear of bears and the scent of a bear can sent them into a frenzy. The horses bucked and reared, and were lashing out with their hooves, striking each other and some of the men. Soon all the men were thrown from their mounts and the horses were crashing through the underbrush in an attempt to get as far from the bear as possible.

The bear charged over the tree slashing at the leader of the men, knocking him to the ground. Two of the men ran off into the woods, chasing the horses, or perhaps fleeing for their lives, or perhaps both, but neither was ever seen again.

The remaining two men drew their long knives. Some Haudenoshonee men of the western lands now carried swords, as the Celts did, but these did not. They used a traditional long knife. The bear reared up on its hind legs before them and roared. They separated to attack, but before they could move forward, two huge Celtic warriors who had clambered over the fallen pine behind them came dashing around the bend.

Erik and Skoth had traveled with seldom a pause throughout the day and had been close enough to hear the commotion on the trail ahead of them. With swords drawn, they charged at the men who were no match for them and who soon fell bleeding to the ground.

The bear had stood watching them as they fought with the Haudenoshonee men. Now it snorted, dropped to all four legs, clambered back over the tree and ambled down the path. With looks of incredulity, the Celtic men looked at each other, then Erik shrugged and looked back to the bloody mess on the chewed up ground of the forest path. The man slashed by the bear was dead. The man Erik had fought was also dead, but the man Skoth had fought was breathing ragged breaths. They leaned over him, asking, "Where are the prisoners?"

His response was one word, "Malsum", and then he breathed his last.

Skoth went back to check on the man and horse beneath the tree. The horse was still whinnying in pain. Skoth took his sword and slashed the horse's throat to put it out of its misery. He leaned in, looking under the branches, to check on the condition of the rider. It looked as though he hadn't suffered long. His head was crushed, and he likely died instantly. Skoth walked back around the bend to where Erik stood scanning the woods on each side of the path.

Erik spoke, "It looks like all the horses took off down the hill, but there are also branches broken on the uphill side. I'd wager some folks went in that direction." Then, without warning Erik yelled, "Ho, you young'uns! Erik's here to save you! C'mon in." In a softer voice, directed to Skoth he said, "If they're out there, that should let 'em know it is safe to come in."

Skoth didn't respond, and when Erik turned toward him he noticed that Skoth's attention was fixated on the fallen tree. More precisely they were fixated upon the eyes surrounded by flowing amber hair that were peering over the trunk of the fallen tree.

Tkaden and Leesha came stumbling into the pathway and Skoth glanced their direction. When he looked back to the eyes, they were gone.

"Where's Enat?" blurted out Leesha, "Have you seen her? Is she all right?"

Tkaden observed, "Looks like you finished these off.

Did you get all six of them?"

"Not six." Erik replied, "Only four here. The others must have run off, or are hiding in the woods. Skoth, I think Tkaden here, is more the woodsman than you, so you stay here with Leesha, while Tkaden and I search the woods." Tkaden picked up one of the Haudenoshonee long knives that was lying on the ground and the two of them carefully stepped through the underbrush into the woods.

Skoth asked Leesha, "Are you all right? They didn't hurt you or anything?"

"No, I'm fine. But I don't know what their plans were. Other than they were taking us to Malsum, that is." Then she saw the wounds on the dead Haudenoshonee leader. "Those are no sword wounds. What did you and Erik do to him?"

"It wasn't us. It was the bear."

"What bear?"

"You didn't see that huge brownish colored bear?"

"No. When the banshee screamed our horses started bucking. We jumped off and scrambled as far into the woods as we could go. They had tied our hands but I pulled out a small blade I had hidden and cut the cords. Since we didn't see Enat, we didn't know what happened to her. We were just figuring out how we were going to avoid the men searching for us when we heard Erik's voice. There was no bear."

"O, there was a bear! A huge, snorting, get down on your knees and beg for mercy bear!"

"Oh? Then where did it go?"

"When we showed up it just turned and walked

away."

"Humph. You're saying you scared it off?"

"Oh, no. I don't think it was scared in the least. I think it did what it wanted to, and didn't want to hurt us."

"Must have liked that rough manly look you have."

"Listen, Leesh. This is nothing to joke about. There was a bear! And there was something unusual about it. How about the maiden at the tree, did you see her?"

"Maiden at the tree? Skoth, are you brain-addled? What are you talking about?"

Skoth pointed at the fallen tree and said, "Right there! She was standing right there behind the tree when you and Tkaden came barging in. I looked away for a second and when I looked back she was gone."

"I saw no maiden. Skoth, are you all right? You didn't get hit in the head did you?"

"No, I did not! She was here!"

"Sure, sure. Whatever you say. What can we do here while we wait?"

Skoth sighed, "Unpleasant as it is, we should gather the dead. We can't just leave them here like this for the carrion to scavenge."

Leesha sighed, "Aye, let's get to it."

They started the gruesome task of pulling the men together and checking them for anything that might be of importance. They talked while they worked but they also kept a watchful eye out for the men that had run off.

Chapter 24 - Fearglas

Erik and Tkaden made their way slowly and carefully down the wooded slope. It wasn't difficult to spot many signs of flight, for the several horses had broken many branches and left many a hoofprint in the forest soil. They had a more difficult time spotting the effects of the men fleeing, and virtually no sign of the light-footed Enat. Tkaden noticed it first and whistled for Erik for come over. There was a drop-off into a deep ravine and it was apparent something, or someone, had recently slid from the edge into the ravine. The brush was heavy and it was impossible to see how deep the ravine was, or what was at the bottom of it. They decide to try to follow the ravine downslope a bit in the hope that they could climb down into it and then work their way back up the bottom of the ravine.

It took some time, because even though the trees were large, the undergrowth was dense and hard to penetrate. They finally found a way down into the ravine and began working their way back up it. The ravine itself was about twenty feet across at the bottom and a small trickle of water zigzagged back and forth across it. The ravine was also filled with scrub brush, though there appeared to be a narrow path that wound through it. Erik cautiously led the way. It could be just a deer path, but one never knew. Then suddenly in a small opening in the brush, next to the trickle of water sat a man dressed from top to bottom in shades of green. Stretched out on the ground next to him, with her head cradled in his lap was Enat. The man lifted the index finger of one hand to his mouth as if to tell them to be quiet.

As they quietly approached they could see Enat's eyes flutter and open. The man in green gently brushed the hair off her forehead and with a cloth he had dipped in the rivulet of water at his side he placed it on her forehead. She focused her eyes on him and smiled, for what filled her vision, as she looked upward, was his craggy bearded face framed by the lush green growth of the trees that towered above him. The image was identical to that on her medallion and cloth. It was the Green Man.

Turning his head to look at the men who now stood above him, the man in green said, "She'll be alright. She just took a little tumble when she lost her footing at the top of the ravine. She bumped her head on the way down. But after a little rest, she'll be fine."

Enat's eyes refocused, taking into her vision Tkaden and Erik. She shook her head, as if to clear her vision, and then winced with the pain of it. She closed her eyes for a moment, took a deep breath, and then reopened them.

Slowly and softly she spoke, "Erik, what are you doing here?"

"Well, I've come to rescue you, my lassie."

"Ohh. And Tkaden, you are all right. What about Leesha?"

Tkaden responded, "She's fine. We're all fine. It seems our captors have all been struck down or run off."

Erik added, as he glanced around, "There's still two of them afoot somewhere hereabouts. We must be careful."

The man in green gave a little shake of his head and said, "You needn't worry about those two. You'll never see them again."

Erik protested, "They're a sneaky lot. Just when you
think they're gone, they sneak up on you. I wouldn't bet on
them being gone."

"Oh, they are gone. Gone for good. The little people
have seen to that."

"Who?"

"The wee little ones, and you'll find they've also
gathered your horses for you. They're tied next to the ones
the two of you who were following rode in on. But more
about that later. First we must move this dear girl to a place
where she can rest and mend for a bit."

The man in green then gently took her in his arms and
started carrying her down the ravine in the direction Erik and
Tkaden had come. They followed close behind.

Several minutes later, they emerged from the
undergrowth were the wooded path made the bend in the
road. Leesha and Skoth, ready with his sword, stood there.
Their mouths dropped open when they saw the green clothed
man carrying Enat. Leesha ran to them asking if she was aye.

Enat lifted her head slightly, saw Leesha, and
murmured, "Mmm. Just follow." She laid her head back on
his chest and closed her eyes.

The man in green told them to follow him now, and
that they could come back for the horses later. He reassured
them they would be fine where they were. He worked his
way around the farthest fallen tree on the path and then
proceeded down the path for several dozen paces. Abruptly
he turned to the uphill side and into a small opening in the
undergrowth. There he followed a trail that went uphill,

between a narrow defile in some rocky outcrops. The space then opened up into a small box canyon, faced on all sides by splintered granite cliffs approximately ten feet in height and topped with the trees that made them seem even higher. One side of the canyon had rocky overhangs, which provided shelter from the rain, and scattered throughout the mostly level canyon were a number of tall hardwoods and pines. On the far side of canyon a small rivulet of water tumbled over the rocks and gathered into a pool at the base of the cliff. As the pond overflowed, its waters then escaped the canyon through some small crevices in the cliff.

When the last of them had emerged from the defile in the rocks, the man in green, with Enat still in his arms, turned to them and said, "Welcome to my home. I'm Fearglas."

Chapter 25 - Evlin

Fearglas carried Enat over to the overhanging cliff wall where they saw that in the rocks there was a small entrance to cave. He didn't take her into the cave, but laid her on a bed of pine needles that was well beneath the overhang. He picked up one of the gourds that was sitting on the rocks nearby and stepped over to the pond. There he filled the gourd dipper with cool water and in the cool waters he wetted again the cloth from her forehead. He carried the water back and held the dipper to her lips for her to drink, then placing the cloth again on her forehead he told her to rest. Leesha sat down next to her sister and took her hand. She patted it and held it as Enat closed her eyes and lay still.

Erik broke the silence, "Nice place, you have here. Looks like you've been here a while."

Fearglas smiled and said, "It is nice. I tend to come and go. But it is always a good place to come back to. I've been here, more than not, for the last several years."

Leesha looked up from where she was sitting and said, "Could someone explain to me what happened. We were behind the bend in the path and couldn't see what went on at the front of the column. Then Tkaden and I were in the woods. Then you two went off and found Enat and Fearglas."

Fearglas answered, "There will be time for the telling when the darkness falls. But before the sun sets we must take care of the beasts. The entrance to my home is too small for them to enter in, but there is a fine and succulent meadow nearby where they can safely spend the night. "If you three would accompany me," he motioned to Erik, Skoth, and Tkaden, "we'll go take them there and get them settled ere the sun sets."

Skoth questioned, "But will Leesha and Enat be safe here? What about the bear?"

Fearglas chuckled, "Oh, the bear. You needn't worry about that. That bear isn't going to come in here and attack them. They are as safe as safe can be."

Without further arguing they left the box canyon and made their way to the horses. They found them all together, the three of those who had been ridden by the captives, and the two ridden by Skoth and Erik. They were all tied to trees where Eric and Skoth had dismounted and run to enter the fray. When Skoth wondered aloud how they all came to be tied, and where were the Haudenoshonee ponies, Fearglas simply told him that the little people had taken care of that. It was also apparent that there were no Haudenoshonee bodies lying about. Again, Fearglas said that was the little people's doing.

Fearglas led them back up the hill for a few minutes and then turn to the side and led them into the undergrowth. Several dozen paces later they came to a secluded meadow covered in lush grass. Erik started to hobble the horses, but Fearglas suggested they just turn the horses loose and not to worry, the little people would watch over them. He also suggested that perhaps since Erik's men would soon be arriving, they could also come up here with their horses and then Erik and his men could camp on the edge of the meadow - as long as they promised not to bother the little people. By now the men had come to respect and trust what Fearglas said, and, to be honest, they were a bit in awe of him, even Erik, so they readily agreed with what he said.

They were about to leave the meadow when Skoth sensed a motion out of the corner of his eye. Quickly turning that direction he caught a glance of a running thin wisp of a figure in a green flowing dress with her dark auburn tresses flowing behind her. Then she was gone.

"Who, or what, was that?" Skoth asked of Fearglas.

After Fearglas had him describe what he had seen, and the others had not, Fearglas said simply, "Well, I reckon that'd be Evlin. Guess she must have wanted to catch your eye. Now let's get down to the path to meet your men."

They had just stepped onto the woodland path when Rolf and Jake on their horses cantered into view. They dismounted and Erik went forward to meet them, telling them simply that everything was all right and they were to follow him. While Erik led them up to the meadow, he explained that they would be setting up camp there but cautioned them that they were to behave themselves and do nothing that might antagonize any of the little people (he referred to them as leprechauns).

After Erik and his men headed up the path, Fearglas and the two young men headed back toward the box canyon. The sun had set by the time they re-entered the canyon through the narrow defile. They went over to the women, where Enat now was sitting up, looking a little pale from her concussion. They had been telling each other their stories, so both knew more of what had happened than either did before.

Fearglas said, "You're looking better, my lady. Took a nasty blow to that pretty head of yours, you did. But rest will make you stronger. You must rest now. We'll start a little fire here and make a little supper for you!"

They soon had a fire going and a pot on the fire with many a wild tuber and fruit in it and another pot with some water set to boil for a fine herbal tea. When the men had come back from the horses they had brought their own and the women's saddlebags with them. They arranged some sleeping rolls under the overhang of the cliff while the food was cooking, and while Fearglas was pulling some fresh fruit and nuts from one of the bags he had hung in a tree nearby. It looked to be a fine supper. The gloaming light was quickly fading in the secluded canyon when Fearglas tossed down woven mats around the fire and invited them to sit and join him for a meal.

They were arranging themselves around the fire when Fearglas said, "You might as well come out now, Evi. Come and enjoy the meal and talk with us, instead of just watching and listening to us."

From the shadows of the nearby trees stepped the young maiden Skoth had seen peering over the tree and running through the meadow. She was slight of frame and stood all of five feet tall. She was clothed in green and moved with an easy grace. As she drew near them, her wavy auburn hair caught the flickering firelight framing her tanned face and green eyes with a tantalizing glow.

"Let me introduce to you my daughter, Evlin, although some of you may have briefly seen her before."

Skoth and Tkaden sat transfixed by her appearance. The beauty of a young woman in the light of fire can paralyze a man. Enat remained seated, still too unsure of herself to stand quickly, but Leesha arose and walked toward her as she walked to the fire. She greeted her and put her arms around her to embrace her. Awkwardly, Evlin returned the hug. Leesha took her hand and pulled her over to the fire finding a place for her to sit on the mat between her and Enat. Enat didn't move much but also said words of greeting and reached out to grasp her hand, giving it a little squeeze as she did so.

Leesha turned to the two men, "Well you big lugs, where are your manners! Staring like that and saying not a word. Pick those jaws up off the ground and say hello to Evlin!"

Fearglas chuckled at the way she upbraided them, but waited to speak until after they mumbled their greetings, "Tis quite a sight to see the effect my lassie can have on the young men."

Evlin, with a tone of exasperation, blurted out, "Oh, Da, enough of that!"

Leesha didn't want there to be any family squabble at the fire, and being curious by nature, commented, "I've never heard of the Green Man, if that be who you truly are, having a daughter."

Fearglas took a deep breath and said, "That is a tale that will take some telling. Before I do that, let's enjoy the food before us."

After they had given thanks, eaten their fill, and supped the heady elixir of the herbal tea, they settled back and were ready to listen to the tale of the Green Man and His Wife. Fearglas surprised them when he looked to Evlin and said, "Daughter mine, would you do us the honor of sharing with our visitors the story of your mother - the Romance of the Green Man and his Sheela."

In her lilting and mesmerizing voice, Evlin gave voice to the lyric of those she loved.

Chapter 26 - The Romance of the Green Man and his Sheela

Through forest and field he wandered,
clothes of green and eyes to match.
Tis said that from his footsteps sprang spring flowers.
Tree and shrub blossomed at his touch.

The animals listened for his voice.
The birds sang melodies to please him.
With open arms and loving touch,
his embrace enveloped them.

He had no desire for a help-mate,
Til one day he saw her running through the meadows
Hair a flying in the breeze, smile shining like the sun
A goddess striding there before him, Sheela Na Gig.

He followed from a distance, ensorcelled with her beauty.
With skin as burnished bronze, and stature lithe and nimble,
she traipsed through fields of blooming flowers,
and danced into his heart, Sheela Na Gig.

Time stood still, and time flowed by unnoticed.
Years felt as but mere moments. Moments felt eternal.
Souls entwined and desires united, they became as one.
Field and forest, creatures great and small, reveled in their
romance.

Green Man and goddess of his heart, lovers of all living,
entwined in love and sparked new life.
The spark became of living flame,
and Evlin was her name.

Mother bear was Sheela, and he was father oak,
fierce and strong as parents be,
None could touch, and naught could harm that child,
wild and free, as bird in flight was she.

But even hearts of green can break,
and Fearglas felt the pain of grief.
For crafty and deceitful Lox, lurking in the deepest shadow,
Sent a curse of dreadful evil to entrap the wild child.

Like a mother bear Sheela rose in her defense,
and gave her life, that her little one might live.
And then that thing of evil fled,
still free to roam, still free to cause great mischief.

For Fearglas stayed to hold his dying wife,
and promised love eternal to her.
Nor would he leave his growing child,
The beauty of her mother that lived within.

But have no doubt of Fearglas vengeance.
For it will come, the mighty oak still lives,
for as the years move on, the broken heart,
embittered by great loss, heals and lives anew.

Autumn brings the dying,

winter waits with promise new,
life bursts forth in spring,
and summer will abundant be.

So dream with me and dance with me,
and chase the hate away,
live life in full embrace,
in honor of the Green Man and his Sheela.

Chapter 27 - Night in the Highlands

When Evlin finished speaking, it was as if the music of her voice lingered like the chord of a lyre that continues to vibrate for a time after it has been plucked. As the sound of her voice slowly faded in their ears, they heard the crackling of the fire and slowly began to register again the sounds of living creatures around them. Still no one spoke.

After a few moments of silence, Fearglas with a discernible sadness in his voice, "Thank you, Evi."

Enat reached out her hand to touch her, and said with gentleness, "That was so beautiful, Evlin. Thank you for sharing that."

On the other side of Evlin, Leesha also reached out and patted her on the knee. Skoth and Tkaden, sitting on the opposite side of the fire, had been enraptured as she spoke, being unable to take their eyes off of her, but now, as if in embarrassment they lowered their eyes and looked into the fire.

Leesha turned to Fearglas, "I don't know what to say, other than I'm sorry."

Fearglas nodded in assent, and then said, "Thank you. But that is time gone by, now it is time to look to the future. Autumn is upon us and winter lies just beyond. Sheela was my spring and my summer. Full of life and beauty. Her death was my autumn. A bitter harvest to be sure, and the last several years have been as winter. New life lies waiting for the chance to burst forth in full bloom." Here he glanced at Evlin, and then went on. "In this natural world around us, the cold of this coming season lies soon before us, but that is only a pregnant pause, before the new springs forth."

Leesha also glanced at Evlin, and then said, "Life is indeed a cycle: life, and death, and life again."

Fearglas nodded, for he felt that Leesha understood what he was trying to say, and then he said to the group, "Night has come upon us. We must prepare for the morrow. Enat needs her rest. Evlin, would you tend to her and get her settled for the night? And Skoth, I must talk with you. Would you walk with me, and come and sit upon the wall?"

"Of course." said Skoth and he arose.

They did as Fearglas had asked. Evlin helped Enat to a place under the rock overhang, but from where one could still set some of the night stars, and she could also see the moon rising in the east. Fearglas and Skoth went out beneath the trees, moving toward the northern side of the box canyon. Tkaden and Leesha sat by the fire for a few moments then went for a walk in the moonlight.

When Fearglas reached the north wall, he made a slight turn and started to ascend a natural rock stairway that worked itself up some crevices in the side of the cliff. The stairway emerged on the top of the cliff on the northwestern edge and there Fearglas invited him to sit on a ledge with him. From there they could see the moonlight reflecting off of the small waterfall and pool tucked into the western curve of the canyon. Soon they were deep in conversation, Skoth listening carefully to what Fearglas' words and occasionally asking clarifying questions or giving brief responses. At first Skoth was somewhat dubious about what Fearglas was asking of him, but soon came to accept and approve of it.

Back at the campsite, Evlin had settled Enat comfortably on a bed of pine needles and then went to the pool to get a container of water. When she returned she poured a small amount into a cup, pulled out a few fresh picked herbs from the pouch she always carried with her, stirred some of them into the cup and handed it to Enat to drink.

Enat sniffed the herbal cup and questioned, "Mint?"

Evlin smiled and said, "A special kind, just drink. Let the water heal you from the inside."

A few minutes after drinking her tea Enat was asleep. Evlin sat beside her for a long time, stroking her hair and murmuring some form of chant over her. Then she went over to the pool. She pulled her dress up over her head and stepped quickly into the pool. She settled herself completely under the water for a few moments and then rose up and stepped back to the shore. From the distance of the cliff wall Skoth could see the waters sparkling as they tumbled down the rocks, and glistening as they slipped from her skin. It was a mesmerizing sight, and if he had not been engrossed in the conversation with Fearglas, he would have been drawn to her. She shook the water from her hair and slipped her dress back on over her head. Then she moved under the canopy of the trees and out of sight.

When Tkaden and Leesha walked away from the campfire they intended to enjoy the walk in the moonlight and to talk about the events of the day in more detail. They found themselves walking closely together as they wove their way beneath the stately pine trees and the branches of the mighty oaks that dotted the floor of the canyon. But there was something magical in the air, and soon they ceased their talking and were walking together silently as they held hands. They came to a slightly larger opening beneath the trees, approximately in the center of the box canyon, and stopped. Standing in the grassy clearing they look up to see the night sky of stars and partial moon framed by the living trees around them. Tkaden pulled her close and she returned his embrace. Time seemed frozen as they lost themselves in each other.

It was far into the night when both sets of people returned to the clearing by the pool and laid down to sleep for the night. Sleep was peaceful for all.

Peaceful, however, is not the word that could be used to describe the night that Erik and his men spent in the meadow with the horses. While the horses contentedly grazed and dozed during the night, the men were anxious and slept fitfully. They kept one man on watch at all times, and saw nothing that appeared to threaten them, but they did occasionally hear strange noises, and sometimes caught glimpses of movement at the side of their vision. It was as though something was out there. Watching. Waiting. But nothing ever happened. It was a pleasant meadow, with sweet grass for the horses, but when morning came, they were ready to move on.

Chapter 28 - Departures

The folks in the hidden valley of the box canyon awoke in the morning to a small fire burning, and Evlin heating up a pot of spruce tea and a kettle of delicious-smelling wild rice and berries. Enat was obviously feeling much better and ready for travel. They clearly enjoyed their morning meal, but when Skoth began laying out his plans after the meal, there were some strong objections voiced.

Skoth told them he was going to be spending the winter with Fearglas. He felt there was much to learn from him during this time. He wanted Leesha and Tkaden to go to Tkaden's home area and to winter with them, seeing if there was any key to what would help the Wabanaki and Celtic people become stronger as the united people of Eirgalon. Enat should travel with Erik back to New Caledonia and rejoin Karl at Tante's. Their task would be to work with Susie and the Women's Circle there. He charged them to focus their efforts to find means that might pull the various kings and chiefs of Celtic Eirgalon into common cause. Erik and his men were to accompany Enat safely to New Caledonia and then they were free to go as they pleased.

They did have some objections to his plan, with Leesha and Enat especially questioning the wisdom of splitting up. Leesha tried to make Skoth understand that Erik would be loath to leave Skoth and she doubted he could be persuaded to leave Skoth here by himself.

At this point, Fearglas interjected, "That may be true, but when you leave this morning and go to meet him and give him his instructions, he will do it. He will be loyal. Even if he should try to find this place, he will not. The entrance will be hidden from him. He must go."

In the end, despite their reservations, they agreed to do as Skoth had asked them. They quickly packed up and said their good-byes.

The farewell between Fearglas and Tkaden held one surprise, for Fearglas made a point of telling Tkaden to share the story of Sheela to Tkaden's father. When asked why, he wouldn't answer, but simply insisted that he be told.

Before they left, Evlin placed a small pouch in Enat's hand, saying, "Here are some herbs. I'm sure you will recognize them, and the woman you call Susie will help you learn more of how to use them. They may look ordinary, but remember that they are a special gift from the Green Man and his daughter."

The final good-bye of the group was said at the narrow defile that led out of the hidden vale. Leesha gave Skoth a long embrace and a few words as well. With tears in her eyes she said to him, "Sko, friend of my childhood. I will miss you."

Skoth, even at this time of serious leave-taking, couldn't help but tease his friend, "I shall miss you, too, but somehow I think Tkaden may keep you occupied enough to take your mind off me. Tho, I'll admit, you have had your eye on me ever since you stole my clothes at the lake."

"Well, it's good to see you haven't lost any of the old Sko since this all began," she said with a laugh, "just make sure you keep it!

"I will."

Then she whispered in his ear, "And do be careful of that Evlin. There's magic in her. Don't let her seduce you."

It was his turn to laugh. He chuckled and whispered back to her, "Aye, careful I'll be. But maybe I'll be the one to do the seducing."

With a "You big oaf!" she smacked him on the shoulder with her hand and then quickly reached up and gave him a little kiss on the cheek and said, "Just be careful." Then she turned and quickly left.

Evlin was standing several steps away, but when she saw Leesha kiss him, a small frown crossed her face. It quickly disappeared as Skoth turned to her and Fearglas and walked back to them.

It was no surprise when the party arrived at the meadow and told Erik of the plans that Skoth had laid out for them, that Erik objected. He said, "That young fool, I'm going to go talk some sense into him. I'm not leaving him alone. The rest of you wait here." With that, he hurried out of the meadow determined to make his way to the hidden valley and to talk some sense into Skoth.

Despite his excellent woodsmanship and tracking skills, Erik was unable to find the entrance to the box canyon. He reconciled himself to the situation, and finally made his way back to the meadow. The rest of the group had the horses packed and was ready to go.

With a frown he said, "I still don't like this. But let's head back to Glenoak, and we will proceed from there."

Chapter 29 - Dunsheelin

Most of the autumn leaves had fluttered to the earth by this cold November day, and the good wives of the isle of Fadis Innis, were bustling about urging the menfolk to get things put away and shuttered up, for they could "feel in their bones, the coming nor'easter." The menfolk often joked about the women and their weather predictions, but they knew with deadly seriousness the power of a nor'easter barreling up the coastline. This type of storm at this time of year could bring waves to swamp any ship and snow enough to cover a flock of sheep.

Teite and Neal were spending this day at the academy, as they had spent almost every day since their friends' departure in the summer. Daily they would pour over volumes of manuscripts. The Dunsheelin Academy on Fadis Innis was known throughout Eirgalon as the largest repository of written knowledge on the western continent. Teite had laboriously been working her way through text after text of the old Celtic texts. She could read Ogham, Old Norse Rune, Modern Rune, and even a form of Latin that originally came from southern Europe, spreading when the Christian religion had touched the Celtic world. Christianity was a strange religion to her. She didn't exactly follow it, though many of its precepts were sound.

The beliefs of the people of Eirgalon were, to say the least, diverse. There were many elements of the old Norse and Celtic ways of understanding the world, as well as certain elements of Wabanaki spirituality. Added to that was the smattering of Christian concepts that had spread when Rome had ruled the European world. But the influence of Christianity was less than might be expected, for when Harold Godwinson had defeated William of Normandy at the Battle of Hastings, the sway of the Christian faith and the power of Rome had diminished in the Anglish Isles. Even though Harold himself had been a Christian, the power of the southeastern European religion grew less the further from the base of its origins and political power.

While Teite continued to study the ancient texts, Neal recently had become fascinated by a new invention that the scholars of the Academy were working on. They called it a "rune press" for it took runes carved of wood, or even formed of metal, set them in a tray, covered them with ink, and then pressed them against a piece of parchment to print the runes. Multiple copies could be quickly made. Neal could sense some of the possibilities for communication that this new invention offered. Teite was heartened to see Neal's excitement concerning this development, for ever since Neal had injured his hand and his friends had left on their adventure without him he had seemed to slip into a melancholia.

As they labored at the academy on that cold autumn day, they heard others talking about the weather comments the good wives had been making. They had also heard the warnings that some of the druids at the academy, who studied the weather of the world, were making as they examined the wind, the sky, and a strange assortment of tubes and bottles they had set up in their workshop.

So late in the afternoon, as was their custom, they

started on the path back to the fortress of Dunsheelin where they had rooms. The sun would have been nearing the horizon, but they couldn't see it for the sky had turned a nasty shade of grey. They hurried down the path for the winds were gusting strongly. Their coats whipped around them. Ahead of them two deer burst out of the woods in frantic flight dashing across the path just steps in front of them.

Startled, Neal and Teite stopped in their tracks. The deer had barely disappeared into the woods on the other side of the road when a huge dog leapt onto the path. The dog noticed them and skidded to a stop. It looked at them and barring its teeth, it growled at them. It took a step toward them as Neal was drawing the knife he wore at his side. As he drew it he winced in pain and shifted it to his left hand. The dog hesitated, glanced at the woods from the direction it had come, and then leapt back into the woods in pursuit of the deer.

Teite said, "What was that about?"

"I don't know?" responded Neal, "but that was one of the biggest and meanest look dogs I have ever seen."

"Was it a wolf?"

"That was no wolf. It had a leather collar on it. But it is a dog I've never seen around here. Let's get moving and get away from it and get out of this wind."

They resumed their hurried walk down the path and to the fortress. The rain was just beginning as they entered the Great Hall of Dunsheelin which was at the center of the fortress, and which was where King Unaine of Fadis Innis, though he preferred to be called simply "chief", held court.

There were no supplicants seeking the king's justice at this time, but Unaine was there. He sat near one side of the hall with his trusted advisor, the old master druid, Theofinn.

The large hearth fire was burning, which gave a pleasant warmth to the hall. It was much appreciated given the cold gust of wind that had entered the room with Teite and Neal. Teite almost ran over to her father to tell him about the strange occurrence with the dog on the path. However, since Unaine was listening attentively to something Theofinn was saying, she patiently waited until he was finished. But before she could begin, Theofinn began talking again. This time, however, his words were addressed to her.

"Teite, so good of you to suddenly appear. I hope you have been studying and practicing the casting and reading of runes. We were just talking about you. We thought we might ask you to use your talents to help us understand some news that has just come to us."

Teite wondered inside what the news was, but held that thought inside and instead reacted with, "I wonder if now is an auspicious time to read runes. The storm, with fury building, is beginning to break upon us. That might influence the guiding of the spirits."

Theofinn nodded with a thoughtful expression and said, "You may be right. I think we can wait till this evening when we are sure all good folks are safely inside, and everything is secure against the fury of this storm. We'll wait."

Unaine now spoke, "Well, there, greetings to you my daughter. And what might it be that brought you rushing over here so quickly when you entered? Surely it wasn't to tell me the storm is breaking upon us. I'm not deaf yet. I can hear the wind and the rain as well as a young man, and maybe even feel it a bit more in my bones."

Teite told her father and Theofinn about the encounter on the path with the dog pursuing the deer. Neal added a few words of description, but tried to shrug it off as nothing more than someone's dog chasing deer.

But Teite was adamant that it must be more than that. She added her reasoning that it was unusual, though not unheard of, to find deer so close to the outskirts of Dunsheelin. She also insisted that the dog stopped and looked back the way it had come before it chose to ignore them and to resume its chase of the deer. That was certainly unusual.

Unaine said nothing, but Theofinn said, "Those are some unusual details. As Neal suggested, there may be nothing to this. However, there have been several strange occurrences in the vicinity of Dunsheelin since Skoth embarked on his quest. They bear contemplation."

Then turning to Neal, Theofinn asked, "Now, young Neal. I'm wondering how that hand is feeling. Is it completely healed and without any pain?"

Neal cocked his head, as if in thought, then replied, "I was going to say it is completely fine and is healed with only a scar. But, now that you mention it, I have felt some pain in the last few days. Occasionally a kind of throbbing pain, but once in awhile a sharp pain shooting through it."

"Any such pains today?"

"Well, as a matter of fact there was. When I drew my knife on the path, after the dog jumped out, I felt that shooting pain. I thought it was probably just because I moved so fast maybe it was pain from the old injury."

Theofinn stroked his beard with his right hand and said, "Perhaps. Perhaps. But I wonder ..." and his words tailed off.

Teite queried, "You wonder what?"

"There seems to be many small unusual occurances. Maybe they can be explained away, but I'm just not sure. I think evil may be afoot."

At that moment the inside shutters of a window on the opposite side of the hall blew open, and the wind and sleet came dashing in. Servants scurried to reclose the inside shutters, and one of the men who had been standing guard rushed outside to seal the outside shutters.

Unaine said in a quiet and calm voice, "I think that later this evening, even though the storm may rage outside, we will have that reading of the runes."

"What about the news? Can you tell me that now?"

"I think that, too, would best wait until we gather round the evening fire."

And so it was, that later that evening, after the shared meal in the Great Hall, and those who helped about the Great Hall and its business had departed, that the four of them gathered together in Unaine's private quarters. His quarters weren't elaborate and had some soft touches obvious throughout the rooms. There were noticeable decorations that Teite's mother had created, and every time Teite entered her father's living quarters she felt again her mother's presence. A small fire crackled in the hearth. Pulled in front of it were a stout table and four sturdy chairs. With the four seated in a semi-circle at the table, the side nearest the fire was open.

161

Unaine asked if she was ready. Teite stretched out the rune cloth with the sacred spiral embroidered into it, on the table and set the bag of runes next to it.

Theofinn commented, "What fine workmanship. Talented was the one who fashioned this. What beauty, and in beauty there is power."

Teite began, "I am ready, but first we must agreed on the question. Perhaps, we are contemplating different affairs. If we are to have some clarity in response, then we must be clear about what we are asking."

Unaine went first, "My thoughts reach out to Skoth. I am curious about him, but I wonder if there is something that we should be doing here."

Theofinn voiced his thoughts, "I also have that curiosity, but I sense an evil nearby. I would like to know about that."

Teite then shared her own concerns, "I worry about my sisters, I'm frustrated that I haven't found anything that might help Skoth, I am troubled about Neal, and I have a similar feeling about the evil Theofinn mentioned. Many are the questions which lie before us."

Unaine looked puzzled, "Neal? Why? What is troubling about Neal?"

"His hand. I think, mayhap, it is worse than he is telling us."

Neal spoke up, "No, no, don't be worried about me. I'm not a problem. I don't think we need to be asking questions about my hand. I'll be fine. It's Skoth I'm worried about. The message you received from Erik said that Skoth was spending the winter in the highlands with Fearglas. If this storm forebodes what this winter will be like, there might be problems for him."

"It's not the weather that will cause the problems for him," said Theofinn, "It is the fact that he is wintering close to Malsum's territory. I worry about that."

Teite brought the conversation back around to the issue of the question, "With all that being said, what shall be the question and subject for the reading of the runes. We need to be clear. We need to be in agreement."

With a bit more conversation they came to the consensus that since winter was breaking upon them and nothing could be done to give or send aid to Skoth at this time, they would seek guidance for how to deal with the situation on Fadis Innis.

They agreed they would be thinking about "What should they do about the evil they sense on Fadis Innis?"

One by one they put a hand into the rune bag that Teite held and drew out a rune. First, Unaine pulled out Hagall and placed it on the cloth. Next, Theofinn drew out Eolh and placed it on the cloth. Lastly, came Neal. He was going to place his "injured and healed" hand into the sack to make the draw, but at the last moment changed his mind and used his left hand instead.

Theofinn raised an eyebrow when he noticed Neal change his mind, and he asked, "Neal, why did you just switch your choice of hands and use your left hand for the drawing?"

Neal, a little embarrassed, said, "When I started to reach out with my right hand, a burning pain shot through it, so I thought I better switch to my other hand. When I did, the pain was gone."

"I don't like the sound of that, young man. But now is not the time to pursue it. You and I will have a look at it later."

Neal assented and then they turned their attention to Teite, so that she could begin her interpretation of the runes. She studied the runes for a period of time, for even the location and manner in which they had been placed on the cloth influenced the interpretation.

She drew a deep breath and began, "The rune Hagall reaffirms what we are feeling, there is a sense of frustration about us as our minds are often elsewhere and strange occurrences happen to us. But it also reminds us to have trust in each other and trust in those things that have made us what we are. Eolh is a rune of protection. There are powers that are protecting us during this time of danger, we should not discard them. There is also the rune of Thorn, which might be called a "helping hand of fate." Perhaps our fate is being challenged, but time weaves a tapestry and though our individual threads may be threatened, the pattern will be accomplished. We need to allow the weaver's hands to help guide our ways."

The storm was building in fury as they began their discussion of Teite's interpretation of the runes. Neal joked about how maybe the danger was just this powerful nor'easter that was breaking upon them. That earned him a baleful look from Teite, and a snort of derision from Theofinn.

Unaine commented on the jest, "No, young Neal, the danger is more than that. Consider your hand, the dog in the path, the fury of the storm, and that feeling of malevolence that sometimes shrouds this pleasant isle. Tis' more than just the weather. Remember the prisoner who threw that knife that struck your hand?"

Neal winced at the memory, and subconsciously flexed his hand.

Unaine continued, "That prisoner mentioned Malsum. He is a real opponent. We may not have seen him face to face, but he is out there, and, for whatever reason, he bears us ill-will."

Theofinn added, "And don't forget the words of the prophecy: *beware the sunset lox a sly and wily fox.* Evil does walk among us in forms we may not see or recognize. We must beware."

When they left for their sleeping quarters that night their minds were troubled, for while the reading of the runes gave them reassurances and called upon them to trust, it also made it clear that there was, indeed, a malevolence directed toward them. Theofinn was worried enough about that, and about Neal's comments concerning his hand, so that he insisted Neal promise to visit him in his workshop on the morrow.

Chapter 30 - New Caledonia

The snow was flying sideways as Erik sat with Karl and Enat, eating the evening meal at Tante's Table. It had been several weeks since they left Skoth in the hidden valley and made their way, first to Glenoak where they celebrated the harvest festival with the townspeople, and then back downriver and to New Caledonia. The late summer days had turned to autumn, and now autumn was turning to winter - with a vengeance! They were glad to be in the safe confines of Tante's Table, enjoying Susie's excellent cooking and the warmth of the hearthfire.

Erik had sent word about the adventures of the young folks across the Fadis Innis Sound to King Unaine at Dunsheelin. Now, for the last couple of weeks, Erik was feeling as though he was an extra oar. There wasn't much of importance for him to do. Enat and Susie were spending many days and evenings with the women of the Women's Circle in New Caledonia. He sure didn't want to get involved with that! It was dangerous to be around the women when they were intent upon their "circle business."

As for Karl, well, Erik had to admit he was a little impressed by the young man. Karl had used his time of healing at Tante's by forging some important friendships. Although, truth be told, it was Susie that had been behind much of what had developed. Susie, and her friends in the Women's Circle, had made a point of arranging for some of the young men of New Caledonia to visit at Tante's Table, where they were, of course, introduced to young Karl of

Fadis Innis. Karl was by nature a friendly and outgoing young man and soon the young men were coming to Tante's not just to eat the fine fare of Tante's Table but also to visit with Karl. And when the time came that Karl could move about as his leg healed, and Susie wisely encouraged him to exercise and rehabilitate it, he was soon enough out about the town with the other young men.

One of these young men was Gunnar, son of Haggar, the local Celtic king. When Gunnar learned that Karl's grandfather had been with the group of Fadis Innis warriors that had fought alongside his own grandfather, when some of the older kingdoms of Eirgalon, to the east of New Caledonia, tried to exert their sway over the westernmost kingdoms, he acted as if Karl were a long lost cousin.

During the weeks of recuperation, Karl made strong inroads into the local community, as he began to spend most days in the companionship of Gunnar and his friends. There were a few times he even missed the evening meal at Tante's because he was supping with Gunnar at the Great Hall of New Caledonia. It was there that he met Gunnar's father, Haggar. In many ways, Karl discovered that Haggar was like Unaine of Fadis Innis. Haggar wasn't one for great formalities or ceremonies, and he was a fair and reasonable man. After meeting him the first time, Karl wondered how a king like Haggar could have an incompetent man like Olaf serving as sheriff of the waterfront. When he later voiced this thought to Gunnar, he had the situation explained to him.

It seems that Olaf is a cousin to King Haggar and Haggar's mother, still living, insisted that Haggar find some post of importance for her dear departed sister's son. So Olaf had been appointed to the seat of the Sheriff of the Waterfront, where hopefully any damage he did could be rectified without too much trouble.

When Karl explained this situation to Erik, after his return from up north, Erik chuckled and said, "Well, that explains a little, but I don't think I'd appoint his pompous ass to a seat anywhere, even to keep the family peace!"

And so it was that this evening, as this gale of November broke over the coastlands of Eirgalon, they sat and enjoyed the evening meal in the warmth of Tante's common room.

As they supped, Karl broached a subject that was on his mind; he wanted to travel to Heilsand, the large Celtic settlement to the east. It was the large harbor city, located to the northeast, around the Vineland Cape.

Erik was a little dubious about the venture, cautioning him, "Well, I'm not the one to be ordering you about, but there are a couple of problems with that. First, not all those easterners have a great liking for those of us who live farther to the west. There was a time when they wanted to rule us. They still bristle at the fact that we stood up to them."

Karl replied, "Yes, I know that. I've learned my history, and Gunnar has shared some of that history from his family's background."

"Then why do you want to go there?"

Thoughtfully, Karl responded, "Well, if there is to be a High King in Eirgalon, don't you think we should be making some contact with those of eastern Eirgalon?

"That's an interesting point. We are all Celts, but we've had our differences over the years and those could cause problems in the future. But I have another concern. Traveling the seas to Heilsand in weather like this is nigh impossible. Even by road it is something best left till spring."

"I don't mean to travel in a storm like this. But when the weather breaks I think we could. There are ships that travel the coast during the winter months, and the roads do clear between storms."

"Aye, tis true. But, any captain worth his salt, won't go beyond sight of shoreline, and will stop at nearly every safe harbor along the way to avoid getting caught in a fast-forming gale."

Enat was silently listening to them go back and forth, but finally she chimed in, "So if you two go off to the east, what about me?'

Erik protested, "I didn't say I was going anywhere. I rather think we should head north myself. In the spring that is. Maybe check in with Tkaden and Leesha. Perhaps even hook up again with Skoth when he comes out of that hidden valley of his."

Karl said, "And I'm only thinking about it. I haven't decided. But, of course, I would want you to go with us."

With mock hurt feelings, Enat replied, "Sure, drag the poor girl along out of pity. Don't tell her what your plans are. Just assume that she'll want to tag along. Perhaps you might be thinking of asking me what I think we should be doing! One says to go east, the other says to go north. Don't I have a say in this?"

Karl was quick to reply, "Of course, we want to know what you think. I was just letting you know what I was thinking. What do you think?"

"Sure, try to appease me. But you asked, so I'll tell you. I think you have done a good job of forging some friendships here. Gunnar and his friends are good people, and it is always wise to have good people for friends. I think your idea of going to Heilsand has some merit, but I don't think we should decide tonight. Let's spend a few days thinking about it."

They discussed the situation for quite some time, but in the end no final decisions were made. They decided to wait on making a decision. Erik helped Karl to postpone his plans by letting him know that although Karl's leg was healing nicely, Karl was still not in "fighting form." So when Erik suggested he speak to King Haggar and ask to join some of his men in practicing their skills and getting back in shape, Karl agreed that would be a good course of action for the immediate future.

Chapter 31 - Tkaden's Hometown - Wausacom

The wind had turned bitter cold, and a driving snow was beginning to blanket the town when Tkaden and Leesha rode into Wausacom, the hometown of Tkaden and the largest Wabanaki settlement in the region. Few people took the time to examine them closely as they wound their horses through the lodges toward the center of the town where Tkaden's father had his lodgehouse. There were several larger lodges where large extended families lived, and even a few lodges where multiple families of one clan might live together, but most of the town consisted of smaller houses where individual families lived as the Wabanaki had come to adopt some of the customs of their Celtic neighbors that intermingled with them. There were a small number of Celts who lived in Wausacom, and there were numerous cases of marriage and offspring between them.

The descendents of the Nordic-Celtic immigrants, who first came to this land more than 400 years ago, had been mixing with the native Wabanaki inhabitants for many generations. While there certainly were varying degrees of bigotry and prejudice in people of both cultural traditions, the truth of the matter was that Eirgalon was developing a blended civilization. People of both backgrounds adopted and adapted elements of the other that they saw as beneficial to themselves.

Tkaden had seen the reality of this blended civilization through his years of growing up in the area of

Wausacom, but Leesha had been, in some respects, more sheltered as she grew up on Fadis Innis. People of both cultures lived on the long island, but the Celts were in the majority and dominated the economic and political life of the island. However, now they were in a region that was often predominantly Wabanaki. During the several weeks that Tkaden and Leesha had taken to travel from Glenoak to Wausacom, Leesha had her eyes opened to the reality of this blended civilization. When they stayed in towns, they visited and stayed as guests with people who were Wabanaki, or Celt, or a mixture of the two.

One thing they did notice is that the towns and villages each had their own local laws and that while there was a general acceptance and sharing of customs and traditions, there was no central authority throughout the land that might mediate disputes. In actuality, there were numerous small chiefdoms and kingdoms, each of which was a law unto itself. Leesha was also surprised by the fact that, generally speaking, people were not unduly concerned about a young Wabanaki man and a young Celtic woman traveling together. Perhaps people simply saw two travelers and assumed that they were husband and wife.

Young love can be a difficult relationship to understand or explain, but it was apparent to those who encountered them during this time that these two were developing a genuine connection to each other. Each felt that they were old enough to do as they pleased, and they were pleased to be with each other. The night before the storm broke and they entered Tkaden's hometown, they were camped in a small clearing that Tkaden had often used when he had gone hunting as a youth.

They had built a small fire to cook their meal and were sitting shoulder to shoulder by the fire as they roasted a small partridge shot by Tkaden earlier in the afternoon. They were talking and joking about what to expect when they entered the town on the morrow.

But then Tkaden turned serious and said with hesitations, "Leesha, I know I should speak of this to your father . . . but he isn't here . . . and I don't think we will be seeing him for some time . . . so there's something I want to say to you . . ."

Leesha, ever the impatient one, interrupted, "Well, you know me well enough by now, go on, I'm all ears!"

"No you're not. All ears, that is." Tkaden was trying to relieve the tension within himself with a feeble attempt at humor.

When Leesha turned a reproachful eye upon him, he stopped with the attempt and returned to the serious, "Leesha, I want you for my wife. I don't know all the customs of your people on Fadis Innis, or if we need your father's permission or blessing, or what, but here is it - will you be my wife?"

She didn't need to answer him with words, although she did say "yes," because she turned to face him, wrapped her arms around him, and gave him a long and lingering kiss, which to him was as the sweetest of ambrosia. When they finally relaxed from their embrace, she did have a few more words for him.

"Our customs allow the woman to choose her husband, I don't need Da's permission, though I will, of course, ask him for his blessing. Since you are the son of a chief and I am the daughter of a king, most people will consider us of equal status, which means that few people of either family can object on those grounds. There might be some political considerations we'll have to make, but I am willing to do so. The truth is, that I have found love with you. I want you. But how about your family? What will they make of this?"

Tkaden smiled, "You already know that my Grandmother, Maedrid, is Theofinn's sister. She will adore you! Others there may be, who might grumble, but I doubt that any of my family will object."

So it was, that as they entered Wausacom, they entered it as intended husband and wife. However, at that moment, the warmth in their hearts was tempered by the cold and snow. The rain had turned to snow an hour before they reached the settlement and they were chilled to the bone. When they reached the lodge of Tkaden's father, they immediately dismounted and tethered their horses. This was a large wooden lodge, which housed the extended family and also served as the meeting place for important town meetings. Its function was much the same as the Great Hall and Keep in Dunsheelin which served as the audience hall and meeting place for the kingdom as well as being the place of residence for the king, his family, and his retinue.

They quickly stepped inside and closed the door behind them. They were greeted by the sight of a welcome fire burning in the center of the common room, with its smoke nicely vented as it was drawn upward into the high vault of the room's ceiling vent. The look and feel of the room was warm and inviting. With surprised expressions, the people scattered about the room looked over to see who had entered. They weren't expecting anyone, since the storm had already driven everyone who should be there inside.

Tkaden's mother was the first to recognize him and came running to him from across the room, exclaiming, "Kade! You're back!"

A flurry of activity ensued that included hugs, greetings, and introductions. Animals were to be cared for, so of course, a younger member of the family was sent out into the storm to get the horses taken care of and bedded down in the stable.

Leesha was warmly welcomed and after the initial greetings, Tkaden's mother, Maeve, took charge and showed her to a guest room where she could get settled in and freshened up from the journey. She also let her know that the evening meal would be served in about half an hour, so she should be sure to rejoin them before that.

Even though the storm raged and the snow was falling at a furious pace, the lodge was filled with joy and celebration that evening. Tkaden had talked privately with his father, Tkomik, for several minutes prior to the meal, letting him know that he had much to tell him about the events of the past several months. But most importantly, he told him about Leesha, and asked for his blessing on them.

As they enjoyed the meal, the gathered family reveled in the tales that Tkaden told of his adventures since he left them last spring. He did leave out some of the more "political" aspects as he told his tales, feeling those would best be saved to share with his father first. They finished the meal and cleaned up, but stayed gathered as a family around the central fire. Storytelling around the hearthfire during the winter months was a tradition of the Wabanaki people, and this night of the first winter storm was the perfect start to the time of storytelling.

Tkaden had told them about meeting a green man of the wilds, but now he wanted them to hear the story that Fearglas had told him to make sure his father heard. Tkaden was a good storyteller, himself, but he knew that his intended, Leesha, had a "gift of gab" as it is said, and so he asked her if she would share the tale of "The Green Man and His Sheela."

Leesha was indeed a wonderful and powerful storyteller, with eyes that capture your attention, words and ways of speaking that wrap themselves around you, and a lively energy that seizes the listener and does not release them until the end.

Many was the time she had gone over the tale in her mind. She recalled every nuance that Evlin had used in the telling of it, and strong in her mind's eye were the expressions she had seen on Fearglas' face at that telling. She entranced them as she introduced it and then began. All other sounds melted away, save for the cracking of the fire and the timbre and tone of her voice. Almost as skillfully as Evlin, she carried them through the story, and then there was silence in the room. The fire crackled and the logs tumbled in upon themselves, as if asking to be given more.

Tkomik let out a deep sigh, and said, "Thank you, my dear, for the telling of the tale. Let all know now, that I claim you as my daughter. Your gifts are many, and I suspect there are many more unseen. Tkaden is a most blessed young man. Welcome to my family."

Leesha, as tongue-gifted as she was, knew not what to say, for she saw a tear in the eye of her father-in-law-to-be.

It was Tkaden who spoke, "We thank you for your blessing, Father. But may I ask why Fearglas would want you, especially you, to hear this story."

Tkomik, now with a look of contentment, replied, "Ahhh. He wanted me to know what happened. You see, his Sheela . . . was my sister."

Chapter 32 - Hidden Valley

Several weeks had passed since Skoth's friends had departed the small box canyon that existed in the highlands of Eirgalon. Many were the hours and days that Skoth spent walking the woods and fields with Fearglas, learning the lore of the land and love of its creatures. For a couple of days they had stayed in the small valley hidden in the highlands of Eirgalon putting up supplies of nuts, berries, and edible plants in preparation for the winter months to come. Skoth was surprised by the incredible energy of both Fearglas and his daughter, Evlin. They were constantly busy and soon it appeared to Skoth that the cave by the waterfall was filled with plenty of food to carry them through the winter.

Fearglas then took Skoth on several long walks through the highlands and valleys, some lasting for days. The beauty of the fall colors that covered the landscape amazed Skoth. He confessed he had enjoyed the bounty of the harvest season on Fadis Innis, but that was nothing compared to the wondrous sights he saw now. As to what Evlin was doing during this time when they were away from the valley, Skoth was unsure. She had not come with them. Fearglas had volunteered nothing about her, and Skoth was reluctant to ask. He had moments he wished she had come with them, for she was pleasant to be with and he did miss her.

Several times during their foray Skoth noticed bear tracks and caught glimpses of what appeared to be a bear similar to the bear that he saw on the day of the attack. When he mentioned these sightings to his guide, Fearglas either ignored them, or said there was nothing to worry about.

They returned to the hidden valley the day before the first winter storm of the season broke upon them. The hardwood trees of the valley had all dropped their leaves, except for a few of the oaks that were steadfastly refusing to shed the final portions of their foliage. The pines and spruce trees still gave color and shelter to the idyllic spot. When they entered into the openness of the valley from the narrow defile, they could see across to the splashing waterfall and pond. Evlin was kneeling next to a small fire from which a wispy tendril of rising smoke was wrapping itself around the tall pines nearby. It may not have had the vibrant colors of the autumn vistas they had seen in the previous weeks, but it was every much a picture of beauty and peace.

She rose to greet them as they made their way to her. She held Fearglas in a fierce embrace for several moments, and then turned to Skoth and stepping forward put her arms around him. He wasn't sure of what to do, for her action caught him unawares. But she smelled so wonderful, and sweet, and full of life, that he lost his thoughts and returned the strength of her embrace.

Slightly embarrassed, he released her, sniffed the air, and said, "Mmmmm. That smells good. It looks like you made enough for all of us."

She smiled at him and said, "Why of course, I know how much both you and Fearglas can eat when you're hungry, and you came a long way today."

Skoth wasn't sure what to say to that. He did wonder how she knew how far they had walked today, or, come to think of it, even that she would know they were returning today, which she obviously knew since she had made such a large pot of stew.

Fearglas simply grinned and stepped into the conversation, "Daughter, dear, you warm my heart, and my stomach too by the looks and smell of it. We are famished. Let's eat!"

They did enjoy their meal together. Skoth and Fearglas ate as if they hadn't eaten for days, though in fact Fearglas had taught Skoth quite well how to live off the land as they travelled. After they ate, Evlin was excited to show them how the cave was now all prepared to shelter them for the winter. Skoth was impressed as she led them through it pointing out the way she had organized it. Skoth had only been in the entrance area of it during his previous time in the valley, now he saw the full extent of it. After rounding a slight bend in the passageway the cave widened into a comfortable sized room. Light filtered into the room through a hole high in the ceiling, which was where the smoke from a fire pit in the center of the room could vent out naturally. There was ample room to sit around the fire and several places to sit and work when the weather outside was inclement. There were several small alcoves around the sides of the large room in which Evlin had arranged sleeping pallets as well as room for some personal space and possessions. Skoth was pleased to see that in the area she had designated for him were the saddlebags and possessions he had with him when he came riding to the rescue of his friends.

The large central space narrowed to a passageway opposite the entrance of the cave. Down that passageway, stored in various bags, boxes and assorted containers were all sorts of nuts, berries, dried fruits, roots, and the like for them to eat during the winter months, as well as a sizable store of dry wood and several containers that Evlin made no explanation of. She did point out one box, however, that surprised and pleased him. It was filled with an assortment of books.

After checking out the cave, their home for the next couple of months, the three of them returned to the fire by the pond. The sun had set and the light was fading fast. There were no stars or moon in sight, for the sky had clouded over and the wind was picking up. The darkness had deepened, and soon there would only be the light of the fire to fill the night.

Evlin turned to Fearglas and said, "It is time to light the winter hearthfire. May I?"

"The honor is yours, my daughter."

"Then let us proceed."

She took a small dipper from the water bucket and walked to the pool. There she knelt by the water and dipped out a small amount of water. Skoth could see she said a prayer as she lifted it from the surface of the pond, but since the wind was picking up, he couldn't understand what she said. She brought the dipper of water back to the fire and sprinkled a few drops over the fire. It wasn't enough to douse the fire, only enough to make it sizzle. Then she reached over a grabbed a large piece of peeled bark from an oak tree that she had obviously placed there for this specific purpose.

Using the shingle of bark she scooped up a number of burning coals and carried them into the cave. She set the bark and coals into the fire pit and then put a few pieces of kindling and a couple of larger logs upon the coals.

She stood before the fire, extended her arms wide, and said, "Creator Spirit, giver of light and life. Bless this hearthfire. During this season of cold and dark, may it give light and life to this place and those who use it. So mote it be."

Fearglas echoed the final phrase, "So mote it be."

Evlin turned her gaze on Skoth and waited. He wasn't sure what to do, so he stammered out the same phrase, "So mote it be."

Evlin continued to stare at him, then made little snort with her breath and turned away.

Skoth thought about that look and that snort for a moment, and then it hit him. The memory of the bear that fought for them and watched them on that day his friends were rescued flashed into his memory. It sure felt the same.

Unconsciously his eyes went wide as Skoth thought to himself, "This is going to be a long winter."

Chapter 33 - Gluskabi visits Theofinn in Dunsheelin

The wind was bitter and the sleet had turned to driven snow by the time Theofinn left the meeting at Unaine's domicile to walk to his tower. With one hand he used his staff for support against the wind, and with his other arm he leaned on the arm of his young assistant druid who had waited for him in the King's Great Hall. Together they made their way to Theofinn's Tower, the tallest building in Dunsheelin.

They were greeted at the door by another of Theofinn's assistants who said, "It's good to have you back home, sir. It is late and I was getting worried about you. The storm is getting worse by the moment."

Theofinn commented, "Not a fit night for man nor beast. Well, I'm back, you can rest easy now."

His young assistant who had walked with him through the storm left him after they entered the tower, and went to his own room. Theofinn made his way to his private quarters. When he opened the door he noticed that there was a fire going in the brazier, which heated the room. His initial thought was how nice it was for one of his assistants to warm his room for him on this cold night. Then he noticed that there was someone sitting in one of the highback chairs near the brazier, but with its back to the door. He couldn't see who it was.

A voice said softly, "You might as well close the door and come sit by the fire to warm yourself." The voice had the timbre of age, yet there was nothing feeble about it.

Theofinn warily made his way over to the brazier and sat in a chair opposite his visitor with the brazier between them. The door was closed on the iron brazier, so the only light in the room was the light from the glowing coals that peeked through the slits in the brazier's door. Theofinn could not clearly see the features of his visitor for, in addition to the dim light, the visitor's face was shadowed by the hood of the robe that he wore.

The voice said, "I've enjoyed watching you, Theofinn."

Theofinn responded, "I tend to be a bit wary when I know someone I don't know is watching me."

"I've noticed."

"Then you'll appreciate my apprehension at this moment."

There was a chuckle to the voice, "Yes, that is wise of you."

"This isn't a night for a man to be out visiting just to make small talk around a fire."

"Not a fit night for man nor beast is a phrase I believe you use."

Theofinn nodded, the dread in him was building, for though as of yet there were no threats in the conversation, he was obviously dealing with someone of power.

Theofinn decided to push on, "You have me at a disadvantage, sir. Perhaps it is simply that I am a forgetful old man, but I neither recognize your voice or your visage."

At this the visitor laughed outright and said, "You are a delight, young Theofinn. How I love the way you have with words. You may have a few years on you, but are certainly not forgetful."

"Yet, I don't recall ever meeting you. Do you have a name that I can use for you?"

"So serious you are now. Ah well, these are serious times. You may call me, Gluskabi."

Theofinn's eyes went wide. Never in his life had he expected to be sitting face-to-face, well, nearly face to face, with a god of legend and lore. If, indeed, this truly was the Gluskabi of the spiritual realm.

The revelation put Theofinn into temporary shock, and his distant childhood years of training in politeness took over. All he could stammer out in his shock was, "It is a pleasure to meet you."

At that the visitor laughed again and said, "It is my pleasure. Now, let's get down to business. I don't intend to stay long, and I have a few words I would share with you."

Chapter 34 - Aftermath of Storm in New Caledonia

For two days the storm battered the port of New Caledonia, dumping nearly two feet of snow upon it. Travel through the streets was limited and the roads were a royal mess, and certain to get even worse should the snow begin to melt. The gale-force winds had wreaked havoc on the waterfront, tearing some ships from their moorings and capsizing others.

The day after the storm broke, Karl and Erik made their way to the Great Hall to volunteer their help wherever King Haggar might want them. He sent them to join a number of his men working at the waterfront with his son, Gunnar. Erik was a little apprehensive about this assignment because he knew that Olaf would be there since Olaf was the sheriff of the waterfront, but was surprised to see no sight of him.

They pitched right in and start to help with the hoisting of one of the capsized vessels. When Erik wondered aloud about where Sheriff Olaf was, one of the other workers replied with derision, "Count yer blessings, man. He's too lazy to do any of this work, and for sure he would be in the way, or mucking up something if he was here."

By noon the sun had broken out, and the temperature had risen to well above freezing. While the warmth was welcome, the melting snow made a mess of the entire waterfront. Erik was impressed by the way Karl worked with the local men. Karl may have injured his leg at the waterfront many months ago, but he was strong as an ox and smart as well. The men remembered how he had been hurt here months ago and they had come to respect him during his time of recuperation and growing friendship with Gunnar. The men followed the leadership of Gunnar as they worked, but Erik noticed they also deferred to Karl as his second-in-command.

Some women had brought bread and stew from the Great Hall, by the order of King Haggar, and the men took a brief break for food. They had finished their lunch and were getting back to work, when Olaf stumbled out of the Hall of Justice. Squinting into the sun and covering his eyes, for the mid-day sun was brightly reflecting off the snow, he made his way to the largest group of workers where Gunnar was giving to directions to get them started on raising the next capsized ship.

In his bellicose way, Olaf said, "You sure haven't gotten much done here. I'll take over now. Now we'll get some work done."

Gunnar looked him over and said, "That's a nice offer, Olaf, but we're doing fine here. This group is toiling here at the command of King Haggar. You'll have to go talk to him if you want it different."

"Why you young pup!" snarled Olaf, "This is my waterfront. I'm in charge here. The old king himself put me in charge. I don't care what kind of orders you think you have, but I'm in charge here!"

The dispute grew more heated and both Karl and Erik sensed more than words might be flying soon. Erik noticed that Olaf's hand was resting on the pommel of his sword as he yelled at Gunnar. Gunnar, and the other workers, had laid their swords to the side to keep them out of the way as they were doing the hard physical labor involved with the ship raisings. Erik had subconsciously reached for his sword when the argument started and was cursing to himself when he saw his sword in its scabbard lying on a barrel several yards away. He was slowly edging his way to it, trying not to draw attention to himself, when he hear the rasp of steel being drawn.

As he lunged for his sword, he heard Olaf's curse, "Go to hell, you young upstart."

Grabbing his sword and turning, Erik's vision turned as if time moved in slow motion, he saw Olaf begin his slashing stroke toward Gunnar. But before the blade could reach the unarmored youth, he saw a thick staff of wood crashing into the hand that held the blade and sending the blade tumbling to the ground. Karl had grabbed an old quarterstaff that lay nearby, that they were using as a lever, and had used it in defense of his friend.

Olaf was howling in pain and holding his injured right arm. He spit a threat at them, "You'll pay for this, you scum!" and began to stumble away.

A couple of men grabbed him, but Gunnar said, "Let him go, he's nothing but a drunken fool. He can be dealt with later. We have work to do."

They released him and he stumbled off muttering curses and moaning in pain.

Gunnar turned to Karl and reached out his arm, saying, "Thank you. You are a loyal and trustworthy friend. Your quick action may have saved my life. I'm in your debt."

They clasped arms, forehand to forehand, and Karl said, "Aw, it was nothing, that's what friends are for. Now that it's over, I'm ready to get back to work. We've got a lot more to do to set this waterfront right."

Gunnar laughed at that, the mood lightened, and as they headed back to work, more than one man gave Karl a hearty thump on the back to say thanks.

Erik stood there for a moment longer. A smile crossed his face and he nodded slightly as he thought, "that young laddie is turning into something, he is."

Chapter 35 - The Bear Clan

Leesha's first evening in the lodgehouse of Tkomik was certainly memorable. She was warmly welcomed, and though the snow fell heavy on the land about them, the warmth of the hearthfire and the telling of the stories had lifted the hearts of all. It was right. It was the way that life should be in the homes of Eirgalon in the nights of darkest winter. This may have only been the first of the winter storms, but with its ferocity it was certain to be one of the season's harshest.

During the course of that first evening, Leesha had been introduced to Maedrid. The old woman had said little other than saying a traditional greeting, but she had watched and listened attentively all evening.

When morning dawned, the people began moving and working about the lodge. Only a few men went outside to check on the livestock in the stables, for the wind was still blowing and the snow was still falling. There was little that could be done outside on a day like this. So the people stayed inside, and many of them began projects that they had set aside to work on during the winter months. Handicrafts of all sorts were often best done during those long winter months.

A young girl came up to Leesha and told her that Maedrid wanted to talk with her. She escorted her to the common room where, seated next to the central fire, was the old woman. She was dressed in plain green and brown woolens, with a light tan shawl wrapped about her shoulders, and sitting crossed legged on a bearskin rug. Her thick white hair was simply braided and pulled forward over her left shoulder. As Leesha approached, she patted the spot on the bearskin rug to her right and motioned for her to sit down.

She spoke with a voice that was softened with age, "Welcome, again, Leesha Unainesdotter."

At first Leesha was startled that she used the old Nordic style name for her, but she recovered, "Thank you, I'm happy to be here, and I must say I am pleased to meet the sister of Master Theofinn."

That elicited a little laugh and a smile from the old woman, "Theo, the master. Why I remember when my little brother was just a little boy running around getting himself into all sorts of trouble. Still doing that I imagine. How is his health?"

"When I last saw him, he seemed fit enough. He walks a little slower than he used to, and he always uses a staff. But he is still as sharp as ever."

"Hah, that staff. You beware that staff of his!"

"I try." she said with a grin.

After a few more comments and pleasantries, Maedrid took the conversation to where she wanted to go all along.

"I thought that I should explain a few things to you, since you seem so love-struck by that young grandson of mine. You make a fine couple, but there are a few bits and pieces of our story you should know. First of these is, that by joining him, you become part of the Bear Clan of the Wabanaki. I'm sure your education has included learning some of the history about the first people of this land, but you probably haven't heard all the legends or understand all of what being a part of this clan means. I know that I didn't, when I married into it."

"Tkaden did mention he was of the Bear Clan, but no, I'm sure I don't know all about what that means."

"Ah so. Well then, listen to the legend of the bear-witch of the Bear Clan. It was many generations ago, when the earth was young and the people were first growing in this land that a young man left his village on a vision quest. Even then our young boys made the step into manhood by going out alone to listen to the spirits. It is said that in his vision he saw a mother bear defending its cub from an attack by wolves. The image vanished to mist before his eyes, and when the mist parted, he saw before him the tracks of a bear, leading into the woods. In his dream, he followed those tracks until they emerged into a clearing in the woods. In the clearing was a pool, formed from the widened banks of a small stream. And beside the pool sat a young maiden. Her beauty was beyond compare, with hair as dark as night and eyes of honey-brown. With open arms she beckoned to him. As he approached her, his vision misted over. He awoke from his dream. He look around and the world was again how he knew it, so he knew his vision was over and that it was time to return to his village. As he journeyed home, from a distant hilltop far above the village, he saw that his people were under attack by fierce warriors, before he could run down the hill and make his way through the woods to help his people, he saw a huge bear run out of the woods, slashing the attackers down. When the attackers fled, the bear began licking the wounds of the injured villagers. Our young man raced down the hill and through the woods. When he arrived at the village, he saw no bear, only a young maiden; the maiden of his vision, tending the wounds of his people. He took that young maiden as his wife. They had many children, and it is said that the blood of the bear-witch is strong in the people of the Bear Clan. And so it is."

Leesha thought a moment and then said, "I'm not sure I understand. Why are you telling me this story?"

"It is a story of the past of the Wabanaki people. I have no blood of the bear-witch in me, though I have my share of other gifts, but when I joined the Bear Clan, I joined their story. So it is with you as you join us. Our story is now your story. If my sight is true, and yet strong, I see this not only as the story of Wabanaki, past or present, but as story of the future Eirgalon. Walk gently around the bear-witch, my dear, for protect her people she will!"

With a wee bit of wonderment and awe at the power and intensity of the old woman's voice, Leesha meekly said, "I will."

Maedrid nodded, paused as though deep in thought, and then said, "And another thing, dear lassie of my blood, or close to it anyway, I'd like to take a look at that little stick of yours."

Leesha was stunned. She had told no one of the wand. Not even Tkaden!

Leesha whispered, "But grandmother, nobody knows I have it, save my sisters and the Women's Circle."

"Dearie, dearie, how are you ever going to use it, or even learn to use it if you keep it hidden away? I don't doubt that it is a powerful tool. But it is just that, a tool. And to learn to use a tool, you must wield it. So go on with you.

Back to your room with you and bring it here."

To Leesha's own amazement, she didn't protest, but sprang up and went quickly to her room to get it. When she returned to Maedrid and sat again next to her, she carefully untied the cord and unwrapped the wand. Gently she held it out to Maedrid, who just as gently and reverently picked up and looked it over.

Maedrid hummed in pleasure to its touch, and then said, "What a beauty this is. Wood of the ancient rowan tree, though many of the common folks call it a mountain ash. And my, the beauty of the gem! Have you been told what the wording is?"

Leesha said, "No one told me, but I did a little research on it and found that it means Spring."

"That it does, but there's so much more to it. Think of the light of the most glorious spring dawn you have ever seen. All the feelings, all the promise, all the power of the springtime and life are all tied up in that ancient word. If I'm not mistaken, this wand came from the lands east of the sea."

"This note went with it." Leesha said as she handed to Maedrid the note that her mother had left with it. "My ma left it for me."

"A lovely lass, your mother was. Your looks favor her. I only met her once, when she was just a lass, but I could tell then she had a power about her. You do too. I can tell. Your natural abilities, together with that wand, can do great good. There is evil afoot in this land. Mayhap you and this wand have a part to play in averting it. What say you, would you like for me to teach you how to use it?"

"You? You know how to use it? You can teach me?"

194

"Achh! Did that worthless druid brother of mine teach you nothing, and tell you nothing about me? Don't answer. I can see, in any case, that there is much I must teach you. Well, we have a long winter ahead of us. Shall we begin?"

Her eyes alive and heart filled with excitement, Leesha said just one word, "Yes!"

Chapter 36 - Winter with the Green Man

Wintering in the hidden valley was anything but harsh. The cave was actually rather cozy as the hearthfire blazed, and the valley floor was bearable, even on the most bitter days of winter. The wind did find its way into the valley but the steep sides lessened its force. Once Skoth wondered aloud why the small waterfall and pond never froze completely, but when Evlin gave him one of those looks he changed the subject of conversation to something else. Later on Fearglas gave Skoth a little more instruction about these sacred waters and their powers.

Fearglas was a good teacher. The Green Man loved this world and he was good at gently teaching Skoth about the powers that lie within it, and about the powers that lay within Skoth. While Fearglas claimed no lordship over anything, he taught Skoth that a true Lord of the Land exists not as master, but as a steward. One does not rule the land, but cares for it. By implication he extended that to the people. A true king serves his people.

In their conversations, and in their journeys, for they did make several forays beyond the confines of the canyon, Skoth learned some of the ways, and what some might be called - some of the magic, of the Green Man. There were also times where either Fearglas or Evlin would suddenly disappear for several days, only to reappear just as suddenly, acting as if they had never been away.

Evlin was his also his teacher, for she had learned of the world at Fearglas' side. Skoth sensed that in some ways she was more powerful than her father, though he could never figure out specifically how that was, only that he felt it. She would often join in their discussions and when Fearglas was gone and it was just the two of them, she would share some of her knowledge. But the learning went the other way also, for Skoth shared with her the story of his people and their ways. And if the truth be told, Skoth came to look forward to those times when Fearglas was gone and he was alone with Evlin. She generally had a warm smile and gentle disposition, although he learned that she could have a fierce temper when crossed. He enjoyed their conversations and he learned he could trust her with anything as he shared the stories of his life with her.

The night of longest darkness came, and passed. Then slowly the wheel of time turned and the amount of daylight lengthened each day.

It was during one of those beautiful days of a late January thaw, that Fearglas whispered a few words in Evlin's ear and then suddenly left on one of his trips. The snow in the valley was rapidly melting and all vestiges of ice that had been hanging around the edges of the pond had disappeared. The waterfall was cascading into the pond with new vigor and the birds and animals were stirring to the music of this mid-winter thaw.

It was shortly after noon and Skoth had gone for a walk about the small valley. He decided to climb the rock stairway on the valley wall where Fearglas had first taken him, and take in the view. As he sat there his eyes were drawn to the sacred pond and the waterfall. Standing at the edge of the pond, he saw Evlin, with arms extended toward the sky, as if in supplication or thanksgiving. Then she lowered her arms and knelt to undo the ties on her leggings and boots. She slipped them off, and then to Skoth's astonishment, she pulled her dress off over her head. She tossed it to the side and, without hesitation or flinching, walked into the pond.

Then she turned and looked directly at him, and motioned for him to come to her. There was no thinking on Skoth's part. The desire was there, but even without that he would have been unable to resist her. He scrambled down from his perch and made his way through the trees and the melting snow to the pond. When he reached the pond, she again motioned him in. He quickly stripped out of his clothing and stepped into the pool. There was steam rising from the water and it felt warm to his skin.

Evlin playfully splashed water at him and he splashed her back, and before they knew it they were in each other's arms. Skoth had kissed a few girls in his life, but none like Evlin. Time, and the world around him, disappeared when his lips touched hers. Her lips left his and she pushed herself back from him enough to touch her finger to his chest where the tattooed king rune was visible upon his chest. She asked him how he had acquired it and when he told her about the water sprite at the sacred pool of Cold Springs on Fadis Innis, she smiled.

Laying her head on his chest, and embracing him fully again she said, "Then tis true. Such a water sprite would never lie."

They were locked in a deep embrace, when something entered Skoth's consciousness and caused him to glance over to the cave. There, sitting on a rock by the entrance to the cave, sat Fearglas. He was leaning back with his arms crossed, smoking on that pipe of his, gazing into the sky, and grinning from ear to ear.

Skoth relaxed his embrace, but Evlin held on as fiercely as before. He was going nowhere, unless he wanted to drag her with him. So Skoth, just said, "Welcome back."

Fearglas, still grinning, said, "Well, thank you. It certainly is getting a little warm today, don't you think?"

Skoth did think that. The thought also entered his mind that this was the second time he had been caught in a pool of water with his pants laying on the shore. He was struggling to think of what to say as an apology - what do you say when a father catches you frolicking in a pool of water with his daughter? But then Evlin started nuzzling his ear and he lost that thought.

Fearglas laughed out loud and said, "Don't mind me, I'm going to go into the cave now and putter about there for a while." And he laughed again as he got up and disappeared into the cave.

After several more moments of enjoying each other, Evlin released him from her embrace. She playfully splashed water at him again and then stepped up and out of the pool. Skoth just watched her, mesmerized by her beauty as she stepped away from him. She picked up her clothes and slowly put them on. Skoth never took his eyes off her, and she knew it.

When she was all dressed, she looked at him and said, "Are you going to stay in there all day? I expect the water is going to start feeling a bit cool soon."

Suddenly Skoth realized that indeed the water was getting colder and he quickly stepped up and out of the pool. He felt no need for modesty in front of her. She had already seen all there was to him. She stood and smiled at him as he dressed, then she took his hand and they walked into the cave together.

Fearglas was sitting on a bearskin rug near the fire contentedly smoking his pipe and they went over to fire and sat down across from him. Skoth was going to say something, but Evlin, who still held his hand, gave that hand a gentle squeeze when looked like he was going to say something, so he wisely held his tongue.

The grin that had been on Fearglas' face had been replaced by a more grim and pensive look. They sat for several moments before Fearglas began.

"I'm happy for the two of you. I really am. But I worry too. I know the time has come for you to move on. I've taught you what I can. I can feel the call of the quest reaching out to you. I would like so much for the two of you to have time for yourselves, to feel the joy of the springtime as once I felt with Sheela. But it is not to be. Or at least not to be at this time. Skoth, you must go to Heilsand. The quest doth call you there."

Skoth doubted not his word, for he had yet to see the green man wrong, and simply asked, "Now?"

"Not this moment. But on the morrow you must depart."

Evlin said firmly, "I'm going with him, father."

With sadness in his eyes, Fearglas replied, "I know, and it grieves my heart to take leave from you. But I must leave also, and tis a different path I take. And I know my Evi, wild and free like her mother, and also fierce and loyal with her passion. You will look out for our young man as no other could."

Turning his gaze again upon Skoth, he said, "And you, who would be high king of Eirgalon, you have walked by my side these several months. You have listened to the land and its creatures. I know your heart but, before you leave, I must hear you say the promise of a true king."

Skoth said, "I know you must. Let us go and kneel beside the pool. I think it best I give my oath there."

The three of them proceeded out of the cave and over to the pool. The waters were cascading down the cliffside, clear and sparkling in the light of the late afternoon sun, and the pool reflected the beauty of the hidden valley. They knelt next to the pool. Skoth was in the center, holding hands with Evlin to his right and Fearglas to his left, as he spoke his promise:

"Hear me, earth and sky, creatures great and small, witness now my solemn pledge.

I promise to protect and steward the land and all who use it, giving thanks to creature and creator for the gift of life. I promise to listen to the land and to the people. I seek to tend and nurture. I seek goodness and beauty. I will serve the people and the land. I ask the blessing of the Great Creator and the Guardian of this place upon my promise and my task."

Then, still holding their hands, he leaned forward till he touched the water of the pond with his forehead. Evlin and Fearglas reached forward with their free hands to touch the water and then lifting their arms, touched their wet fingers to their mouths, in witness said, "So mote it be."

Later that evening, after the sun had set and the winter chill was settling back upon the earth, they were in the cave discussing what supplies they might need for their journey. Fearglas would not tell them where he was going or what he was doing, other than to say "something that needs to be done." He did make a point of telling Skoth several times, "that when the need arises, call upon me."

About their journey, Fearglas told them, "Sorry I am, to not allow you to make a leisurely trip to Heilsand, walking hill and dale and celebrating springtime breaking out around you as you travel, but of necessity you must travel with all speed. I've arranged for the little people to allow you the use of a couple of their horses for a brief time. The snow has melted enough for travel by horse to be your fastest way to start your journey. Go to the headwaters of the River Oustona. Evlin, you know the spot. There will be a canoe waiting for you. Travel as fast as you can down the river. This warm spell has opened the waters throughout its length. At the seaport, find the fastest ship on which you can book passage to Heilsand. With good fortune you will arrive before the vernal equinox. Beware those who would stop or slow you. Malsum was on your tail last fall, but that sly fox has lost the scent by now."

Fearglas paused for a moment and went to the back of the cave, where he retrieved the oaken walking staff that he had been carving and polishing for the last couple of months. Handing the staff to Skoth, he went on, "You've seen me working on this staff as we sat around the fire. You may not have realized I was fashioning it for you, but it is for you. When you hold it you will feel the strength and power of the earth and all its creatures. You are of this world, and you have kingly power, but this can make you stronger. As you travel, get to know the feel of it. Ask Evi about it if you have questions, she may be able to help you get the feel of it."

They spent a last peaceful night in the safety of the valley cave, and then when morning broke they put out the hearthfire and bid farewell to the cave and the glistening waters of the waterfall and pond. When they exited the narrow defile that led into the valley they stopped and Fearglas and Evlin gave each other a long embrace. After a brief hug and farewell with Skoth, Fearglas turned one way down the path to the west, and Skoth and Evlin turned toward the meadow of the little people. Their journey had begun.

Chapter 37 - Neal's Hand

The storm was still blowing over Fadis Innis and its capital of Dunsheelin the night after Gluskabi's visit with Theofinn. When Theofinn woke, he had to shake himself to reality. For a moment he wondered if it really happened. Did one of the gods, truly deign to visit him, or in his fatigue had he just dreamed it so?

He looked about his room, there was no evidence of his visitor, but Theofinn knew he had really spoken with Gluskabi. Even if he had just fallen asleep in his chair by the fire, which he was certain he had not, and Gluskabi had spoken to him in a dream - it would still have been a visit from a being beyond the physical realm. He chuckled to himself when he recalled how he had said that "it was said that old Thorfall had spoken with the gods," and now the same could be said of him.

Dismissing the satisfaction of that thought, he turned his mind to more pressing matters, especially the matter of Neal's hand. It troubled him that Neal still suffered effects of the knife wound to his hand, and it troubled him more that Neal had been so secretive about it.

It was the middle of the morning before Neal showed up at Theofinn's door. Theofinn was in his workshop and had left instructions with his assistants that Neal was to be brought to him when he arrived.

He asked Neal to come and sit at the worktable and put his hand out so he could examine it. What he saw alarmed him. The hand that had looked like it was healing nicely several weeks ago was now inflamed along the scar and was tender to the touch. Laying Neal's hand gently back on the table after touching it. Theofinn got up and went over to the washbasin and washed and rinsed his own hands. He then dried them and returned to his chair.

"I have a few questions for you. Relax and answer me the best you can." said Theofinn. "First, the wound healed normally those first few weeks, right?"

Neal, leaving his hand laying on the table as if he didn't want to pull it back to himself, responded, "That's right. It was a clean cut. Deep enough to slice some muscle. But there was no infection, and it seemed to heal well."

"And then you went through a time of exercising it and rebuilding its strength back. Did you do all the stretching and exercising of it like you were told?"

"Well, I was pretty faithful about it. Once in awhile I neglected doing the exercises. But it felt fine and it was like it was back to normal, so I didn't think it mattered too much."

"When did you start noticing the redness and the pains?"

"It was around the time of Samhain. About a month ago."

"Can you describe the pain?"

"Well it normally doesn't hurt. Occasionally there is kind of a warm throbbing, but then that goes away. When the real pain comes it is like a sharp stabbing feeling."

"Is it like the moment of the original injury?"

"Why, yes, that describes it!"

The questioning went on at some length. After several

minutes, Theofinn called out to an assistant who was working in the back of the room. He told instructed him to get a helper and go to the locked storeroom and get the locked crate that had the assailant's knife stored.

A few minutes later the two helpers returned, carrying the crate between them. They set it on the worktable in front of Theofinn, who pulled out his set of keys and unlocked it. As he did so, he noticed that Neal was flushed and breathing hard.

He opened the case, and there, tied into a sheath was the knife. Theofinn took a piece of leather into his hand and reached in to lift the weapon. Before he could touch it, Neal leapt to his feet and struck Theofinn to the floor. He grabbed the knife and bolted to the door. The young assistants stepped forward to block his way, but he charged through them pushing them aside and ran out of the workroom. He ran down the hallway and dashed through the outer door and disappeared into the snowstorm. The assistants ran to help Theofinn as he lay on the floor, but he yelled at them to stop Neal. They turned and ran after him but soon returned to report that they had lost him.

An exasperated Theofinn asked, "Didn't you follow his tracks? You should be able to follow them in the snow!"

The disappointing answer was, "Yes master, but he stepped into the tracks others had made and we lost him. We are sorry. Should we arrange a hunt?"

"Of course, we need to find him before he hurts others or himself. Go to Unaine and tell him what has happened. Ask him to organize the hunt."

Unaine was sitting in the Great Hall talking with a

couple of his men when Theofinn's assistant came rushing in and told him the news. He dispatched his men to go out and hunt for Neal, warning them to be careful.

In the woods near the edge of town Neal huddled under the protection of a copse of large spruce trees that were heavy with snow, where at least he was somewhat protected from the wind. When he fled from Theofinn's Tower he had not grabbed his winter cloak and now, although he had been flushed with the activity of running to escape, he started to feel the chill penetrating his body. He untied the sheath and pulled the knife out. He smiled as he saw the gleam of the blade and sighed in satisfaction when he stroked it. He furtively glanced about himself as he suddenly realized that people would be looking for him. His mind frantically searched for a place where the blade could be hidden before they found him. Suddenly he looked up, and then began to scramble up the branches of the tree. He had worked himself about twenty feet off the ground when he found a place where he could tie the sheathed blade without someone seeing it from the ground. He quickly fastened it in place and then scampered back down the tree. He looked around to make sure that none could see he had been there. Other than a few scratches on the tree, which even a squirrel might have made, the place seemed undisturbed.

He stepped out from under the trees and noticed that that his earlier tracks were already almost drifted over, so he grabbed a fallen branch and retraced his path, trying to smooth it over with the branch by brushing the snow behind him as he went. Soon the fresh fallen and drifting snow would cover it again. When he had retreated this way for several yards, he tossed the branch to the side and then veered a different direction, so that if anyone should find his steps in the snow, they wouldn't trace it to the trees. He headed back into town, running in a haphazard fashion. And so it was that after several minutes a couple of Unaine's men spotted him and caught up to him. They warily circled him but he held up his hands and allowed them to capture him. Hands tied they took him to The Great Hall.

In spite of the snowstorm, there were now several people gathered in the Great Hall including Unaine, Teite, Theofinn and several of his assistant druids. A handful of Unaine's men that had been sent out on the search had already returned. They sat Neal, with hands still tied, on a stool before King Unaine. As a matter of respect and care for the old druid who had been knocked to the floor by Neal, a chair had been brought forward and was placed near to the King's large chair.

It was a serious and dangerous offense to strike the Master Druid, perhaps not as dangerous as raising a hand against the king, but still dangerous. The king deferred to Theofinn in the questioning of Neal.

Neal tried to explain that he didn't know what had come over him. His story was that when he saw the knife the pain in his hand was excruciating and that he knew the knife was causing it. So he grabbed the knife, unaware of who he struck he just knew he had to get rid of it. He said he ran out of the Tower and ran to the lakeshore where he threw the knife as far as possible into the lake, which was still open of ice this early in the season.

Unaine and Theofinn conferred quietly with each

other, before Unaine declared, "The deed was against our code, but I'm not sure if Neal did it out of evil, or foolishness, or out of a sickness that lies within him. Before I pronounce a final sentence, I declare that Neal shall be sequestered under watch in the Tower of Theofinn. Until we determine what is behind what was done, no one is to harm him. Everyone is to be watchful of him, for we want to take no chances that he will harm others."

Chapter 38 - Heilsand

It was well after the end of the Yule celebrations, nearing the end of January, when Karl led a group to Heilsand. The group included Gunnar and a number of his men. They took one of the karvi longships used by Gunnar's family. It had eight rowing benches on a side, and all seats were filled with Gunnar's men, friends of Karl. It was loaded with trade goods, but the mission was reconnaissance as much as trade, for Karl (as well as Gunnar and his father, King Haggar) wanted to know about the state of affairs up the northeastern coast. Enat had persuaded Karl that she should go with him, because after all, women can go places and hear conversations that men cannot. Erik was going along, under the pretense of watching out for Enat, but he wanted to do some scouting of his own. When Erik's men, Rolf and Jake, just happened to show up at Tante's Table the night before their planned departure, it was quickly arranged for them also to go along.

They shipped out in the morning, but the journey took much longer than expected. Several days of inclement weather, adverse winds, and a couple of Atlantic storms kept them closely hugging the coastline and frequently running for safe harbor. They spent more time in harbor than at sea and it was the final week of February before they sailed into the Heilsand harbor. They arrived at the docks of Heilsand shortly before nightfall. Several men would stay the night on ship, covered by a sealskin tarp that stretched over the deck like a tent. Sealskin, heavy woolen and leather clothing, and a small brazier to heat them were plenty to keep them warm. The presence of several armed men on deck would also suffice to protect their trade goods.

Erik and his men would be taking Enat to stay at a lodging house he knew. Enat had come to wonder about Erik, did the man know people in every village, hamlet, and city? Karl, Gunnar, and the rest of the men were going to the Harbor Inn, which was the large hostel for sailors on Harbor Row that had dormitory style rooms. In the morning, Gunnar and Karl would make a courtesy call on the chief of the Heilsand Celts, King Ragen. It was the proper sign of respect for the son of a chief to do.

The lodging house that Erik took Enat to was more an inn than a tavern, which did surprise Enat, since she knew Erik's proclivity for a good tavern. It was a large two-story building and had a sign that said "rooms available" hanging by the front door. When they entered, they came into a large dining room that was already half filled with people. There were mostly men, but there were a couple of women, and also a few children with them. It was much more of a family-type establishment than Erik usually frequented. But Enat did notice, as she looked through to the kitchen, that there was a dream-catcher hanging on the wall. She felt assured that she could quickly connect with the local Women's Circle.

Enat and Erik's men waited by the door, while Erik started working his way across the room towards the kitchen. He was only mid-way through the room when a middle-aged woman, carrying a couple of baskets of bread as she came out of the kitchen, screamed out, "Erik!" and putting down the baskets on the nearest table, ran to Erik, throwing her arms around him. Erik returned the hug with gusto, lifting her off the ground and turning a circle with her in his arms.

Enat thought, "Oh, my goodness, another one of his lovers."

But circumstances are not always as they seem.

Setting her down Erik brought her over to Enat. There he said, "Everyone, I'd like to introduce you to my little sister, Fiona." His men nodded, each saying a polite, "Mam."

Enat was tongue-tied momentarily, and then said, "Pleased to meet you. I'm Enat."

With a cheerful smile and a laugh, Fiona replied, "Oh, no, the pleasure is mine. But my, Erik, you are robbing the cradle with this one."

Erik was a little flustered, and stammered, "No, no, Fiona. You have it all wrong. This is Enat, Unaine's daughter. You know, Chief Unaine!"

Fiona, still teasing said, "Ah, sure. And these two handsome boys with you are her bodyguards, sent to protect her from you, no doubt!"

Fiona quickly arranged for them to have rooms, and got them seated at a table saying, "Now, I'll be wanting to talk with you and hear the story behind this visit, but first I have a room full of hungry people, and a meal to serve. I can't expect my girls to do it all while I'm sitting here gabbing. Enjoy the meal. We can visit later."

They enjoyed a fine home-cooked meal, one of the best he'd had in a long time in Erik's decidedly biased opinion. But even Enat, Jake, and Rolf would not have disagreed.

They observed the people around the room as they

ate. The atmosphere was friendly, but subdued. Perhaps they were more used to the boisterous atmosphere of a tavern and its common room, but there seemed to be something that held gaiety in check, even in this friendly room.

In conversation at the table, Enat remarked to Erik that she didn't know he was from Heilsand. He wasn't, he explained, but he had been here a few times. The reason his sister lived here was that she had married a man from here. He had been a fisherman, and quite successful, until he was lost at sea in a violent storm several years ago.

After supper the other borders went to their rooms, while Fiona's daughters, twins in their early teens, cleaned up. Fiona took her newest guests upstairs to get them settled in their rooms. On the way upstairs, Enat commented on how she admired the dream catcher hanging on the kitchen wall and wondered if she might be able to meet with someone who knew how to make one. Fiona responded to her with a wink and said that she was sure she could find some one.

Erik asked Fiona where his nephew was, he would be just a couple of years older than the twins, and Fiona told him that he was serving as an apprentice shipwright down at the docks. At that moment, alarm bells starting ringing.

Chapter 39 - The Summons to Heilsand

Out west of Heilsand in the Wabanaki settlement of Wausacom on that very night, Maedrid was saying a prayer for her grandson and his intended. The formal wedding would take place in the lands and hall of Leesha's father, as was proper for her people, but the handfasting ceremony had taken place before they left. Winter's harshness had broken, and there had been several days of near spring-like weather during month of February. Maedrid's weather-sense could feel that there had been some coastal storms, but the weather this far inland had remained relatively mild.

A fortnight ago, Tkaden had come to Maedrid seeking her advice. He had been having nights of troubled dreams. At first he thought that the dreams were probably caused by concern for his new friends, including Evlin, his recently discovered cousin. He was also in turmoil because he had struggled through several conversations with Dakatomi since his return. In those conversations he had withheld information about Fearglas and Evlin, and that was troubling him. He didn't like to lie, or to be deceitful. But he had also grown to sense that Dakatomi wasn't telling him everything either. It was obvious that Dakatomi was negative about his relationship with Leesha. He also kept getting images of the city of Heilsand flashing in those dreams. He had been to Heilsand once, a couple of years ago, but there was no reason he knew of why he should be thinking, or dreaming, of it now.

Maedrid was sometimes called "a seer" by the people

of Wausacom, because of her visions, but the truth was that she also had considerable talent and skill in reading and understanding people and situations. It was perhaps a combination of these that allowed her to help Tkaden understand that he and Leesha were being summoned to Heilsand, and that they should arrive before the spring equinox. Maedrid had spent the winter days instructing Leesha in how to call upon her own powers in wielding the Eostre wand, and was confident in the young woman's ability and discretion. She knew that Leesha and Tkaden would be a formidable couple in years to come, but she was sad to see them leave because she felt she didn't have much time left and might not see them again. Ah, well, she sighed to herself, she had done what she could.

Family and friends had wished them well, and they had departed for the coastal city to the east. They entered the western edges of Heilsand the same afternoon that Karl and the others made port from the sea. They made their way to the home of some friends of Tkomik that lived near Heilsand. They were millers at a water mill that had been constructed on one of the small streams that ran into the river, which then flowed into the nearby harbor. The Wabanaki had learned to grow corn from the Lenape people to the south, and had learned some of the mechanical aspects of milling from the Celtic "newcomers," so this family of millers from Wausacom were widely accepted by all people in the area.

In this home, Tkaden and Leesha were warmly welcomed and enjoyed a fine meal and conversation around the table. They had just settled into bed for the night when they heard the alarms in the far distance, sounding from

Heilsand. Tkaden immediately sensed that whatever was causing the alarm to sound, was something that involved him, so he and Leesha quickly dressed, and made their way outside. To the east they could see an orange glow to the skyline. Something was on fire. The further east they walked the greater the glow. They knew it must be a large fire.

Chapter 40 - Great Heilsand Fire

At this very moment, Skoth and Evlin, were sitting in a vessel anchored in the Heilsand harbor. They had made their way down the Oustona River as planned and had then taken a fast merchant vessel coasting eastward along the coast of Eirgalon. They disembarked on the western side of the Cape Vineland isthmus and crossed by foot to the east side where they had arranged passage on a vessel heading up to the Heilsand harbor. This allowed them to avoid having to travel slowly around the Vineland peninsula and islands in inclement weather. It ended up cutting several days of travel off their journey because of the coastal storms that had plagued the area.

The sailors on the trading vessel were roused by the alarms and saw the flames of the fire licking the sky all along the harbor. They knew their help was needed. In a settlement like Heilsand that was constructed mostly of wood, fire was a dangerous development. The captain of the ship decided to have them oar the ship south of the city's main harbor and run it up on a strip of sandy beach near the isthmus that connected Heilsand to the mainland. From there the ship would be out of danger and they could make their way to the harbor on foot and help in any way they might be called upon.

In the harbor area of the city, bedlam and chaos reigned. There were several unconnected buildings on fire. When Erik ran outside in response to the alarms, he immediately knew this was no random accident. Those buildings had been deliberately set on fire. But now was not the time to seek out the perpetrators - unless they could be seen starting new fires. Now was the time to fight the blazes that, if unchecked, could burn down much of the city. The waterfront was already alive with people passing bucket after bucket of water from the shore to the buildings on fire. Some men had already grabbed long hooked poles and were trying to pull down the buildings on the edges of the fires to prevent the fire from spreading. In spite of the recent rains, the buildings were blazing because they were constructed of dried and seasoned timber and once ignited burned with a fierce intensity. It was going to be a long night.

The men, women, and children as well, all pitched in to do battle with the fires. They had no idea how far afield the fires were spread about the city, or the other battles that were being fought that night. They only focused on what was flaming in front of them.

On the western edge of the city, Tkaden and Leesha had left the safety of their lodgings and were hurrying to the city. In order to get into the city itself, where fires were burning, they had to cross the narrow isthmus on the western edge of the city. As they came up to the isthmus they expected there to be a watchtower and guards. Eirgalon was generally at peace, and had been for decades, but the Celts had a long history of disputes between chiefs and kings, and even a large and powerful city like Heilsand would be protected. In fact, there was a fortified tower and substantial log wall that ran across the approximately one hundred foot wide neck of land.

The large gate in this wall, which would normally be

closed at night, was open and no guards were to be seen. This seemed suspicious to Tkaden, but Leesha reasoned that the men must have gone to fight the fires, leaving the gates open so that others could come to help as well. They didn't have time to waste investigating the unguarded gate. They felt themselves pulled to get to the fire that they might help in any way they could. They were on the main thoroughfare that passed by the city commons and then came to the major fortress of the city. It bordered the city's central market square and then veered to the right and ran down to the harbor.

As they hurried toward down the street, they noticed that the mass of fires were coming from the harbor district that lay to the south and east of the fortress. There were a couple of fires also to the north of the fortress, and as they ran, more fires began to light the sky beyond the commons which they had just past. These were no chance fires; someone was setting them. They had nearly passed the fortress when Tkaden grabbed Leesha by the hand and pulled her to a stop.

"Look!" he said, pointing to the watchtowers on the walls of the fortress. The watchtowers were empty, but as they watched they saw a few men emerge along the top of the wall. It was dark, but Tkaden had good vision, and with the skies alive with flickering light from the fires, he could see clearly. He continued, "Those are no warriors of Heilsand on that wall!"

The gate to the fortress was closed tight. One would expect the gate to be open and the warriors to be out fighting the blaze, but that was not the case. In front of the gate he could see a number of bodies lying on the ground. And at some distance from the gate, huddled behind an unhitched merchant's wagon waiting to be loaded with its morning goods, were a couple of men carefully peering around and over the wagon, looking at the gate.

One of them shouted at Tkaden and Leesha, "Get out of arrow range! Now! Move!"

They quickly ran down the street away from the fortress. At the first corner they came to they ducked around the corner of the building.

Once around the corner, they stopped. Tkaden peered back around the corner and yelled to the men at the wagon, "What's going on?"

"Skraelings!" a yell came back. "They're in the fortress and have closed the gate against us! Go help with the fires. We can't attack the fortress now. We've been ordered to keep an eye on the gate to see what happens. Go help with the fires."

So they turned away and hurried into the harbor district. When they reached the harbor road, they saw how terribly serious the situation was. Nearly every building that fronted the harbor was ablaze, and even some of the second street of buildings were catching fire.

"What can we do?" Tkaden said aloud, but thinking that it was hopeless.

With determination in her voice, Leesha said, "Follow me."

She worked her way carefully, yet quickly, through the people and lines of water buckets to the nearest dock, and continued walking until she had reached the end of the dock.

She turned and faced the scene for a moment and then asked Tkaden to stand between her and the fires, and to not let anyone bother her.

Pulling the Eostre wand from her cloak she turned and faced the open waters. She reached down to touch the waters and then raised her wand to the sky and began chanting a prayer. The winds shifted slightly and grew stronger. A storm, which had been several miles offshore, now began moving toward land. But could it come soon enough and would it rain enough to make a difference?

Coming up the beach from the south, Skoth felt the power of the storm change, and he could see the center of that power. To his eyes the figure at the end of the dock looked as though there was a nimbus around it. It fairly seemed to glow with power and the storm moved at its beckoning.

He recognized Leesha, standing there with the wind whipping her hair and clothes, and he saw Tkaden standing between her and the crowd of people scrambling to fight the fires. He knew what he should do. Standing at the water's edge, he took hold of Evlin's hand with his left hand and holding his staff in his other hand he touched it to the water of the sea. He sent his power into Leesha's spell.

On the dock, Leesha's eyes went wide as she felt the power of the storm surge within her. Wildly she looked around her, and her eyes found Skoth a hundred yards away on the shoreline. Now she held both hands high to the sky calling even more strongly for the rain, and the rain came pelting down. The storm had moved completely onshore and was drenching the fires. It was as if unending buckets of water were being poured unto the flames, which were now hissing and sending up vast plumes of steam.

People ran for cover to the buildings that had not yet been consumed by fire. The fires began going out and the rains doused the torches. The deluge continued unabated until the only light was from a few glowing embers that had been hidden at the bottom of the blazes, and the light that spilled from the doorways of buildings where people stood in amazement. Then, as if the water bucket had run out of water, the rains suddenly stopped.

Leesha lowered her arms and felt like the proverbial wet dishrag as she released the power of the storm. The glowing nimbus around her faded. Tkaden put his arm around her and helped her down the dock back to shore. At the end of the dock he met Skoth and Evlin. They were all drenched to the bone, but they were smiling.

"Well done, Leesha!" said Skoth with a hearty laugh, and then he joked, "They always said there was a tempest raging in you! Guess they were right!"

Leesha, still feeling dazed, "You know it wasn't just me. I was doing what I could, but I don't think it would have been enough. But when you joined your strength in, it was like the whole world was moving."

"I only added to what you were doing. You were guiding this gale. Not I."

A small number of people carrying torches from inside the closest remaining building came splashing their way through the drenched waterfront street towards them. It was a dirty and bedraggled group that confronted them at the water's edge.

One of them, a tall and muscular fellow, who seemed to be in charge, said, "Strange things are afoot tonight. And you are one of them. Some of us noticed that young man try to shield you from our view out there on the dock, but we know what we saw. You somehow called that gale from offshore onto these fires."

Leesha hesitated and glanced at Skoth before saying, "Well, ahh, I, ahh . . ."

The Heilsander went on, "Don't be modest. Some of us here know druid work when we see it."

Another of the town's people, this time a strong, heavy set woman, turned her gaze to Skoth and said, "And some of us of the Woman's Circle can recognize a man of strength and power when he wields it. You are one of those. We want to know who are you, and what you are doing here, and why."

Before he could respond a young soldier came running up to the man in charge and panted out, "Drottin Tyg, Drottin Tyg, you've got to come right now. The Skraelings are threatening to kill the king."

At this point Skoth realized the man standing in front of him was a leader of the military forces in Heilsand, for "Drottin" was the old Norse term that some chiefdoms used to refer to the leaders of the fighting forces.

Skoth quickly said, "I'm Skoth, from Dunsheelin. I'm here to help you. Let's go!"

Trottin Tyg led them as they moved into the street and started toward the fortress that Tkaden and Leesha had passed earlier. Men, who had been fighting the fire, grabbed weapons they had laid aside and joined the procession. Skoth was pleased when Erik and his men, Rolf and Jake, came up and joined in as well. And then Karl, with Gunnar and his men, joined in.

Erik made his way over to Skoth and as they walked he said, "Well, we meet again, young Chief Skoth. Looks like you are in the thick of it again. Got any bears to protect you here?"

Evlin, walking on the other side of Skoth, loudly cleared her throat and leaned around Skoth to give Erik a glare that stopped him in mid-thought and that he wisely decided not to react to.

Chapter 41 - The Fortress of Heilsand

In short order they arrived at the corner where Tkaden and Leesha had hidden, and they saw that the Heilsand warriors had pushed some wagons further into the public square some thirty yards distance in front of the fortress' main gate. They had also set up a number of shields on the wagons to form a protective barrier for those who were negotiating with the captors.

Under protection of shields, Drottin Tyg and the runner who had come to get him, made their way to the wagon barrier. Tyg talked for a few moments with some of the warriors there, and then sent the runner back to the waiting group with some orders. Most of the men were to remain there, ready for more orders. A couple of men were sent back to the waterfront to make sure all the fires were out, or under control so they would not reignite neighboring buildings. The last order was that he called for Skoth to come up to join him. Skoth motioned for Erik to join him and the two of them went forward to the wagons. Evlin, Leesha, Tkaden, Karl, and the rest all waited at the distant gathering point. Some of the Heilsand men worked their way around the first set of streets that bordered the fortress, so they could make sure that any other fires were out and so that the Skraelings could not escape the fortress by another means.

Tyg called Skoth up to him and said, "I have seen, and I know, that you are a man of power, and if you represent the isle of Fadis Innis, your advice is welcome here. I heard Wild Erik call you 'chief' - be you King of Fadis Innis?"

"This may take some time to explain."

"Then let's use the time of waiting here to begin your tale. Those Skraelings on the wall have threatened to kill King Ragen lest we allow them to leave. I plan on doing nothing until the light of day, if I can hold them off. Tell me your tale. Mayhap we will have time to hear it all."

Skoth told him as much as he thought was important for him to know. There were some details he left unsaid, such as his relationship with Evlin, but he did share with him the history of the prophecy and the action of Chief Unaine in naming him High King. Skoth did say that he wasn't claiming to be lord of Heilsand and its people, but only that he was trying to follow the quest laid out before him and if he could in any way be of service in this situation he would do it.

Tyg was thoughtful as he listened, as were the small group of men around them in the forward position of the wagons. During this time, Erik said nothing, though he did nod in affirmation when Skoth recounted some of his adventures to date.

Finally, Skoth ended saying, "So there it is. I know it sounds strange. A year ago I would have thought this was a child's fairy tale. But I've seen too much in this past year. I don't blame you if you don't believe it all. However, I do assure you that I am here to help you and I will do it in any way I am able."

Tyg was quiet for several moments, then nodding he said, "I am a man of action, that's why I am Drottin of this domain. King Ragen trusts me, and the men respect me. I say this now, in front of you and witnessed by my men, that I believe your words. Your quest seems honorable and true. Bold you are to share it with me. Simpler men might have thought you in league with those Skraelings in there and seeking to usurp our king. Actions prove, where words but promise. Mayhap the time will come when I shall call you High King."

Thereupon Drottin Tyg extended his arm and clasped Skoth's arm, forehand to forehand, in sign of a promise.

After that, Tyg asked, "I noticed that one of the men walking with us, one of your friends, is obviously Wabanaki. How sure are you that he is not one with those Skraelings in the fortress?"

"His name is Tkaden, from the town of Wausacom. You are right, he does have Wabanaki blood, but he also has blood of ours coursing through his veins. I am sure of him. He has nothing to do with the men inside the fortress. I suspect most of the Skraelings inside the fortress are Haudenoshonee. I've had dealings with them already. Unless I am mistaken, we are dealing with followers of Malsum. They do not wish us well."

"Malsum. I've heard that name, and never in a good context. I've heard he wants to rid this land of any and all of us who have ancestors who came from the eastern lands."

"That is he. He speaks word of division and destruction for Eirgalon."

"Well, when the morning light comes we will see what can be done about his men."

The small group of men fell silent for a few minutes, each of them traveling deep in their own thoughts. Then Skoth said, "I arrived on your shores only when the fires were blazing high. Can you tell me how they came to be, and how it came to be that the fortress was taken by our foes?"

Tyg shook his head in frustration and said, "I know not how it all transpired, but the Skraelings came by stealth among us. I suspect that over several days they entered our city and plotted, and planned, and made their preparations. Then, at an appointed hour, they secretly set fires in buildings along the waterfront, and in other parts of the city. There is nothing so dangerous to us as fires that go unchecked. You can see that most of our homes and buildings are made of wood. When the fires began, many of the men left the fortress to fight the fires. I suspect that we had a couple of traitors amongst our men who stayed behind, and that allowed the Skraeling host to enter and subdue those few that remained. So now we have our own fortress in their hands."

Skoth nodded his head in understanding. He asked, "What do you intend to do? Will you allow them to escape in order to save your king?"

Tyg frowned and said, "They killed some of our people with the fires, and they have certainly killed some of our men who tried to guard the fortress." With that he pointed toward the gate where a couple of the fortress guards still lay dead on the ground near the gate, because every time someone ventured forth to get the men they had been met with several arrows which drove them back.

Tyg continued, "By rights, I can't let them go. They must pay for their crime. But I will follow the orders of my king. If King Ragen commands us to allow their escape, I will do so."

They waited.

It was in the hour of the wolf, that hour of deepest darkness before the first light of dawn, that the captors tried to sneak out on the far side of the fortress by letting down rope ladders, but watchful eyes saw them and raised the alarm. They quickly pulled the rope ladders back to the top of the wall.

Several minutes after the failed escape attempt they tried again to parley at the front gate. One of them shouted out, "Let me speak to your commander!"

Tyg stood forth, clad in the helmet and armor his men had gotten for him after the fire and shouted back, "You may speak to me!"

"Are you the coaster in charge here, or are you just a mouthpiece?"

"I'm the one you speak to. What is it you want?"

"We want safe passage for our men out of here, and your promise to leave us be. The true people of this land want nothing to do with you and your coaster ways."

"Where is King Ragen?"

"He is sitting on his throne waiting for you."

"And what about the rest of our men?"

"None of your men are in here with us. They deserted their posts to fight the fires."

"What assurance can you give us that you will give us our king and leave us in peace. You have attacked us unprovoked. You make war on us."

"War? This is not war. This is but a small warning. Malsum is telling you to go back to the islands across the waters in the sunrise lands. You are not wanted here. This land belongs to its true people."

Skoth softly called and motioned for Tyg to return to the safety of the wagon shield, which he did.

Skoth said to him, "Allow me to speak to them. I've had some dealings with Malsum's people already."

He had scarcely gotten those words out of his mouth before Evlin was at his side, and not far behind her were Leesha and Tkaden.

Leesha was apologizing profusely, "I'm sorry, Skoth. She was standing there right beside us and before we knew what was happening, she had taken off. We couldn't catch her. The best I could do was to cast a shadow of darkness over us to protect us from their eyes so they couldn't see us and get a clear shot at us."

"Hmmn," said Skoth, "a shadow of darkness? That might come in handy."

He reached out his hands to Evlin and took her hands in his, then for several moments looked deeply into her deep brown eyes flecked with streaks of gold. Smiling and turning away from her toward the others, he said, "You couldn't have stopped her if you had tried. You don't know my Evlin."

Tyg looked over the new arrivals, "Some of your people, I presume?"

"Yes. They have been companions on my quest."

"So what is it you intend to say?"

Skoth smiled an enigmatic smile and replied, "I intend to provoke them. They have a plan laid out in their minds. I am not in that plan. When they know I am here they will change what they try to do. They won't have a well-thought out plan for attacking me. They will simply react, and that won't be good enough for them, because that will give you the opportunity to deal with them."

They spent the next several minutes making plans and Tyg sending orders to his groups of men surrounding the fortress. Leesha used her wand to call up what she had called a "shadow of darkness" spell to cover the arrival of Erik's men, and Karl with his men (Gunnar and his crew).

Light was beginning to brighten the eastern skies, when Skoth stood up and stepped to the side of the shielded wagons. He had his wavy black hair covered by a helm that one of the warriors of Heilsand had procured for him, and he was dressed in his simple traveling leathers. His shield was still slung over his back and his sword was in its scabbard on his left hip. In his left hand he held the oak quarterstaff given him by Fearglas.

His voice deep and projecting, he shouted, "Servants of the false shaman, Malsum: come and listen to the truth."

Several more faces peered over the parapets of the fortress.

"Do any of you know who I am? Do you know why your shaman fears me?"

A response was hurled from the fortress walls, "Malsum fears no one! You are just another coaster dog! Are you here to free your king and to let us go?"

Skoth glanced and nodded to his friends behind the wagons, and then he spoke again, "He has sent his assassins to kill me. They have failed. He has failed. His plot to burn this city has been foiled. You know he fears me. I am Skoth."

Upon revealing his identity, he quickly stepped to the side behind the cover of the shielded wagons. Which was a wise move, since as soon as his name was proclaimed, more than a dozen arrows tore through the space where he had stood.

Howling voices went up from within the fortress as the gates were flung open and men began rushing out. At that moment some of Tyg's men sent flaming spears crashing against the walls of the fortress near the gate. They did no damage to the stone walls of the fortress, but they did serve to illuminate the attackers streaming out of the gate. Arrows from Tyg's men who were stationed behind barriers across the square to the sides of the gate flew into the attacking Haudenoshonee host. Erik, Karl, Gunnar, and the rest of the soldiers ran out from the sides of the shielded wagons and rushed into the attackers, slashing at them with a vengeance. Another troop of Tyg's men rushed in the open gates to deal with any of the warriors who might have remained inside the fortress. In the public square before the fortress gates a couple of dozen Haudenoshonee warriors battled more than a hundred Heilsand defenders. The battle didn't last long. Within minutes all of the Haudenoshonee host were down. The dead and dying littered square. No quarter was asked for and none was given.

It was still before dawn, but the sky was clear because the winds had come in from the west and blown the clouds away. In the rising light one could see tendrils of smoke still rising from the smoldering fires that still remained, and the burnt smell of the many fires still filled the air.

Chapter 42 - The Aftermath of Battle

They walked among the slain and Tyg observed, "These men are dressed in Wabanaki and Celtic attire. Yet you have said they are Haudenoshonee."

Skoth, walking with him, said, "They are not Wabanaki. I'm sure a closer examination will prove this true. Tkaden, will you examine these men, for me. Gruesome work, but we must see if there is any evidence of where they come from."

One of Tyg's men came running out of the fortress, "Drottin! You must come. There is something you must see."

Quickly, Tyg and Skoth, with Evlin at his side, made their way into the fortress. Erik followed close behind, with Karl and Gunnar, but Leesha and Tkaden stayed behind to do their appointed task.

Walking through the gates and into the inner courtyard of the fortress, they saw the bodies of several Heilsand defenders lying where they had been cut down. They had obviously tried to defend the fortress but were overwhelmed. The heavy rains during the night had washed the blood from them, but they not been moved or cared for. No respect had been shown them. There were even two of them who had their hands and feet bound and then had been shot by several arrows, as if in cruel sport by their attackers.

The warrior led them into the Great Hall of the Fortress of Heilsand. This was not much larger that the Great Hall of Dunsheelin, but it was more elaborate. The floor was of polished tile, and had the same sacred spiral as that of

Dunsheelin. There were a number of tables and chairs throughout the room and the hearthfire still burned. The major difference from Dunsheelin was that at one end of the hall there was a raised dais and a large carved oaken throne. It was to the throne that he led them.

On the throne was old King Ragen, dead, with his hands bound and with his own sword plunged into his heart. Lying upon his lap was a note, written in Old Norse runes, which said, "Take your kings and leave our lands." It was signed, "People of the Dawn Land".

"Cursed Skraelings!" Tyg said with disgust. "They will pay the price for this deed." Turning to Skoth he asked, "Do you still, standing here with me before my dead king, assert that these are no Wabanaki, for they call themselves the 'People of the Dawn Land'?"

Skoth sighed, "It is a sad day. I mourn the death of your chief. But I am sure. The men who did this are followers of Malsum from the Haudenoshonee lands."

"So you say. But where is your proof?"

"They seek to throw us into dissention. We of Celtic blood and we of Wabanaki blood are becoming one people, the people of Eirgalon. Malsum likes that not, and seeks to make us question each other. He seeks to divide Celt from Wabanaki, inlander from coaster, shaman from druid or priest. If he can divide us, he can defeat us."

"Again, so you say. My heart says to believe you, but for my people, I need proof."

While they were so discussing, an elderly woman was brought before them. It was the mistress of the kitchen crew. She lived in a small suite behind the kitchens, and rarely left the fortress, even when the rest of her helpers had finished with the daily work and departed to their homes at the end of the day. She would retire to her rooms and enjoy the satisfaction of a day well lived in service to her lord.

When ushered into the Great Hall she saw the body of King Ragen, and she fell to her knees with a wail. Tyg allowed her a few moments of grief and then reaching down and taking her by the arm he helped her stand.

"Good woman," he said, "how is it that all others in the fortress are gone, or dead, and you lived through this ordeal?"

"Drottin Tyg, you know me. I'm too old to go out fighting fires. Little or no help, I would be. Late as it was when the alarms first went off, there were still folks here. All who could went off to fight the fires. Only the King, so frail he was, and a few of his men remained. And me, of course, little was there I could do, I stayed here too. Then I heard a ruckus in the courtyard. King Ragen, may the gods receive him, ordered me to quick go hide. You know me, I have a mind of my own, and I'd have stayed and fought to protect my king, but he ordered me to hide. So I hid. Oh, what a terrible deed. Oh, poor Ragen."

"Yes, indeed, good woman. We all grieve for our king. But the fires are extinguished and the attackers are now all dead. We live and the city lives. Is there anything more you can tell me? Where did you hide? What did you see and hear?"

"Well, good Drottin, you know that I know this old fortress better than anyone else. My whole life I have lived here. I know every nook and cranny there is. The pantry has a secret panel that leads to a small passageway, well, I need not tell you more in front of strangers, but there I went. Quiet as a mouse I was. I listened to those Skraeling wretches as they searched for others, and then as they shouted at our king!"

"And what language did they speak?"

"Well, as they spoke to good King Ragen, may the gods receive him, they spoke in our tongue, but as they spoke to each other they spoke a tongue I know not."

"Was it Wabanaki?"

"No, no, none of their dialects. My sister, dead now for four years, married a Wabanaki man in her youth. I know and speak their tongue. It was not that."

Drottin Tyg looked at Skoth.

Skoth said, "From the start they intended no one to live. If so they would have spoken Wabanaki in front of Regan and any witnesses to deceive them, just as they dressed in Wabanaki and Celtic fashion to deceive us."

Tyg nodded and said, "Here is proof enough. Never would I doubt this good woman's word. These devils were from the western lands. I doubt it not that Haudenoshonee was what they spoke."

Tyg then turned and gave instructions to his men to take the king from his throne and to have men at the waterfront prepare a funeral ship for the king. He also told them to use partially burned wood from the fires that had been set to build the pyre on the ship for "the king gave his life as we fought those fires." He asked the Mistress of the Kitchen if she needed to time recover, but she insisted that what she needed to do was to supervise the scouring of the Great Hall.

Leaving the Great Hall in her capable hands, Tyg led the way back to the square in front of the fortress. Skoth and Evlin walked with him. Evlin had said nothing through all this and said nothing now, but she slipped her hand into Skoth's hand and gave his hand a gentle squeeze.

Dawn had fully broken upon the city by now and since the fortress' main gate faced the southeast, the March sunrise was hitting it directly and bathing it in light. Nothing to identify precisely where the invaders had come from was found on their bodies, though some of their weapons did not appear to have been made in Eirgalon, and were likely of Haudenoshonee construction. Their bodies had been taken to one end of the public square and the shielded wagons had been disassembled and removed.

Drottin Tyg motioned for the crowd to assemble. Warrior and common folk, alike, gathered before him. They were murmuring and talking to each other, but when he raised his hand to speak, silence fell upon the crowd. He spoke.

"People of Heilsand. King Ragen is dead. He died in defense of his people. This evening, at sunset, we will send his funeral ship to the sea. So we honor his kingship. The King has left no descendants to lay claim to the kingship of Heilsand. I have been his Chief Drottin for more than a score of years and he often entrusted me with the affairs our people. Until the meeting of our people at an Alting to name our new king, I claim command of this city and its people. There I will ask to be named your king."

The people were subdued, they were grieving the death of their king, but they gave affirmation by pounding staffs to shields, stomping the cobbled stone of the square, and clapping their hands.

Tyg wasn't finished, and when their affirmations died out he went on, "Also standing here before you is a man who in no small measure enabled us to overcome the tragedies of the night and defeat our enemies. His name is Skoth of Dunsheelin, and he has claim to be High King of Eirgalon. We have never had a High King over the people of Eirgalon. We have had generations of chiefs and kings, and often we have had times of bitter battles and rivalries with our neighbors. But times have changed and forces unknown in their power threaten us. Forces from outside our land. Should you proclaim me as your king, know that I will support his claim to be to be our High King!"

This pronouncement took the people by surprise. As Tyg gave Skoth an embrace of thanks and then lifted Skoth's arm high in victory, the many who had seen or heard of his involvement in the actions of the night gave again a sounding of acclamation, though not as long or prolonged as for that of Tyg as King of Heilsand.

Erik, standing slightly behind and to the side of Skoth and Evlin, said quietly, "Well, I'll be!"

Chapter 43 - Funeral Pyre and Future Plans

As difficult as that day was for the inhabitants of Heilsand and its surrounding territories, it was also a day of new beginnings. Under the leadership of Ragen, whom some had come to question if his mind was growing as feeble with age as was his body, the city had lost some of it vitality. Under the leadership of Tyg, there was every indication that that situation would be remedied. The waterfront would be rebuilt and renewed energy in expanding innovation, exploration, and trade would likely happen.

It was also a day of reunions. The travelers that had set out with Skoth on his quest were reunited. They didn't have much time to share their stories with each other that day because they were busy with helping the people of Heilsand clean up from the fires and the attack of Malsum's men. However, after the send-off of the pyre-ship that sunset, and for the next several days until the Alting, on the day of the Vernal Equinox, they found times to reacquaint themselves and to give each other updates on what they had done.

It is often in the simple and ordinary activities of daily life that people develop respect and appreciation for the talents and abilities of others. It is true that in the moment of crisis, Skoth and his people acted decisively and bravely. The people saw that, and were even awed by the power of what they had done. But it was in the physical work of cleaning and rebuilding the city that the common folk of Heilsand came to know them. They worked side by side with the workers on the docks, the soldiers at the fortress, and the laborers on the buildings. They talked and joked and treated the people with respect. In so doing they earned the admiration and respect of the people. Soon the people began calling Skoth "Chief" when they addressed him. He was puzzled where that came from until one day he mentioned it to Karl, and Karl told him that ever since people overheard Erik calling him by that name, they started to use it also. Karl also told him that Erik was thoroughly amused by this.

They did find time to pursue some leads that they felt might be related to helping Skoth on the task of his quest. Enat, accompanied now by Leesha, followed up on her connection to meet with the Women's Circle. The Women's Circle of Heilsand was just as anxious to meet with them as they were to meet with them. King Ragen may have known at one time that the Headmistress of his kitchen was a member of the leadership of the Women's Circle, but it was doubtful that Tyg was aware of it.

In those Women's Circle discussions Erik's sister Fiona asked Leesha and Enat how the women of Heilsand might help. The sisters made two requests. First, they asked to be given any information that might pertain to Skoth's search for identifying the key of his quest. Second, they appealed for a commitment to making contact, and establishing a relationship, between the Women's Circles of the Celts and the Wise Ones of the Wabanaki people.

Tkaden and Evlin got acquainted with each other as cousins. Tkaden enjoyed telling Evlin about the Bear Clan of Wausacom, and some of his family stories, but he had to confess to her that his father had never told him much about his aunt. He did know that Sheela was Tkomik's half-sister, and that she had disappeared before he was born, but there was little else he could share about her.

Karl had spent most of the time of the quest apart from his boyhood friend. In effect, he had been on a journey of his own, growing into his own manhood, without dependence on another. Skoth was happy to see Karl's leg had healed so well, and was as impressed as Erik had been by the relationships Karl had formed with Gunnar and the people of New Caledonia. Karl had developed a small following of his own. While Gunnar was in command of his men from New Caledonia, the men looked to Karl for direction. In addition, two days after the fire, four men at arms of Fadis Innis just happened to show up in Heilsand and gave their service to Karl. They didn't say much about what had brought them to Heilsand, only that Unaine had sent them on their way a couple of weeks ago. Rolf and Jake, Erik's men, tended to still take direction from Erik when he gave them special orders, but otherwise they also followed Karl.

Erik, being Erik, would have enjoyed a few days of tavern visiting in the fine city of Heilsand, but since the city was so focused on the efforts of rebuilding and since his appointed charge was back in view, he suppressed that urge and worked at being the best bodyguard and aide that he could be for his Chief.

The people of Heilsand were fascinated by the exotic beauty of the woman who had stood at Skoth's side that tragic night and who now worked at his side. Her looks certainly captured their hearts: flowing dark auburn hair, fine features and soft brown eyes flecked with gold, skin of honey gold, and a smile that melted hearts. However, it was her fierce protective nature for Skoth and her compassion for those who were hurting that impressed both the man on the dock and the woman at the hearth. In the conversation of the people in the street there were comments that if "Chief Skoth" was to be their High King, then this was a woman worthy to be their queen.

The day of the equinox was fast approaching, and with it the day of the Alting to declare the new King of Heilsand. There didn't seem to be any doubt in the minds of the people that Drottin Tyg was the right person for the job. He had held the city and its towns and villages together in the old age of King Ragen, and if given the responsibility of King, he would be a strong leader for their future. Skoth, and the other folks of his quest, were making plans to head back west, but when Tyg invited them to attend the Alting as his honored guests, they knew they must accept.

The day of the Alting arrived with horns being blown and bells sounding from the ramparts of the fortress. Joyous sounds these were when compared to the sounds of the alarms from a few short weeks ago. The city was soon teeming with people on this fine spring morning. The druids of the kingdom had observed the morning equinox ritual on the heights of the hills to the south of the city and had returned in procession across the narrow neck of land to the city gates. They had then processed down the main thoroughfare and come to the Fortress of Heilsand and entered through its main gate. The important personages of the land were now assembling in the Great Hall.

The Great Hall had been thoroughly cleaned was

richly decorated for the occasion. All vestiges of the attack had been removed. Even the grand throne where Ragen had been slain had been removed. It had been placed on the funeral ship and gone up in flames at sea. Today, there was no throne, although the raised dais remained and on that dais sat a simple, though substantial, chair. Whoever was chosen to be the king would commission artisans to make a new throne. The sacred spiral on the floor in the center of the hall was open for all to see. Around the spiral were arranged more than thirty chairs with an open space at the end that led to the raised dais. In those chairs were the leading men of the city and the neighboring towns and territories that made up the kingdom of Heilsand. It was they who would choose the king.

Skoth, and his people of the quest, were seated in chairs near the hearth fire of the hall, which was opposite the main door. In the kitchen door, stood the mistress of the kitchen, a smile on her face as she surveyed the scene. She gave a knowing wink to Leesha and Enat as they came in and took their seats - Women's Circle business, no doubt.

The Master Druid of Heilsand gave an invocation from the center of the sacred spiral and then asked any claimants for the kingship to stand forth. Two men stood and stepped forward. One was Tyg. The other was tall, broad-shouldered man with red hair and beard to match.

The Master Druid asked each man to briefly describe why he made his claim.

Tyg went first, "I am Tyg. I have served as Chief Drottin of our men-at-arms for fourteen years. I claim no noble blood, or land holdings. I claim only a life that has

243

been lived serving our people. King Ragen trusted me to lead his men. He trusted to me to make decisions for our land when he was unable or unsure of himself. In the wake of the tragic events of the fires and his death, I have led the people to begin the process of rebuilding. I will be faithful to the land and our people."

Many of those around the circle of chairs nodded in agreement with him as he spoke. From those sitting and standing in the areas of the Great Hall outside of the center circle, one could hear murmurs of assent.

When Tyg was done speaking, the other man spoke, "I am Leif, son of Bjorn, holder of the estate of Darby, in the western reaches. I am Marchwarden for the western lands of our kingdom. I have served and ruled. You know me to be an honest and fair man. Ragen was of the coastal lands. Tyg is of the coast. We need a man that will be for all the people and lands of Heilsand, not just the coast. I will be that king."

Skoth observed the crowd as Leif spoke. He saw many with thoughtful looks, and some with heads nodding in agreement. When the two claimants were finished speaking the Master Druid stepped around the circle, asking each man in turn who he supported. Most of the responses were for Tyg, but there were a handful of men who voiced support for Leif. When all had spoken, The Master Druid followed the long path to the center of the sacred spiral.

There he stood and called out, "Tyg, we call upon you. Come forth to be our king."

Tyg stood, and following the same path, made his way to the center of the labyrinth. There, in the center of the sacred spiral and in the center of his people he gave his oath and promise. Then he knelt and the Master Druid took a torc with the King rune of Heilsand engraved upon it and placed it around his neck. The druid then took his staff and striking the floor three times declared "So mote it be."

King Tyg rose and walked to the dais. He turned and faced the crowd, and then as they shouted words of acclamation and stood for him as he sat down upon the chair, signifying that he assumed his place of leadership.

When the shouting had died down, he held up his hand for silence and motioned for the crowd to be seated. The crowd obliged. Then he spoke, "I want all of you to know that I hear and understand what my friend, Leif of Darby says. This must be a kingdom for all of its people. My first action is to appoint Leif as my Chief Drottin." Turning his gaze to look directly at Leif, he asked, "Do you accept?"

Shouts of "Ja! Ja! Ja!" echoed through the hall when Leif nodded in acceptance and then walked to stand by the side of Tyg, but off the dais.

When the voices had tied down, Tyg held up his hand again, and again the crowd went silent. He looked at Skoth and motioned for him to come forward. When Skoth had come and was standing in front of him, he spoke.

"We owe a debt of gratitude to you, and your people, for all you have done for us in these trying times. Heilsand thanks you!" Again sounds of affirmation filled the hall. Tyg did not stop them, but let their voices linger on. When the cheering finally died down, he spoke again, "I know you make no claim of lordship over Heilsand, but I know you have claim to high kingship over all of Eirgalon. In the centuries that our people have been in Eirgalon no Alting has yet been called to name a High King. Now is the time. Our people and land need to be as one. I, as King of Heilsand, pledge our support and aid in your quest. I will stand for you as High King of Eirgalon."

Skoth smiled that disarming "aw shucks" smile of his, and said, "Thank you King Tyg. You will be a good king, and may the gods that be, bless you, your people, and all the lands of Heilsand. I understand that this is no small pledge that you have given. As I strive to fulfill my quest, much might be the cost of fulfillment. I ask you to look around this circle of men, they represent the people of your realm. Now look over at my companions on my quest. We are people of this land, Celt and Wabanaki. As High King, I would be king of all the people, creatures, and lands of this realm. If we are to be one Eirgalon we must be indeed, one, as Leif has said. We must be one, as people of the coast and people of the interior, but we must also be united as one. That means people of Celt heritage and people of Wabanaki blood as one people. Our blood is already mingled in the veins of so many of us. From now on, we must see ourselves, not as Celt, or Wabanaki, but as the people of Eirgalon. Will you follow me in this?"

Tyg was not one to make rash decisions. A thoughtful expression covered his face. His gaze circled the room, taking in the expressions on the faces of his leaders who were seated as well as those who sat and stood outside the inner circle. For a moment, for some unknown reason, his gaze settled on the face of the Kitchen Mistress of the Great Hall. He saw her smile and nod her head in approval. Something in that look gave him the answer he needed. He stood to answer.

"What you say is wise. We are in truth one people, and we shall be one in name and deed. I do so promise. I stand now, and I will stand in the future, for you as our high King!"

Again Skoth gave another one of those "aw shucks" looks of embarrassment and stepped forward to take Tyg's arm in a strong and sincere arm clasp. The day of celebration was just beginning.

Chapter 44 - Evil Attack in Dunsheelin

Warm weather had chased the last of the winter storms away from Fadis Innis and the grasses of the island were greening out, although the trees and not yet begun to bud. There was a positive feeling in the air that Spring was close at hand as the sun neared the vernal equinox and the daylight hours increased.

Unaine's thoughts frequently were about his girls and the others on the quest. While he had received a number of reports from Erik during this time and he knew that all was well with his two daughters, he couldn't help but have feelings of fatherly concern filling his mind. He repeatedly told himself that they were adults and that they could take care of themselves, but they were still his little girls. Nothing would ever change that.

The winter months had been hard on Unaine. He had missed the vitality of the young folks that were so dear to him. Yes, he still had Teite and Neal with him, but Teite was engrossed in her studies and research at the academy, and Neal was still under the watchful eye of Theofinn. The escapade with that accursed knife troubled Unaine. Neal talked and acted normal for the most part, but often were the times that Unaine noticed Neal flexing the long ago injured hand. Perhaps it was just a habit Neal had developed while recuperating the muscles of the hand, but Unaine wondered if it could be something else. There was also something about the look in Neal's eye. At times there was this far-off and wild look that Unaine had never noticed before.

The last message Unaine had received from Erik said that they were on the way to Heilsand. Undoubtedly they had arrived by now and he wondered what was happening. He wondered also what had become of young Skoth. Was he still hidden away with Fearglas as Erik had reported? What was he learning of his quest?

So it was that in the late afternoon of one of the warming days of mid-March that a messenger arrived in Dunsheelin. He went to the Great Hall, but was told that Unaine was out for a little while, so he sat down at a table in the hall to wait. The ladies in the kitchen saw him waiting, and brought him food and drink. They knew where Unaine had gone. Out of respect for him, they gave him privacy. Unaine was sitting in an arbor that he had commissioned to be constructed on the shores of Lake Ronkonkoma many years ago for the pleasure of his wife. It wasn't far from the Great Hall, but it was a peaceful and private place. He often sat there and remembered the times he had shared with Jeni. The vines, which shaded the arbor in summer, had not yet leafed out, so he sat in the glow of the late afternoon sun, enjoying its heat. With him sat his trusted advisor, Theofinn.

Teite, escorted by Neal, came hurrying down the path. She was obviously excited about something. With animation in her voice, she blurted out, "Father! I think I may have a clue about the key to Skoth's quest!"

Neal stumbled for a moment and she turned her attention to him. He was doubled over holding his stomach.

He said, "I feel sick. Wait. Don't tell him anything. Let me relieve myself. I'll be right back."

Then he turned and ran back down the path and out of

sight.

Theofinn said, "Where is his watcher? He was supposed to have someone with him, looking out for him, at all times, even at the Academy."

Teite answered, "Oh, don't worry about that. He's been fine. I told your assistant to go back to his work, that I would watch him."

"Young lady, that was his work for the day. And now Neal is alone, isn't he?"

A look of alarm crossed her face.

"I'm sorry. I didn't think. But he just went to relieve himself. I'm sure he'll be right back in a minute."

"Perhaps. Perhaps. But just to be sure . . ."

Theofinn left that comment unfinished, pulled a small whistle from his tunic pocket and blew it. Within moments one of his other assistants came running up to him. He told him to get a couple of Unaine's men and to go search for Neal, and also they should send a couple of the Chief's men to the arbor.

Unaine said to Teite, "You have such a trusting heart, my dear. You are so much like your mother was. But she learned to temper that trust, and to guard her ways when needed. You must learn that too."

Teite sat down in the arbor between the two men, on a chair that was nearest the lake and that was furthest from the path, but from where she could see Neal when he returned.

It wasn't long before they saw Neal hurrying back up the path to the arbor. The Chief's men were already there and standing guard. When Neal got to the arbor, they stepped in front of him.

Neal stammered, "What? What's going on? Why?"

From behind the guards, Theofinn said, " You know you were never to be alone, my boy. Then you go running off by yourself like that."

"But the cramping was so severe. Would you have had me soil myself as I stood in front of you?"

"Of course not, Neal. Come, have a seat with us. Let him through, men."

The guards took a step apart and Neal walked between them. As he stepped into the arbor, he reached into his cloak. Pulling out a dagger, he dove at Teite. He was driving the dagger straight for her heart, but before he could reach her, Theofinn's staff came crashing down on his arm. The guards jumped forward to grab him as Unaine threw his body up and out of his chair. They all tumbled to the ground in the middle of the arbor. In short order they had Neal pinned to the ground. The dagger lay on the ground in front of Teite. It was the very dagger that had injured Neal last summer, and that he had claimed to have thrown into the lake.

Teite was stunned, but kept saying, "Why? Why?"

Neal grimaced in pain, saying, "I can't breath. It hurts. Can't breath."

"Back away from him, Teite. And don't touch the dagger. No one touch that dagger," ordered Theofinn. Then he said to Neal, "Where does it hurt?"

"Chest... heavy weight... can't breath."

"Try to relax. I'll see what I can do."

Theofinn turned to his assistant that had returned and ordered him to run to the Tower and get his Bag of Potions -

and to hurry!

Teite, who had stood and backed away from them, cried, "Why? Why would you try to kill me?"

Neal looked up at her. He struggled to get the words out as he struggled to breath. "I didn't want to. But you said you knew how to find the key... Can't... let him find... the key... Sorry... Forgive me."

Neal's arms then went limp against those he struggled against and his eyes rolled up in his head.

"Do something for him!" Teite wailed.

Theofinn knelt over him with his hands on Neal's forehead and chest. Softly he chanted, but nothing happened. Soon the assistant returned with the bag. Theofin reached in and pulled out a small bottle and poured a few drops from the bottle into Neal's mouth, but still nothing happened. Theofinn continued to chant. But nothing happened. Finally, Theofinn sat back and sighed.

"There's nothing I can do. He's gone. Whatever has possessed him, is gone too."

Unaine sighed and said, "At heart he was a good man. I'm sorry, Teite. I know how much he meant to you."

She burst into tears and threw herself on him. The guards had released him and now stood to the side, waiting for Unaine's orders. Theofinn reached into his bag and taking a cloth, carefully wrapped it around the dagger and tucked it securely into the bag. Handing the bag to his assistant he ordered him to take it to the Tower and not to let anyone near it.

They patiently stood by as Teite gave vent to her grief. When she finally raised herself from him, Unaine reached out his hand to help her stand.

Unaine said, "He was a good man. We'll give him an honorable sendoff. Come, let us leave this place. My men will take care of him and will arrange for the funeral pyre." With that he nodded to his men, and they nodded back.

With Unaine on one arm and Theofinn on the other, they walked back down the path to Dunsheelin.

Chapter 45 - The Clue to the Key

There was sadness in Dunsheelin that evening. Word had spread quickly of young Neal's death. Plans were made for his cremation. Unaine insisted to all that although Neal had been under suspicion because of the taint of the dagger upon him, he was to be given the respect and honor of a warrior's funeral. Unaine made sure that it was proclaimed that Neal had died as a result of his involvement in the quest.

Teite was taken under the care of the Women's Circle, and Unaine and Theofinn returned to Unaine's private quarters at the Great Hall. The messenger was brought to him there. The message from Erik recounted the events of the Heilsand fires, the Haudenoshonee attack on the fortress, and the death of the king. While Erik did not give all the details of the events, he did make it clear that the new king, Tyg, had promised to support Skoth as High King. After the messenger left, they discussed the news.

Theofinn smiled at this news. "Well, well, well. It seems our young man has come out of seclusion and made quite a stir."

"Yes," said Unaine, "in spite of what has happened here. That is good news. Evil is abroad. They have confronted it there and pushed it back. But what of here? What is happening to us? Spring is upon us, but dread and evil seem to seep around us. One of our talented youth is dead. And we couldn't stop it."

"My friend, we can only do our part. I, too, grieve for Neal. He had the potential to be a fine scholar and druid.

What would you have me say?"

"I know you are right, Theo. But it still grieves me. And it makes me wonder about the timing of events. Teite was coming to tell us of finding a clue to the key of Skoth's quest. She sits in mourning tonight. I have no desire to intrude upon her sorrow, but I think we must talk with her, and soon. Our adversary attacked in broad daylight today in order to try and keep her from sharing it with us."

"You're right, of course. But I don't think we have to be over-worried about Teite. She is with some of the ladies of the Women's Circle, and they are fierce in loyalty to their own. They also, how shall I say it, have certain abilities and skills which even I would not want to challenge. I think she is safe. But you are right. Any information about a clue to the key must be shared so that we can get it to Skoth."

There was a knock at the door. The men looked at each other, and Unaine said, "Come in."

To their surprise, Teite walked in. Gwen, who worked in the kitchen of the Great Hall, and Katie, escorted her. The fact that two of the leaders of the Women's Circle were with her indicated either that this was a matter of importance, or that they were concerned about Teite's well-being. Or perhaps it was both.

Upon seeing his daughter, Unaine immediately arose from his chair and went to her. He embraced her for a long moment.

She said, "I'm alright, Da. But I thought it was important to come and talk with you about this afternoon."

Unaine nodded and with compassion in his voice, responded, "Aye, a grievous loss it is. Come sit. Ladies, you too, please join us."

When they were all seated, Teite went on.

"My heart aches so. But we must rise above our private pain. I must share with you the discovery I made while I worked today. I fear it was this very information that drove Neal to his death. Whatever power it was that had control over him didn't want us to know it. It drove him to try and silence me before I could share it. And it killed him as a result."

Unaine glanced to Theofinn and said, "We were just thinking the same thoughts, my daughter."

"That means it is vital information. And it means I must share it. If only I know this clue, then I am in danger. If I should die, the clue dies with me, or until someone else figures it out. It also means that whoever I share it with will also be in danger."

"We all are in danger here, dear daughter. Dangerous times are these. Yes, in sharing it, you will take some of the direct threat from yourself. The danger shared might lessen the threat to you. But, you will still be in danger."

"Da, I trust you more than anyone. Who should I share this with? Who else should I put in danger? Oh, I wish Ma were here to give us her advice."

Unaine sighed and said, "So do I, Teite. So do I."

Theofinn spoke up, "There are two considerations. First, yes, anyone you tell will share the risk. But for only one person to have the knowledge would be foolish for if that person dies the knowledge could be lost, so it must be shared in spite of the risk. Second, if this is information our adversary would desire, the people who have this knowledge must be people who would never share it with our enemy. In any situation!"

"Who then should we trust? When next I see Skoth, I will share it with him, but before then, with whom should I share this burden?"

Unaine nodded thoughtfully, looked at Gwen and Katie, and then turning his gaze back on Teite he said, "I assume you have shared this dilemma with the Women's Circle, but yet have not confided the information with them." Teite nodded, and then Unaine went on. "I'd be interested in knowing what the Circle recommends."

Gwen glanced at Katie, who nodded, and then began, "You are right, Chief, in your assumptions about she has shared with us. And Theofinn, you might be surprised to know that we agree with your analysis of the situation. In fact, that is why we have come here. We need to make sure this information is shared with our High King, and we need to protect it from our adversary."

She paused and looked at the people around the room, but no one else spoke. So she continued, "It is our suggestion that Teite share this information with you, Unaine, and you Theofinn. Both of you can be trusted, if anyone can, and both of you are already targets and have your defenses. We also suggest that she confide it with one member of the Women's Circle. That suggested person is I. I am a simple worker in the kitchen of the Great Hall, the suspicion that I would be privy to such important information is minimal. That makes me a good backup repository for the knowledge."

Unaine smiled and nodded in agreement. It was a good plan. When they agreed that it would be so, old Katie excused herself from the meeting and left. The four of them sat in silence for a few moments. Teite drew a long breath before she began to tell her story.

"For months I have been looking at every old manuscript I could get my hands on, thinking there it must be something in one of the oldest of texts from this land. You know I can read scripts from all of the languages that have been in use in our culture: Old Ogham, Norse Rune, Modern Rune, and Latin. I found nothing that I thought was helpful. Then I considered the fact that perhaps the key was something that our Wabanaki, or even the Haudenoshonee, might have written. But they have no written language of their own. What they have written is in one of our languages, usually in our modernized Ogham script. So all their writings are recent. I felt that I was at a dead end. But then I had an idea. Why would it have to be an old writing? The Wabanaki are great storytellers. They have a wonderful oral tradition. Some of their stories go far back in time. Many of them are even stories of the creation, and have come down through many, many generations. There are several variations of this tale, but this one that I found, which was first written down a couple of hundred years ago, seems to me to reveal the key to Skoth's quest. It is the story they call: Medawisla and the Loon's Necklace."

Unaine and Theofinn leaned forward in their chairs. Theofinn glanced at Unaine, and said, "Medawisla is said in Wabanaki legend to be the messenger of Gluskabi. I would be most interested to hear you tell this story."

Teite smiled, "Yes, he is the messenger. Here, then, is the story."

Chapter 46 - The Loon's Necklace

Once upon a time, when the people were new in the land, there was a young man of the people whose grandfather was blind. Since his father had died shortly after he was born, he was responsible to help find food to feed his grandfather and their clan. Sometimes there was so little food for the people, that some would have to do without. Some would sacrifice for the good of others, but some would fight and steal from others so that they might have more to eat.

The young man wanted to get food for his people so that all would have enough to eat, so he would take his father's bow and go out hunting. It was a strong bow, and as he grew the young man's strength grew so that he could pull it with ease. But his father was not there to teach him the skills of the hunt, and his grandfather was blind, so often, even though he knew there must be game, he could not find it and he came home with little or nothing.

One evening, while sitting at the fire with his grandfather told him, "I can not teach you the way, but call on Gluskabi for help." He lifted a fine necklace of shells from around his neck and handing it to the young man, he continued, "Take this to Medawisla, his messenger, the one with the wailing and laughing calls which echo across the lakes and woods. He often takes the form of the diving water bird we call the loon. Give this to him and ask for his help."

The following morning, in the growing light before the dawn, the young man took the necklace to the nearby lake where he could hear the echoing laughter of Medawisla. He stepped into his canoe and paddled out unto the lake where he could see the form of the diving water bird in the morning mist.

There he made supplication. He asked for help to care for his people. When the loon came close, he removed the necklace of his grandfather from his neck and tossed it toward the loon. It fell around its neck and lay upon its back. The loon said to him, "Jump into the water. Put your hands around my neck and hold on tight as I dive."

He did as he was told. They were long under the waters and when they surfaced they were near the far side of the lake.

"Look to the shore," instructed the loon, "Can you now see the game upon this shore?"

"Yes, I can."

"Then hunt here. There is game for your people here."

To each of the shores of the lake the loon carried him. It dove beneath the waters, and the same scenario was repeated. When it finally returned to the shore where the canoe was, it repeated the same promise, but then it added, "There is game enough for all your people. Care for all of them. You have given me this necklace. When your people are in need. Remember the necklace."

So the young man climbed back into the canoe and returned to the shore. There he found abundant game. He took it to his people. He taught them how to work together and to see the abundance that lay before them. There was enough for all. And so it is.

When she ended the story there were several moments of silence before Theofinn broke the silence by saying, "That is indeed an interesting tale. Gluskabi certainly is a benevolent being, and Medawisla is his messenger. You would have us believe that this is a message for our time?"

Before she could open her mouth to speak, a distant sound came though the open windows. The breezes of that warm spring day had diminished into stillness during the evening hours. The temperatures had remained relatively warm, even through the day had descended into darkness of night. The nearly full moon was rising as the echoing laughter of a loon bounced of the waters of Lake Ronkonkoma.

Gwen said, "It seems abundantly clear to me. I'm no scholar, like Teite here, but the story fits, and I'd say that voice we just heard proves it."

"Trust me," said Theofinn, "I'd be the last one to doubt Gluskabi would send a message to us if he chose to. It is my opinion that you are right. The key for Skoth's quest involves the loon's necklace. I'm not sure how we should interpret this. That job belongs to the High King. It is our job to get this story to him."

So at the end of that tragic day in Dunsheelin, they lifted themselves momentarily out of their grief for a young man they loved, to pledge themselves to the task of communicating this story to High King Skoth.

Chapter 47 - The Call to an Alting for the High King

It was mid-morning on the following day when a rider on horseback came galloping into Dunsheelin. When he reached the Great Hall he quickly dismounted and asked for an audience with King Unaine. Within moments he was ushered into the Chief's presence where he handed him a sealed pouch. The messenger declared it to be a message from King Tyg of Heilsand. Unaine opened it and read it to himself. He ordered the messenger to go and make plans for taking a message back to the coastal port. He was to acquire a fresh mount from the king's stable and to return in one hour's time for the message.

Unaine then sent for Theofinn, Teite, and the others of his council of advisors. Within the course of a half an hour, they had all assembled in the Great Hall. By that time, Unaine had written his reply and was prepared to seal it.

Unaine invited them to sit around the council table, which was actually just a couple of the tables of the Great Hall pulled together. As they were getting themselves seated, he noticed that Gwen, from the kitchen, was cleaning around the hearth. He caught her eye and smiling, he nodded at her. Once seated, the eyes of all council members looked to Unaine with questioning expressions, for they were seldom called to a meeting in this manner.

He announced to them, "I have just been informed by messenger that an Alting for all of Eirgalon has been declared by King Tyg of Heilsand. The purpose of this assembly is to do something that has never been done in the past. It is to declare a High King of Eirgalon. In the message he also says that he, and Heilsand, will stand for Skoth Brianson of Fadis Innis as High King!"

He let the enormity of that proclamation settle into the minds of the Council members before he went on. Heilsand was one of the more powerful of the kingdoms along the coast, and the support of its king would carry a great deal of weight.

"It is also declared that this Alting for the High King shall take place during the observance of Beltane, the first day of May, at New Caledonia."

Several heads nodded at that. Such a location would make sense. It was somewhat centrally located along the coast. Many of the kingdoms of the interior could access it by descending the riverways of Eirgalon and then skirting along the coastline to New Caledonia. But Chief Unaine wasn't yet finished with relaying all the details.

"King Tyg also declares that since this involves declaring a High King of all Eirgalon he has invited ALL the people of Eirgalon to send their kings and chiefs to this meeting to stand, or to refuse to stand, for someone as High King. He makes it clear that this includes the Wabanaki chiefdoms. The voice of Fadis Innis needs to be at this High King Alting. I will be going, with my daughter Teite, to be our voice. We will travel to Riverhead and then depart with the King's Fleet. We will take three of our finest longships and two hundred men-at-arms to honor our king. However, we will not leave our lands undefended. Theofinn will remain here, and act as Regent until I return."

The discussion that followed affirmed the decision Unaine had already made. More detailed decisions as to which specific men would be going with Unaine, and which would be staying on Fadis Innis were worked out. The days of departure were planned. Out of respect for Neal, it was determined to wait until after the funeral to make leave-taking from Dunsheelin. But once the rites of the death passage had been observed, full preparations for the departure were commenced. The activities of those days helped to momentarily distract Teite from her grief, but many times during the traveling her thoughts turned to Neal, and she resolved to get revenge upon the perpetrator of his death.

The physical details of the response of the other Celtic kingdoms of Eirgalon were similar in many ways to what occurred at Dunsheelin. Plans were made and men were on the move to New Caledonia. Some had heard rumors of Skoth's quest and of recent events, but some were unaware and were going to protect their own self-interests. For if someone was to be declared the High King of Eirgalon, they wanted a voice in the decision.

When the message from King Tyg reached the Wabanaki chiefdoms of the interior lands, most of the leaders called for councils to discuss the matter. The results of these councils were predominantly that decisions were made to send delegations to the alting, although there were thoughts and comments made about "coaster plots" and there were some serious reservations about what this might mean.

From Heilsand, Karl and Enat left with Gunnar's crew and ship as soon as they were able to make arrangements and leave the port. They planned on making a fast trip to New Caledonia and then to help Gunnar's father, King Haggar, make arrangements for the alting.

King Tyg insisted that Skoth and Evlin ride with him aboard his flagship as his guests of honor. Of course, Erik and his men, as Skoth's bodyguards, were also aboard as passengers, along with Leesha and Tkaden as part of his retinue.

Skoth felt a little bit embarrassed by it all. From the very first day that Unaine had thrust this quest upon him he had been uncomfortable with the importance that others had placed upon him. He had been learning how to deal with it and accept it, but at heart he still felt himself just a simple fellow. He remembered that once, when he was just a child, he had gotten into trouble by leading his friends in maneuvering a heist of some bread and cheese from the Great Hall kitchen to take on one of their adventures. In the course of getting caught and punished, he recalled Erik saying to him, "When you take the leadership, both good and bad come your way. You might as well get used to it now." Getting used to it he was, but he still wasn't comfortable with it, and in a way he hoped he never would.

The word of an alting for a High King spread throughout Eirgalon. There were many who questioned what was going on. There were some, like the blacksmith of Glenoak, who simply smiled a knowing smile to themselves when they heard the news. There were some who said that they didn't know who the High King should be, but it was high time that Eirgalon be united under the guidance of such.

However, not all was positive. There were places throughout the land where agents of Malsum had been at work. When word of this alting spread, they countered words of optimism and hope by sowing seeds of distrust and doubt.

Dakatomi, head shaman of the Wausacom chiefdom, was one of those who accompanied its chief, Tkomik, to the alting. Dakatomi's influence was powerful among the Wabanaki. While he had never spoken against Skoth publicly, he was one who often insinuated that there were "other paths" that could be followed. Murmurs and mutterings about "those coasters trying to boss others around" were commonplace.

Springtime was in the air as the temperatures were warming, and trees were beginning to green the landscape. The final weeks of April saw folk from far and wide making their way to New Caledonia. It was sure to be an interesting Beltane celebration this year.

Chapter 48 - Arrival at New Caledonia

The docks and river quays of the city that were in the estuary of the River Oustona were already filled when the three Fadis Innis longships approached. They beached them on the sandy shores to the south of the city near the forested point of land that jutted out into Fadis Innis Sound. Unaine gave the order to set up camp on the edge of the woods, and to make sure that if there were any local inhabitants in the area they would be compensated for any inconveniences the Fadis Innis contingent caused. No need to cause hard feelings by being inconsiderate of any of the locals.

As they were setting up their camp, the four longships of the Heilsand group arrived and beached just to the south of them. Skoth joined the other men in jumping out and pulling the ships onto the shore. In short order, the Heilsand ships were ashore and men began offloading supplies and setting up their camp.

Once ashore Leesha quickly made her way to her father and her sister. Tkaden followed closely behind her but before he could say anything, Unaine wrapped his arms around him and said, "Welcome to the family and good luck to you with this one! She has a mind of her own, you know!"

Tkaden laughed and replied, "Thank you, and I already know that!"

With mock indignation, Leesha, "Well now, if you two aren't a couple of pots calling the kettle black!"

After those pleasant greetings, Leesha went off in private with Teite that she might console her and share her sorrow as they talked of Neal's death.

Then Skoth came striding down the beach, with Evlin at his side and Erik a couple of steps behind them. Skoth carried no shield, but had his sword slung on his back and had the sturdy oak staff in his hand. Evlin was wearing her normal softly muted green and tan woolen clothes, but on this fine spring day also had a vibrant green hooded cloak of fine and sturdy linen that was a gift from King Tyg. It was embroidered with gold threaded Celtic knotwork around the wrists, hood, and hems. King Tyg had insisted that the partner of his High King wear something more fitting of her importance than the simple traveling cloak that she had been wearing when she came to Heilsand, and so had given her this gift.

Unaine extended his arm to clasp Skoth by his arm and said, "It sounds like you've had some interesting adventures. Your father would be proud of you!"

"Yes, sir, and thank you," responded Skoth, "this certainly is quite some quest you have sent me on!" Turning toward Evlin he went on, "I'd like you to meet Evlin. She is . . ." he paused and then said, "Well, she is Evlin. I've never met anyone like her."

"Ahh, so this is the one. Eyes that sparkle rivaling the sunrise and hair that challenges the glory of the setting sun. Your beauty overwhelms me, my dear. But I hear there is much more to you than meets eye."

Evlin smiled at the old chief and said, "Thank you, sir, but my father told me to watch out for men with such a silver tongue. And especially those who have aged like a fine wine."

They heard Erik, who was standing behind them and to the side, give a snort.

Unaine glanced at him and asked, "Do you have something to say, Erik?"

In response, Erik said, "Not much right now, Chief. But I think the silver-tongued and silver-haired fox has more than met his match."

Unaine gave a laugh, ran his hand through his graying hair, and said, "You may be right. But in any case, let's get this camp set up and get settled down for the night. I'd also like to met King Tyg this evening and get his measure. Tomorrow we go to pay a courtesy visit on King Haggar."

As he said this he looked north, up the shoreline toward the city of New Caledonia. A small procession of folks was coming towards them from the city. At the front walked Karl, with Enat on one side and Gunnar on the other. Behind them walked a troop of warriors, one of whom was carrying the standard of New Caledonia. On the standard was the Tree of Life, which symbolized the ancient forests of Caledonia across the seas, and the forest lands of New Caledonia in Eirgalon. The presence of the standard indicated that this was an official welcome from the leader of New Caledonia.

Unaine stepped forward to make the formal exchange of greetings with Gunnar as the representative of New Caledonia. After the formal exchanges were completed, the informal greetings between long absent friends and families began. Enat hugged her father and then asked about her sisters. Upon being told where they were, she immediately left to join them. Karl and Skoth greeted each other with bear hugs and slaps on the back as best of childhood friends might do. At this point Gunnar excused himself and his men that they might go further down the beach and make official greetings with King Tyg of Heilsand.

Chapter 49 - The Three Sisters

Enat found her sisters sitting on a log at the edge of a small clearing several yards into the forest, where they could have a little privacy from the activities of those establishing the beachhead camp. Teite was softly sobbing as she had her head on Leesha's shoulder and Leesha had her arms around her sister. Enat came up behind them, and bending over them, she wrapped the two of them in her arms. No words needed to be shared. In sorrow, it is enough to be present and simply share the grief.

Several minutes later, Evlin stepped into the clearing. The three sisters looked up at her as she walked toward them. They could see tears in her eyes. She knelt before them and took Teite's hands into her own. Looking into Teite's eyes she said, "The story of your loss has been shared with me. Grievous it is. Without a doubt this was Malsum's doing. The same Malsum who killed my mother. I promise you, he will not go unpunished."

Teite spoke, "Neal died because he was hurt by, and then possessed by, the power behind the tainted knife that was intended for Skoth."

"So I have heard. And it is by Malsum's will that the knife was thrown."

"If he had not been with Skoth that night, he would still be alive."

"Aye, and my beloved would be dead. I would have never met him. His quest would be over and Malsum would be working his will. But by chance, or fate, or other mystery, your Neal paid the price of friendship. Great honor belongs to the one who lays down his life for his friend. I promise you, neither Skoth, nor I, will ever forget his sacrifice."

"Thank you. It was so hard to see him die. There was nothing we could do."

"No, there wasn't. But we can do something now. We can thwart the evil foe's plans. We can help Skoth on his quest."

Teite's eyes lit up. "Yes, we can. And I have information for Skoth that might help. I must share this information about the key to his quest with him as soon as possible. Neal, well, not Neal, but that which possessed him was trying to kill me to prevent it being shared when it caused his death."

"Then tonight, we'll gather together - the sisters and their men, and we'll hear of this key. Together we fight our foe."

So it was, that later that evening, after camp was set, a meal was shared, sentries posted, and the campfires burned low, that the four young women met with Skoth, Tkaden, Karl, and Chief Unaine in the Chief's tent. Erik was also there, just inside the entrance of the tent. Every so often he would part the flap of the tent and glance outside. It wasn't an ostentatious tent, because that wasn't Unaine's style, but it was large because it was often needed to host a meeting of several men. A small lantern was hanging from the center pole of the tent to give a sliver of illumination to their meeting.

Skoth started the meeting by thanking them for their help in his quest and then he recounted some of the details about what had happened to him since the rest of his party had left him in the hidden valley. Of course he didn't tell them everything, especially about his time in the sacred pool with Evlin, but he told them as much as seemed reasonable at the time. Once he had shared some of the events of the past months, he shared his belief that his quest involved the unity of Eirgalon. But he felt there was more to it than that. He expressed his hope of finding the key to his quest, but, in spite of the good that had come out of his time with Fearglas, still had not determined what that might be.

This is when Teite spoke up, "I think I know the key. Maybe not all the details. But my research has turned up what might be your key. I think this legend from the Wabanaki is crucial information for your quest. Or at least that it is a clue."

Thereupon, she told them the tale of the Loon's Necklace. They were silent for a few moments before anyone spoke.

Tkaden was the first to speak, "I remember this story. At least a version of it. It is one the elders used to tell as we sat around the fire during the winter evenings."

Skoth asked Teite, "Why is it that you think this story is the key?"

Teite nodded and said, "I know, at first it seems a little far-fetched, but I'm not saying that the story is the key. I think the story is a clue to finding the key."

"It sounds like you have thought this through. Can you explain more?"

"Well, the need of the people and their dissension, the young hero, the communication with the gods. All of these are at least slightly analogous to our situation."

"So, if I understand you right, you are suggesting that my quest to find the key to guard our humankind, as the prophecy declared, involves the loon's necklace?"

Unaine interrupted at this point. "You ask good questions, Skoth. Here are a couple of more bits of information that might help. On the night of Neal's death, the day Teite shared this story with us, Teite had just finished telling us this legend. We too were questioning in our minds is this were a clue. At that very moment, in the stillness of the night, Medawisla laughed at us."

Teite nodded, "It's true. Even Theofinn agreed it was Medawisla. He is the messenger of Gluskabi. I believe he sent us this clue."

Skoth looked thoughtful. "Hmmm. Chief, you said a couple of bits of information. Is there more?"

Unaine said, "One more. This is something I have shared with no one. Theofinn confided in me, before we left to come here, that he had been visited one winter night by Gluskabi himself. He sat with him in Theofinn's private quarters. By the light of the brazier they sat and talked."

From the doorway, Erik snorted, and spoke, "Maybe the old coot was just dreaming. He does that sometimes. Just dozes off. Did anyone else see this Gluskabi?"

Unaine answered him, "Erik, I know you don't always believe these types of things, but to answer you - no one else saw him and Theofinn said he couldn't remember all of the conversation, but he told me one point that was important in the conversation. And remember, he told me this before Teite shared her story with me. Theofinn said that

Gluskabi told him that Medawisla would bring us a message, and that we should listen to it. Perhaps he did dream it, but even the dreams of a druid are not to be ignored."

Erik gave a little harrumphing sound, but said nothing.

Skoth half asked and half commented, "Then my quest is to find the loon's necklace for that is the key to preserving our humankind."

There were a few moments of silence as the group of them let that idea settle in their minds. Then Teite spoke, "I talked with Theofinn about this. We concluded that it is highly unlikely that the loon's necklace is a physical artifact. We think that it is a figure of speech and that the loon's necklace symbolizes something."

"And what did he think it symbolized?"

"You're not going to like this, but he said that you would ask that. He also said that it would be your job to figure it out."

Skoth sighed.

Teite offered, "You could cast the runes and I could give you an interpretation of them."

"No. Not that I don't think you are good at it, but this is something I have to see on my own."

They continued their discussion of this for several minutes before their discussion turned to a sharing of the events each of them had been through in the last few months and to thoughts of what might happen on the morrow. Finally they went their separate ways into the darkness of the night.

Chapter 50 - Meeting the Six Kings

Two days before the alting was to meet on the day of Beltane men and women from the Celtic kingdoms near and far were still arriving in the city. Contingents of folk from the Wabanaki were also arriving, and for the most part they were making their camps to the north of the city.

The formal meeting would be held in the Great Hall of New Caledonia, but prior to that, King Tyg of Heilsand wanted to introduce Skoth to some of the kings of Eirgalon. He requested that King Haggar of New Caledonia invite a select few of the leaders to meet in what the folks of the city called the "lesser hall" of the fortress. As was the Great Hall, the lesser hall lay within the fortress keep of the city, but it was smaller and less elaborately decorated. Its primary use was normally as a lunchroom and assembly hall for the people of the keep. It was an interior room with no outside windows, lit by slits high in the walls where the room rose beyond its neighboring rooms.

A spring thunderstorm was rolling into the area and lightning occasionally flashed in the sky as the participants of the meeting made their way to the hall. Skoth and Evlin, followed by Erik and a couple of his men, arrived at the requested time. Evlin wore the cloak of green that Tyg had given her, and Skoth wore a similar cape of green with the Celtic knotwork (also a gift from Tyg). Skoth's sword was slung in its sheath on his back and with his hand he held the oak staff.

As the doors to the hall were opened before him he

could see six men seated in a semicircle facing the door. Skoth recognized Unaine and Tyg, and assumed the others were kings and chiefs of their own lands. Two chairs were placed before these men. No doubt they were intended for Skoth and Evlin. Side by side, they momentarily paused before entering the hall. Erik and his men stopped behind them. They would wait outside. Taking a deep breath, Skoth and Evlin stepped into the room and started walking to the chairs intended for them. They heard the doors close behind them and heard the wooden door bolt set into place.

One of the men in the center of the semicircle rose as they reached the chairs. He was about to speak when Skoth and Evlin heard from behind them the sound of swords being drawn from their sheaths.

The standing man in the front of the room raised his voice to say, "Olaf, what do you think you are doing?"

Skoth and Evlin whirled to face the back of the room. Standing in front of the door and along the back wall where they had been posted as guards when they had entered were six men with drawn swords. One, that Skoth assumed was Olaf, spat out these words, "By the will of Malsum, all of you will die! Now! Say your final prayers to your gods!"

With that said the armed men raised their swords to attack. Before they moved more than a step, Skoth slammed his staff on the floor with a resounding crack and shouted in old Gaelic "DORCHADAS" which means "darkness." The skies above the city cracked with the fury of thunder and lightning, but darkness enveloped the lesser hall. Added to the sound of the thunder were the sounds as of a roaring beast and the groans and gasping of men in pain.

The roar of thunder diminished, replaced by sounds of men flailing about in pain and splashing in blood. Then in the room was the sound of a staff striking the floor. The word SOLAS, which means light, was heard, and slowly the natural light of day again filtered into the room. The kings were stunned by what they saw.

In the middle of the room, arms around each other stood Skoth and Evlin. Her head buried in his chest. They were soaked in blood. Skoth still held his staff in one hand. Around them lay the bodies of the six guards. Plunged into the chest of Olaf was Skoth's sword. The men were slashed and torn apart as if a great beast had ripped into them. The coppery tang of blood and death filled the room.

There was a pounding on the bolted door. Erik and his men had heard the awful sound and on finding the door bolted from the inside had grabbed a trestle bench to use as a battering ram. The door flew open, with Erik running in right behind. He slipped on the bloody floor, but maintained his balance. He came to a stop and stood still, and said, "Bloody hell!"

Unaine was stepping forward and as he moved, he said, "Hell it is! For these traitors!" Looking to Skoth and Evlin, he asked, "Are you two injured?"

Skoth and Evlin released each other from their embrace, but Skoth kept hold of her hand. Skoth was breathing heavily and had a wild look about his eyes. It was a look that none of them had ever seen on him before, but Erik recognized it from his days as a young warrior. "Berserker" was his name for it. It was when a warrior slipped from his normal self into a battle fury of inhuman proportions. That wild look was ebbing from Skoth's eyes when Evlin lifted her face towards Erik, and he saw that same wild look as her eyes flamed with fury. They too ebbed when she recognized Erik, and then she looked down at her clothing soaked with the blood of her attackers. She muttered something like "oh, my" and seemed embarrassed.

Skoth answered Unaine, "No, we're unharmed, but it looks like we've made quite a mess."

Tyg came up to him and said, "I'm not sure exactly what exactly has happened here, but I am sure that you saved our lives. None of us were armed, and against those six we wouldn't have lasted long. But let's get you out of here and into some clean clothes."

From that point on, King Haggar took charge, giving orders to his people to "get rid of those dead vermin on the floor," to get the hall cleaned up, and to take Skoth and Evlin to his own quarters to get cleaned up.

It was mid-afternoon before a messenger came to King Haggar's private quarters, with a request that Skoth and Evlin join him and the other kings at a table that had been set up in the Great Hall. During the intervening hours, while Haggar was dealing with the aftermath of the incident in the lesser hall, Haggar's wife had taken charge of Skoth and Evlin. She provided them with fresh clothes, a private place to collect their thoughts, and a few bites of food to nourish them. The blood-soaked clothing would have to be thoroughly washed to remove the blood, so she arranged clothing for them that she thought was appropriate. Skoth was of a build similar to Gunnar, so she simply appropriated some of her son's clothes for him. He certainly looked like more a prince of the realm than he had previously.

Evlin was another matter. Hilda took over like a mother hen taking a chick under its wing. Evlin tried to protest, but Hilda would hear none of it. She had her maids get Evlin stripped out of her bloody clothes and into a bath where she could scrub the blood and filth from her skin and hair. She raved about Evlin's beautiful auburn tresses as they rinsed the blood from hair, scrubbed it clean with soap, and then rinsed it with rosewater.

She gave Evlin an undershift of fine linen to wear while she sent a maid with instructions of what to get and where to get it. She went on about how she would like for Evlin to wear one her best dresses, but Evlin's figure was far too slim for her matronly clothing. Her maid returned, out of breath and carrying a satchel of clothing. Evlin had never had someone help dress her before, other than her mother when she was just a child, and at first she protested. But Hilda was a strong-willed woman and those kinds of protests fell on deaf ears.

The final result was stunning, and when they brought her into the sitting room of Haggar's private quarters where Skoth was waiting, his jaw dropped open in shock. He had seen her without clothing, and he knew her beauty, but now he was dumbstruck for she appeared before him as a vision of a fairy queen. Hilda had kept the themes of the tan and green clothing that Evlin had been wearing, but had dressed her in the finest of linens. The pale misty green linen dress she wore was formfitting from the shoulders to the hips and then flared widely. The low-cut neckline was embroidered with gold Celtic triquetras. The sleeves of the dress were of thin beige linen that had a trail of gold embroidery running from shoulder to wrist. Around her neck she wore a thin gold necklace with a triquetra pendant, and around her waist was wrapped a pale gold silk cloth. Her dark auburn hair was unbraided but tied together in the back with a gold cord and flowed in loose waves to the middle of her back.

Hilda, hands on hips, looked them over as Skoth stood there, mouth agape and staring at her, and she said, "Well, man. Don't just stand there. Say something."

Finally he said, "You're beautiful, Evi." Then, because he started to over think he started to over explain, adding, "Not that you weren't beautiful before. I mean, you always look beautiful, but now, cleaned up and, I mean you are always clean, but …"

"Oh, be quiet, you big oaf. I know what you mean," she said as she went forward and into his embrace.

Chapter 51 - The Kings Meet Again

Six men were sitting at the table in the Great Hall when Skoth and Evlin entered the room. There were others in the hall, including Erik, but some were seated and others were standing around the fringes of the room at least several yards away from the table. This was no longer a totally private meeting for what was said here could be heard by others and would, in all likelihood, quickly spread as gossip throughout the city.

The men stood as Skoth and Evlin approached the table and then sat after the couple was seated. They introduced themselves: Haggar of New Caledonia, Tyg of Heilsand, Duncan of Glesga, Leif of Straumford, Collin of Rekvik, and of course, Unaine of Fadis Innis.

Haggar invited them to be seated and then he started the conversation. "Welcome. On behalf of the people of New Caledonia, I thank you. Gunnar and Karl have told me much about you, but what happened this morning reveals what power you possess."

Tyg shared his welcome, "Well met again, my friends. I witnessed your actions in Heilsand, and now again today. How grateful I am to call you my friends."

Leif spoke next, "I've never met you, young man, but I recognized that sword when I saw it this morning. That sword belonged to my friend, Brian the Bold. You carry it well."

He was followed by Collin, "I'm still not sure of all that transpired here this morning, but I do know that the two of you have earned my respect and gratitude."

Then Duncan spoke, "When that man named his leader as "Malsum" and that he was calling for our death, my heart chilled, for Malsum is growing strong in the west. He is speaking against our people and trying to drive us from the land. I fear that the fertile valley to our north, and even my own city may soon be under attack from him."

The last king to speak as they went around the table was Unaine, who was seated to their right. "My faith in you as the one named in Thorfall's prophecy is stronger than ever. I knew not what might befall you when I first placed the king rune in your hand, but you have not disappointed me. Would you please draw forth the rune, crafted and consecrated by Theofinn, the Master Druid of my land?"

Skoth pulled the rune from under his tunic and lifted it, still on the simple leather cord, over his head. The other king rune, the one hammered of iron by the blacksmith of Glenoak, he left beneath his tunic. He held the runestone of Theofinn in his open hand and looked at it for a moment before handing it to Unaine. Unaine had a quizzical expression on his face as he examined it.

After examining it for several moments, Unaine said, "This is the same rune, I see Theofinn's mark upon it. Yet when last I saw this, it was of polished grey. How did it come to be this amber color?"

He handed it to Duncan, seated to his right, that he and the others might pass it around the table and examine it.

Skoth replied, "Now that's a story to tell." He went on to tell them the story of his encounter with the water sprite at the sacred pool of Cold Spring on the isle of Fadis Innis, concluding by opening his tunic enough to show the mark upon his breast.

Collin asked, "How do we know this is true? And if it is true, how do we know that the water sprite might merely be playing a trick on you, or that this might be one of Malsum's machinations?"

Skoth had no chance to reply, before Evlin spoke. "Such a water sprite can not deal in falsehood!" For a moment, that stopped the conversation, for all saw the fire that flared within her eyes.

Skoth then spoke calmly and with a tone of understanding, "When first it happened, I too wondered about it. I was early on my quest. Still trying to find my way. But I have no doubts now."

Now Tyg spoke, "And neither do I! I called for this alting. I know we have a High King. Again I pledge to you, that at the alting, I will stand for you as High King of Eirgalon!"

By this time the king rune had been handed all the way around the table and was in the hands of Haggar, seated next to Evlin. Haggar handed it to Evlin and said, "I think this pendant deserves a better chain than this piece of old cord, but it will do for now. Evlin will you please restore this rune to its rightful owner and place it round the neck of the man I will stand for as our High King."

The other men around the table nodded in affirmation, and discussion shifted to the times and procedures for the meeting which would happen the day after tomorrow. At the conclusion of the meeting the men rose to go their separate ways. Haggar invited Skoth and Evlin to stay in the fortress of his Great Hall, but they declined saying that they thought it best to head back with Unaine and stay in his camp.

Erik came up to escort them out of the hall and back to the camp, but before they left, Hilda came to them and said, "I'll have those clothes of yours washed and spotless, and then sent out to your camp. And you keep what you are wearing. Consider it a small gift from me. I may not be able to do much for you, but what little I can do, I will."

Chapter 52 - Visit with the Wabanaki

On the morrow, the day prior to what was now being called the day of the High Alting, Skoth and Evlin made their way northward around the city to the camps of the Wabanaki chiefs. They took with them, Leesha, Tkaden, and Karl. Of course, Erik also went along. Trailing in the distance, trying to be unobserved, Erik had his men Rolf and Jake shadowing them. After the previous day, Erik had no doubt that Skoth could defend himself, but just in case Skoth didn't see something amiss, Erik wanted to be there. After all, Skoth had walked right into the trap that dim-witted Olaf had set for him. Sure, Erik thought, you could argue that the other chiefs should have seen the danger too, but they didn't. Sometimes the high and mighty, especially the young ones, get to thinking their high and mighty thoughts and then the low lying branches can trip them up. Best if he was around to watch out for them.

The spring thunderstorms of the previous day had pushed eastward and the day was blessed with a clear blue sky. The morning was still a bit cool, so Evlin was wearing the green cloak and Skoth was wearing the cape that Tyg had given them. Hilda, true to her word, had returned them cleaned and spotless!

They had only walked a few steps when Erik offered, "I've a little experience with this town. If you let me lead, I'll take you the quickest way through these streets to their camps on the north."

Karl, in a jovial mood, said, "O, that's a good one.

Experience with this town. I wonder what Susie would say about that?"

Evlin turned to look at Erik, "Susie? Who is Susie?"

Erik, a little flustered, snorted, "Someone I've known since before you pups were born. Now enough of that. Follow me."

With that he ended the conversation and started walking down the street. True to his word, he adroitly maneuvered them through the city to the Wabanaki camps on its northern fringe. Once there, they located the Wausacom camp of Tkomik and found him sitting with a group of men around a small campfire, upon which a kettle of water was heating.

Erik noticed that the shaman, Dakatomi, was one of the men in the group. He felt the hair on the back on his neck prickle and he resolved to keep at least one eye on that man. Tkaden led Skoth and Evlin forward to meet his father. Tkomik stood as they came forward. He held both hands forward and clasp Skoth by the forearms when introduced to him. When Tkaden introduced Evlin, he stepped forward and embraced her with both arms. Softly he spoke to her.

"Daughter of my sister, with open arms and open heart, I welcome you to the clan of your mother."

A small tear appeared in the corner of her eye that no other could see as she settled her face upon his chest, returning his embrace. "Uncle. Thank you."

"You understand, that I knew nothing about you, or what happened to your mother, until Tkaden and Leesha came home and told us of meeting you. Had I known, I would have searched you out."

"Aye, I know. But father deigned not to tell you. His reasons for that are unknown to me, but he is good, and what he does he does for good cause."

"I know that well, my niece, though bitter was it to lose my sister, knowing not what befell her. I see now that it was fate; both of wonderful and beautiful. You are a witness to that."

Throughout this conversation, Skoth just stood there. He felt a bit ill at ease, like he was too close to an intimate conversation but having no way to unobtrusively remove himself from it.

Then Evlin reached out to Skoth and pulled him closer.

"Uncle, here is Skoth, my beloved. He is now one of us. Whether you stand for him as High King, or chose not to you, that is your decision to make. But he is mine, and I am his, and nothing will change that."

"I would expect nothing less from you, daughter of the Bear Clan. He is a fortunate man to have you at his side. And as for you, young man, I hope you know how fortunate you are."

Skoth smiled as he nodded and said, "I'm beginning to."

Erik noticed that Dakatomi, who was sitting on the opposite side of the fire, was leaning forward and attentively listening to this conversation. So Erik spoke up and said, "Ho, there, Shaman Dakatomi. How good it is to see you again. Be careful not to tip forward into the fire."

Dakatomi responded by sitting back and saying, "Why, hello again, Erik. I didn't expect to see you here. I figured you'd be off with Unaine."

"Unaine's here, alright, along with almost every other chief in the land. I thought I'd just tag along with my young friend today. Interesting events seem to happen around him, and I like to keep my life interesting."

The people of Tkomik's retinue were arranging for places for their visitors to sit as this discussion was going on, so when Tkomik invited them to sit they promptly joined the circle around the fire.

Erik was in the process of seating himself, when Dakatomi added, "It seems to me that the interesting happenings, always seem to occur when you show up. I wonder why that is?"

None of the young people who were present wanted to seem impolite and to interrupt the verbal sparring between the two older me, but Tkomik had no qualms about it.

"Yes, yes. the times are interesting. And the two of you have both seen your share. But what I want to hear is from our young man who would be High King. I deem it good that Tyg of Heilsand has invited us to participate. So I ask you, Skoth, why should I, or any of the chiefs from the Wabanaki lands, participate in this decision? Why should we have a High King?"

Skoth took a deep calming breath, and began, "First, one of lessons I learned from Fearglas, but also what I experienced as a boy at the knees of Chief Unaine, is that while a ruler may seem to make the decisions and command the people, their true role it to serve the land and its people. Make decisions? Yes. Give directions? Yes. But these are not done for the well-being of the king. They are done so that the people and the land will prosper."

Tkomik nodded thoughtfully and said, "And, second?"

"It is time for us to be the people of Eirgalon. We are no longer Wabanaki, or Celt. Or for that matter of Celts of Eire, or Scot, or Viking blood. We have mingled our blood and we will continue to do so. All who live here should be recognized as belonging to this land. The High King will be a symbol of that truth. He will be the promise of that unity, and he will come to be the realization of that unity."

He paused, and Dakatomi spoke, "I have heard this before. In the Great Hall of Dunsheelin, the Celts offered you forth as their High King. I'll admit there lies an aura of magic about you, but this is no proof that what you say is true. You may claim the mantle of High King, but claiming something doesn't make it so. Why should the people of this land from the beginning of time, follow you, a Celt born of people of other lands? Where is the proof?"

Skoth could sense the ire rising in Evlin sitting next to him and imagine the fire growing in her eyes. He reached out his hand and gently placed it on her arm. Then he replied.

"A good question, that. Part of the proof will be if the kings of the Celtic lands stand for me. They know the message of unity I proclaim. If they stand for me, they accept the call for unity in Eirgalon. It will mean they accept my message that this land is a land for all of its people. As for deeds? I have done to date, what I have been able. Only time will give the proof you ask for. Would you deny us this time?"

A smile crept across Erik's face. He had to admire the

way Skoth had turned the tables on Dakatomi. He was even more pleased when Dakatomi sputtered out a response of, "Hmmph, we'll see." Not very convincing words from a tricky shaman, he chortled to himself.

Conversation and discussion of the situation of the Wabanaki people in Eirgalon and the alting to come on the morrow continued for a while longer. The water that had been boiling on the fire was used to steep some spruce tea that was served to the guests. The tone of the conversation between the Wabanaki and Skoth's people was cordial, and even friendly. Peasantries and farewells began to be exchanged when finally Dakatomi spoke again.

"By the way Skoth, do you still have that fine tabac pouch that I gave to you at the beginning of your quest?"

That was a question that caught Skoth by surprise. He thought back to that discussion he had with Dakatomi on the road just outside of Dunsheelin, the fine pouch and the tabac it held, and the blacksmith he gave it to at Glenoak.

"Why, no, I don't. As you say, it was a fine pouch, and I enjoyed the tabac. But I gave it to a gentleman in Glenoak. I wanted to say thank you to him. It seemed the right thing to do at the time."

With a slight sneer in his voice, Dakatomi said, "I wondered as much. I entrusted you with my finest pouch, and you gave it away."

"I meant no offense, Master Shaman. I thought you had given it to me as a gift. I had little else on me of value, and I thought it was mine to give."

"No matter, "Dakatomi said with noticeable disdain, "it just shows how you handle your responsibilities."

"I thought it was a gift freely given. I apologize for the offense that my sharing it with another has caused."

The younger visitors in the group were uneasy about Dakatomi's comments, but not wanting to show disrespect to an elder by challenging him, they said nothing. Erik was about to say something, but was forcing himself to stay quiet. However, Chief Tkomik was slightly annoyed by what he felt was the disrespect that Dakatomi was showing Skoth. Wanting to smooth the disagreement over, he interrupted the conversation. "Now, now, old friend. You are always generous with your gifts. It was a fine and generous gesture you made when you shared your tabac and pouch with our young friend. We can't begrudge him the right to try and be as generous as you. Now, let's allow these good folks to leave and to make their preparations for tomorrow. It's going to be a big day."

His intervention ended that conversation, and shortly thereafter Skoth and his group left. They began making their way back to camp as Erik led them by circling through the western outskirts of the city. Their discussion went back to the comments that Dakatomi had made at the end of the visit. Skoth asked Tkaden what he made of the old shaman's comments.

Tkaden said, "They baffle me. He always was one to try and make you think. You know the type, they ask more questions than give you answers. But it seems to be like he has gotten harsher, and even mean lately. When we spent the winter at Wausacom, I didn't spend much time with him, but he just didn't seem his old self anymore."

Karl jokingly added, "That's called getting old. Right,

Erik? Sometimes when folks get old they just get all sort of crotchety."

Erik responded with a, "Hmmph" and was going to add more, but they heard some shouting behind them. A young man was running towards them from behind and calling to them as he ran, "Wait. Wait. I have something for you."

They came to a halt and waited for him to catch up to them. When he reached them, he held out in his hands a nicely beaded tabac pouch. It was similar to the one that Dakatomi had given to Skoth many months ago.

Breathlessly, the young man said, "Shaman Dakatomi told me to run and catch you and give you this. He said to tell you that he was sorry for the way he spoke to you and that he wished to give you this gift to replace the one that you gave away. Please accept it from him."

Skoth looked at him, and looked at the tabac pouch in the young man's hand. Skoth thanked him, but before he could take the pouch Erik had reached out and grabbed the pouch and quickly slipped it into a pocket in his cloak.

Erik directed his words toward Skoth, saying, "Allow me to handle that for you Chief Skoth. Ye've got yer hands full with that staff in one hand and with yer young lady's hand in the other."

Skoth said to Erik with a slight hint of amusement in his voice, "Why thank you, my good man." He then turned his head and dismissed the young messenger by saying, "Go tell your master that you have delivered your package, and that I thank him for it."

After the youth had departed and they had

commenced on their journey, Skoth asked the rest, "Well, what do you make of that?"

Leesha said, "Well, it could be a sincere apology."

Tkaden affirmed the same, as did Karl, but Evlin said, "I don't trust the man. It doesn't smell right to me."

Skoth cocked an eye at Erik and asked him, "So, Erik, what do you think? You sure were quick to grab it."

"I'm with Evlin on this, this smells like that polecat you shot when you were just kid. Phew. It let loose its spray and you smelled for days. First he makes a big deal about you not having the original pouch and then we are hardly out of sight before he sends you this one. It's almost like he had planned it out so that you would have this in your hand. I don't like it. I'd as soon through it in the river, if you'd let me."

Skoth said, "You may be right. I wish Theofinn was here to examine it."

Leesha suggested, "How about if we have Teite and Enat take a look at it when we get back to camp?"

Skoth agreed to that course of action. Perhaps their fears would be allayed, or perhaps they would find something.

Chapter 53 - The Eve Before Beltane

The High Feast of Beltane was a celebration that the ancient Celts had observed in Europe for centuries prior to their settlement in the western lands of Eirgalon. It was a time to celebrate new life and fertility. In Eirgalon it had blended with some of the features of Wabanaki spring and planting observations to become a festival similar to, yet distinct from, old Celtic rituals. The evening before the celebration had come to be a time of somber prayer and invocation of the divine powers upon the fertility of the land, while the actual day and eve of Beltane were a time of gaiety and joyous celebration of the budding life which surrounded them.

The sun was soon to set and the evening fires had been lit, but the rites of prayer had not yet begun. The full moon was rising on the eastern horizon when the three sisters and Evlin emerged from Unaine's tent with the tabac pouch they had been examining. The looks on their faces were anything but happy.

Skoth was seated under a large oak tree near the edge of the woods. He was in conversation with Unaine, Tkaden, Karl, Gunnar, and Erik. The women joined the men and Leesha took the lead.

"You won't like to hear this, but we are sure there is something amiss here. Both Enat and Evlin are sure there are other herbs mixed in with the tabac. We suspect that the tabac has been soaked in the liquid of the cowbane plant. We're not sure what would happen if you smoked it, but we're sure it wouldn't be good for you. Besides that, I have a sense that there is some sort of shaman spell on either the tabac or the pouch. I can't tell what it is, but there is something wrong."

Teite added, "I'm not sure what there is about it. The designs on the pouch all seem to be traditional Wabanaki ones. It just that looking at it makes me uneasy, the same way that looking at that accursed knife that infected Neal made me feel."

Skoth asked, "So what do you recommend we do with it?"

Leesha answered, "It was given to you as a gift. But a gift given, be it by nature evil or by intent evil, is no gift. We say it should be destroyed."

Erik didn't hesitate, he stood up and started reaching for the pouch, and said, "Let's take care of that, right now. We'll throw it in the fire."

Almost in unison, the four young women shouted, "NO!"

Erik, who had seldom had women say "no" to him during his life, stopped in his tracks when the women shouted at him.

"What? Why?" he stammered, and then it dawned on him. If, indeed, the tabac was laced with poison, or the pouch was cursed, then igniting it in the fire would most likely trigger the evil. Anyone who breathed the smoke, or was touched by the fumes, or perhaps was even in the vicinity might well be affected by it.

Skoth asked, "What do you suggest would be the best way to dispose of it?"

Teite answered, "Certainly not by fire. We think there is a real chance that might trigger the poison in it. I suggest we take it out to sea, scatter the contents, and place a rock in it to sink the pouch to the bottom."

Evlin said, "A second option would be to scatter the contents in the surf along the shore, the saltwater of the estuary will dilute the poison of the cowbane to levels where it can't hurt anything, and then throw the pouch into the latrine where it will rot away."

Skoth thought about it a moment and said, "It think it is best to take care of it as soon as possible. Since I don't want to send a crew out to sea tonight, let's do it Evlin's way. Erik and Karl, would you do the honors of walking it down the shoreline, beyond where anyone has beached their ships and dispose of it?"

"It'd be my pleasure, Chief. Can't think of a finer place for it to end up than in a pit, covered with waste."

Erik and Karl took the pouch, which was wrapped in a piece of leather and left on their task. While they were gone the others prepared for the evening fire and rituals. When they returned all were ready to begin with more pleasant activities. Erik concluded that aspect of the evening by making a motion of wiping off his hands and saying, "Hope that foul piece doesn't stink up that hole too much."

Chapter 54 - The High King Alting

The spring day of Beltane dawned with clear skies and heavy dew upon the ground. The men and women of Eirgalon that had gathered in and around the city of New Caledonia had spent the previous evening devoted to the more somber prayers and rituals of the festival. Today they would conclude the observance of Beltane with joyous bonfires into the night.

Early that morning, when light had first begun to brighten the eastern horizon, Evlin had slipped from Skoth's side. She fastened her cloak about her and went outside to walk the in the woods and to observe the Beltane tradition of women gathering the early morning dew and washing in their faces in it. Noticing Teite, Leesha, and Enat leaving their tent, she motioned for them to follow her. She led them to a path in the woods that led them uphill under oak and maple trees and then through a grove of towering pine trees. The path then opened up into a grassy knoll that overlooked the estuary where the river met the sea.

Carefully and gently they wiped the dew from the plants into the small bowls they had brought with them. They filled their bowls, for the dew had fallen heavy that morning. Evlin then called them together and raising her arms to the heavens, said before them, "Daughters of dawn and lovers of life, wash your faces with the waters of the new day. May the dreams of field and forest, creatures great and small, awaken now. Bring hope. Grow in beauty. Grow in love. Grow strong in truth and purity. Wash and be renewed."

Each of them said, "So mote it be."

Thus, prepared for the day, they followed the path back to the camp and assembled with the others to enter the city and attend the Alting for naming the High King of Eirgalon.

At noon the leaders met in the Great Hall of the Fortress of New Caledonia. The fortress courtyard outside the Great Hall and the public square outside the main gates of the fortress were crowded with the common folk who could not gain admittance to the Great Hall. There was a festive air of excitement and anticipation amongst the people, which far exceeded the normal observance of Beltane. No doubt, this would be a Beltane that would be long remembered in the history of the people of Eirgalon.

The Great Hall of New Caledonia was arranged in a similar fashion to the other great halls of the Celtic kingdoms. However, there was one difference. The sacred spiral that was inlaid on the floor was not a labyrinth of the Baltic fashion, but was a winding "seed spiral" of seven rings. For this alting there were eighteen large chairs placed in a circle around the outside edge of the spiral. Eleven of the chairs were for the kings of the Celtic kings present, six chairs were for Wabanaki chiefs who had come, and the final chair was for the man that King Tyg had put forth to be the High King - Skoth Brianson of Dunsheelin. The advisors and followers that each leader had brought with them would be seated in chairs behind them. Skoth would have Evlin, Erik, Karl, and Tkaden behind him. Unaine would have his three daughters behind him.

The participants were in small groups and making

conversation when Skoth entered the hall. Soon he noticed that Dakatomi was with Tkomik, so he made his way over to them. Skoth noticed a sort of quizzical expression on Dakatomi's face. That, in itself was strange, since in the previous encounters Skoth had with the man, Skoth had always felt it was difficult to read the man because of the lack of expression his face normally revealed.

Skoth started the conversation by saying in a voice loud enough so that others nearby could hear it, "Shaman Dakatomi, I wanted to thank you personally for the gift of the fine pouch and tabac that you sent me after our meeting yesterday. It was most interesting."

Dakatomi hesitated in his response, "Ah, why you're welcome. You sampled it then?"

"Sampled it! Why we emptied the entire pouch! I must say, we were all quite impressed by it."

Again Skoth saw a flicker of puzzlement cross Dakatomi's face, but before the shaman could respond, the horn sounded for the beginning of the alting. Quickly the folks in the room made their way to their appointed chairs. Skoth and his delegation went to their places and were seated. The horn sounded again and all conversations in the hall ended.

King Tyg of Heilsand stood and spoke, "I declare this Alting to proclaim the High King of Eirgalon to be in session. This is my duty and responsibility as the one who sent forth the summons to you kings and chiefs of Eirgalon. I thank King Haggar and his realm of New Caledonia for hosting this gathering. These are dire times for our land. We have grown and prospered for generations. There are those who would say we have done so without the presence of a High King, so there is no need for one in this time." He paused and looked around the hall, and then continued.

"This may have been true. But the times have changed. We have resolved our differences and disputes throughout the generations past by conflict, as well as by negotiation. Today, a new and different kind of challenge confronts us. It is twofold. First, we are a mixed people. The blood of Celt and the blood of Wabanaki are mingled. Few are the families where this is not so. But politically we are separate. A Wabanaki in Celt lands is often not seen as a citizen of that land. A Celt in Wabanaki lands is similarly, often not seen as a citizen of that land. Coastal and interior people share distrust and animosity toward each other. A High King for all the people and lands of Eirgalon would be a symbol and promise of unity among us." Again he paused for effect, and then went on.

"The powerful second reason to declare a High King is to meet the challenge on our western borders. As some of you know, my own land and its king were attacked a few short months ago. Those attackers killed King Ragen. Malsum of the Haudenoshonee has vowed to destroy us and drive us from our lands. He has united the people of the western lands and is moving against us. One by one we would fall to his warriors. But together we can stand against him." A third time he made a long dramatic pause, and then he finished his speech.

"There is a third reason, but I will let Unaine of Fadis Innis, explain that in greater detail. When it comes time to stand for the High King, let it be known that I will stand for the man I place in nomination before you, Skoth, son of Brian, who saved us from Malsum's storm in the attack on Heilsand! I yield to King Unaine of Fadis Innis."

Unaine stood and looked about the room. He held his gaze for a moment on Skoth, and smiled like a father smiles upon the son in whom he has great pride.

Unaine spoke, "I heartily agree with King Tyg, concerning the first two reasons, but for me the third is even greater. Hard it is, for us mere mortals to understand events that transpire around us, though try as we might. Many of you know that I was trained in the druid ways since my youth, thinking I'd be serving my brother, Rian, when he became king. But he died an untimely death, and then my closest friend, Brian the Bold was also cut down. I was called to lead my people. My knowledge of our history and study of the druid ways has given me insight into ancient prophecies. When the Celts first settled in this land, mixing with the Wabanaki, the great druid, Thorfall, in conversation with the gods, foretold:

> *The arrow's flight replaces death with life*
> *a double week of generations and new lands are filled*
> *with strife*
> *the east moves west and north moves south*
> *unite as one to meet the test*
> *beware the sunset lox*
> *a sly and wily fox*
> *a youth, son of bold*
> *must lead the fold*
> *a kingly role to search and find*
> *the key to guard our humankind.*

I have no doubt that this prophecy is about young Skoth. It, and he, have been tested and found true. Under his leadership we are to be united. We are being tested as a people. He is on a quest. In his hands lies our future. I, and Fadis Innis, will stand for him as High King. I ask the alting. Be there other men to choose from as our High King?"

Unaine was silent as he looked around the circle. None spoke. Unaine nodded to Tyg and then sat down.

King Tyg stood again and declared, "There is before us but one who would be High King. As is our custom when standing for our kings, we now ask him to speak to us of kingship, and then we will give each lord here, a chance to speak and say his mind before we ask who would stand for this man as king. Skoth, son of Brian the Bold, speak now to us."

Tyg sat down and Skoth stood. He took a moment to look around the room, looking at each of the kings and chiefs in turn, but also looking at the men and women who sat and stood behind them. Then, taking a deep breath, he spoke.

"I am honored and awed by your gathering here today. Having this quest and this responsibility is not something that I have sought, but I have been taught and I believe that one should not shirk from one's duty. I will not turn from this responsibility.

I do not know all that is to come, but I do believe that what the kings of Heilsand and Fadis Innis have told you is true. I believe we are in the process of becoming one people. Yes, we have come from many roots with many names: Celt, Eire, Scot, Viking, Wabanaki, and more. But we are the people of this land, and this land is the home to all of its people. I tarried this winter past with Fearglas, whom some of you call the Green Man. With me today, is his daughter, Evlin, who carries in her blood the truth of who we are in this room: Wabanaki and Celt. You have heard stories of how the Green Man loves this land. Those stories are true. And before I left him, I made a solemn promise before earth and sky to serve the land and its people. Should you stand for me as High King, I will stand for you. I will serve you and our land. I will confront our enemies. I will seek the key to our future."

His speech concluded, Skoth turned to sit down and was warmed by the smile that Evlin gave him. King Tyg then declared, "Skoth, son of Brian, has spoken. We have heard his words, and now he will hear ours. It is our responsibility to discuss and accept or reject what he has said. Proceeding in an orderly fashion around this circle, let us now speak our piece. King Unaine and I have already shared our words. I ask King Haggar of New Caledonia to speak next."

Around the room they went, some made strong affirmations for Skoth, but there were some who were less warm to the idea of a High King. Legitimate issues were raised as to just what it meant for there to be a high king, what kind of loyalty was expected, what would be some of the practical aspects of how one would exercise such high kingship without already having a realm of their own. There were also comments made concerning the need for reconciliation between coastal and inland people, as well as Celt and Wabanaki.

After all of the leaders present had their say, King Tyg gave a nod to the herald near the door. The herald again winded the horn. King Tyg then said, "All have had their say.

Now is the time for action." He then stood and said, "I stand for Skoth, High King of Eirgalon."

Unaine followed suit, and one by one the men stood to make their declarations. Tkomik was the first Wabanaki chief to stand. Though Dakatomi sat behind him with a baleful look upon his face, it was Tkomik's place to make the decision. The other chiefs with great solemnity, also gave their assent.

At the end, all seventeen of the gathered leaders were standing. Tyg again nodded to the herald, and again the sweet clarion call of the horn sounded forth.

Tyg then spoke to Skoth, "Skoth, son of Brian, you have been called by the people and lands of Eirgalon to be our High King. Will you walk to the center of the Sacred Spiral and give your oath?"

Skoth stood and then walked to the center of the Great Hall following the path of the labyrinth as it wound back and forth around the room. Once there he lifted his arms in supplication, "Hear me, earth and sky, creatures great and small, witness now my solemn pledge.

I promise to protect and steward the land and all who use it, giving thanks to creature and creator for the gift of life. I promise to listen to the land and to the people. I seek to tend and nurture. I seek goodness and beauty. I will serve the people and the land. I stand for them. I ask the blessings of the Great Creator, and all spirits good and true, upon my promise and upon my task."

The horn sounded again, and King Tyg asked, "As High King of Eirgalon, what shall we call you?"

Skoth smiled and chuckled, and said, "I never thought

about that. Just call me Skoth. The name I was given at birth is the name by which I will serve."

King then directed the herald and announced, "Sound the horn again and have it proclaimed to city and the land: We have a king, High King Skoth of Eirgalon. Let us celebrate this new beginning. I declare this High King Alting concluded. Long live the King."

The horn blew and announcements were made to the cheering crowd outside. Inside the hall, the people applauded and Evlin ran to Skoth and threw her arms around him in an embrace. Others moved forward to congratulate him and wish him well. Small groups formed, and people moved about as they talked with friends from far away, and as they started heading to the events they had scheduled to celebrate Beltane.

Skoth and Evlin had received congratulations from several people when Dakatomi came up to Skoth. The elder shaman said quietly, "Don't think this is over."

Dakatomi was then noticeably startled when Erik's deep voice right behind him said, "That's one thing you have right. It's just beginning."

Evlin narrowed her eyes as the shaman retorted, "You don't know the powers you have become entangled with."

Evlin stepped toward him with a fire flaring in her eyes, "Perhaps you are the one who doesn't understand. You should know better!"

"Bah!" was his response as he turned away and slipped into the crowd.

Skoth pulled her back to his side and said, "Enough of his unpleasantness. It is time to go and join the festivities."

Later that evening, after the dancing around the Maypole, the passing between the bonfires of Beltane, and all the feasting and revelries, they were escorted by their friends back to their camp outside the city. King Haggar had invited them to stay in the fortress, but Skoth felt that spending the night in the countryside was an action that symbolized his belonging to the land of Eirgalon. They had been pleased to see their friends enjoying the celebration, and when they returned to the camp they were not surprised to see Karl and Enat pair up and go one direction, and Leesha and Tkaden go another. But they were surprised to see that Gunnar, who had accompanied the procession back to camp, and Teite had walked away together down the beach. Perhaps it was a time of new beginnings.

Chapter 55 - Sunrise

Before dawn the next morning, Skoth and Evlin made their way up the forest path to the grassy knoll where Evlin and the sisters had been the previous morning. They spread a blanket and sat down to enjoy view of the rising sun as it would break the eastern horizon over the river estuary.

As they sat, Evlin leaned over and laid her head upon his shoulder. He could sense her contentment. The moments stretched into minutes as the sky brightened from rose to gold. And then the orb of light broke the skyline and enveloped them in blazing luminescence. Young lovers on the height in the bright sunshine of a new day.

On the distant beach below them, two men walked the shoreline. The rising sun had not yet broken upon them, but as they turned west and looked upward to see the first rays of the sun striking the tops of the towering pines, they could see above the pines the very top of the grassy knoll and the young couple seated there. And in the first light of that new day they had hope for the future of their land.

Unaine turned to Erik and said, "The sun rises on a new era in our land. What do you think of our young Skoth now, my friend?"

"Tis a strange thing to have the one, who when little, was constantly getting into trouble under our feet and who we had to be looking after, now be the one who is looking after us."

"So it is. So it is. Through it all, he has turned out all right. But there is more to come. There are huge challenges before him. I think he is going to need someone by his side."

"A right fair beauty she is! And powerful in her own right!"

"True. But, I was referring to you."

"Me? Awe, chief, you don't mean I have to keep tagging along and watching over him."

"Indeed I do. More than ever he needs someone to keep him humble, and to watch his back at times. You are the man for the job."

Erik gave a long, deep sigh and then said, "As interesting as life has been, I suspect it is going to get even more so."

Unaine laughed as he patted him on the back and said, "Like it or not, we live in interesting times."

High above them, on the grassy knoll, the two gloried in the light of the sunrise. As they watched the sun reflect off the waters of the estuary that stretched before them, Evlin questioned Skoth about the key to the future.

"I know you have been thinking about the story of the loon's necklace. Teite and the rest seem to think that it is symbolic. But I wonder . . ."

Skoth turned from looking over the waters to look into her eyes, and said, "You think elsewise?"

"I'm not sure. It may be true that the symbolism of the linked shells on the loon's necklace are a way of describing the tying together of the people of Eirgalon into one realm. But what if there is more? What if there is a physical object, a real necklace?"

"I know what you are saying. I have wondered the same. The prophecy sends me on the quest to find the key to save our humanity. We have begun the work of uniting the people of Eirgalon. We have recognized that as a people we have enemies that seek to destroy us, and that we must be united against them. Therein could lie our salvation as a people, but what if there is more?"

"So will you search for such a key? Will you seek the loon's necklace?"

"I must. It was the quest bestowed upon me. Somehow I must both lead our people as we confront the foe from the west, and I must find the key."

"And how do you intend to do this?"

"I'll follow the story. Trace its roots to the place where it began."

"How shall you begin?"

"By taking the first step. We start at the beginning. We make preparations to leave and then we head west and north - to the lands beyond our sunset."

Coming soon

Book 2 in the Chronicles of Eirgalon

The Land of the Sunset Lakes

Prologue

*By mere tendrils of thoughts do the gods shift, ere so
slightly, the dream of a single man,
and so is altered the course of human history.*

In realms which lay beyond domains of men, exist
such beings called by mortal man, "the gods." Be they gods
or demons in the thoughts of men matters little, for truth be
told, to some they may be gods and to some they may be
demons. Be that as it may, at times they touch the human
world, and in their touching they move and turn that world
into different outcomes and alternate timelines.

One of theses beings was known as Lox. Some
claimed he was the alter image of Gluskabi, as malevolent as
the former was benevolent. He saw that Gluskabi had altered
human history merging Viking and Celtic settlers with the
native Wabanaki inhabitants of what was now called
Eirgalon. Lox determined to bend this human history his own
way. In Gluskabi's timeline of possible human history, the
Haudenoshonee man, Deganawida (Two River Currents
Flowing Together) received a vision from the Creator. It was

a vision of peace and cooperation among all the Haudenoshonee causing them to form a great lodge of the people some would call the Iroquois confederation, but the crafty Lox had different plans.

And so it was that thirty years before the Alting for the first High King of Eirgalon that Lox stepped into human time and gave to Deganawida a different vision and so created Malsum. His vision was to unify the land, but with terror and might against the people from the east, in determination to drive the invaders and their collaborators from the land.

Chapter 1 - Vision

Deganawida was a young man born to the Huron people who lived in the western lands of Eirgalon. He was born west of the valley of the Mahakentuck on the north edge of the great lake his people called Ontario, which means beautiful waters.

The vision quest is a sacred rite of passage for the young men in the land of Eirgalon. They lay themselves open to the spirit world seeking dreams to guide their lives. When it was time for young Deganawida to make the passage to manhood, his elders prepared him by guiding his fast and sending him alone to a quiet place to wait for his vision to come. None of them could know of the great vision that the Creator intended to give this talented youth. He was to be the Peacemaker, uniting the people of the region in peace and cooperation. That vision, however, was not to be, for the spirit of Lox, in his malevolence intervened, and came to Deganawida before the Creator could complete the Peacemaker vision.

Lox twisted the tendrils of this dream. It was still a dream of unity for the great people of the beautiful lakes, but this dream was twisted to become one of unity under his watchful eye as the people joined together to confront and destroy the dwellers of the lands to the east. Deganawida was to become Malsum, the incarnation of the malevolence of Lox. He would drive his people to unity against their common foe: the descendents of the European invaders.

When Deganawida, now called Malsum, returned to his village he shared the dream of his vision quest. The old Huron shaman of his village was troubled by this vision, and so he sent Malsum away from them. Malsum wandered for a time, and traveled to the southern shores of Lake Ontario, where he came to live among the Mohawk people. There was power in the young man, for Lox dwelt within him, and soon he rose to leadership among his new people. He called them forth and from the quarreling tribes of Mohawk, Oneida, Onondaga, Cayuga, and Senaca, he formed the mighty Haudenoshonee. He united them in their hatred of the Celtic people of Eirgalon, as they called their land.

For several years he sent agents sowing discord and dissention among the Wabanaki and Celtic people of the lands to the east. When he heard rumors that the one who would be unifying all the people of eastern Eirgalon had been revealed by his adversary, Gluskabi, he made plans to destroy him. Those plans had come to naught, and now he was confronted by people who claimed to be one people, and who were ruled by High King Skoth.

It was an early day of summer-like weather in late May, only a few short weeks after the Alting that had proclaimed Skoth to be the High King of Eirgalon. The loyal minion of Malsum stood on the bluffs on the western shore the River Mahakentuck and watched the longships of King Duncan of Glesga returning to their port on that isle near the eastern shore. Ayenwatha was his given name, but Malsum called him simply Ayen, and he was Malsum's warchief.

Ayen had hoped to attack this Celtic stronghold before Duncan and his men had returned, but now he must make different plans. Nodding to his men, they stepped back from the bluff and began to make their way back to camp. Ayen took one last look across the river. He cleared his throat and spat at the sight, and then followed his men.

The People of Eirgalon:

Collin, King of Rekvik
Dakatomi, Shaman of the Wabanaki
Duncan, King of Glesga
Duncan, Blacksmith of Glenoak
Enat, daughter of Unaine
Erik, Chief Unaine's friend and man at arms
Evlin, daughter of Fearglas and Sheela
Fearglas, the Green Man of legend
Fiona,Erik's sister
Gunnar, son of Hagar
Haggar, King of New Caledonia
Hilda, wife of King Haggar
Karl, close friend of Skoth
Leesha, daughter of Unaine
Leif, King of Straumford,
Malsum, Haudenoshonee leader
Neal, childhood friend of Skoth
Rolf and Jake, a couple of Erik's warriors
Ragen, aged King of Heilsand
Sheela, mother of Evlin and wife of Fearglas
Skoth, son of dead Brian the Bold
Susie, owner of Tante's Table
Teite, the eldest daughter of Unaine
Tkaden, young Wabanaki man
Tkomik, Chief of Wausacom
Tyg, officer in Heilsand and new King
Unaine, King of Fadis Innis